Fish Perfume

A Romantic Comedy

by

Sammie Grace

To My Baby Brother Tom,

With Much Love
and thanks!
Sammie Grace

Copyright © 2012 Sammie Grace
All Rights Reserved

This book or any portion thereof may not be reproduced or used in any manner whatsoever without the express written permission of the copyright owner except for the use of brief quotations in a book review.

This is a work of fiction. Names, characters, places and incidents are either the product of the author's imagination or are used fictitiously, and any resemblance to actual persons, living or dead, business establishments, events or locales is entirely coincidental.

Paperback ISBN 978-1480121478

Cover Illustration by Mike Stricklin/stricklinstudio

This book is dedicated to my mom.
I love you and miss you every day.

ACKNOWLEDGMENTS

I would like to thank Carol McCune, Cathy Wareham and Laura Harris for all of their enthusiasm and support. Huge thanks to my beautiful gang of Philly girls who have been there for me for decades through life's ups and downs. Thank you to my book club girls in Rhode Island for all their wonderful thoughts and suggestions. A special thank you to my husband who is my biggest fan no matter what I do. You're the best.

A warm thank you goes out to you. Thank you for taking the time to read my book. I hope you enjoy it.

CONTENTS

CHAPTER ONE

Three days ago was the last day of school. I teach ninth-grade Social Studies at Girls Catholic High School, otherwise known as the Whore House on the Hill. As an alumna myself, I personally feel it is unfairly nicknamed. It's not that much of a hill.

Once again, I'd lined up a summer job at the local garden center and, on my days off, I planned to visit the Jersey shore as much as possible with my friends.

I wiggled out of my shorts, ready to jump in the shower, when the phone rang.

"Meggie, is that you?"

I recognized my grandmother's New England accent at once.

"Of course it's Meggie, Gram. How are you?"

"Good, honey, but I need a big favor."

Hmmmm…Gram asking me for a favor.

"What's up?" I asked.

"Well, I know you probably already have plans for the summer, but I was wondering if you would like to come up to Rhode Island and run the marina for me."

I had to sit down on my bed as thoughts of Gram being sick swirled through my head. My heart leaped into my throat. I choked out, "Are you sick?"

"No, darling. I'm fine. I just want to take a nice long vacation out west."

"Of course, I'll come if you need me but can't you find someone more qualified?"

"You'll be fine," Gram reassured me. "You've been up here enough over the years to know how I operate things. It'll be a piece of cake for a smart girl like you."

She went on to tell me about the marina and whom to ask for help if I needed it. I was half listening as my mind reeled with thoughts of all the things I could screw up. Then I heard her say, "I'm leaving tomorrow. When do you think you can be here?"

"I have to close up the house and pack. I could be there the day after tomorrow."

"Great, honey. I'm sorry it's short notice, but I just made up my mind today. I'm afraid if I don't get out of Dodge soon, I'll never go."

"Gee, Gram, I wish I could be there tomorrow to see you before you leave."

"I'm leaving you plenty of notes and I'll be in touch. Bye, sweetie, and thanks."

Before I could say another word, Gram hung up and panic took over.

Gram never left during the summer when her marina was in full swing. I knew why she asked me. I'm the only family member left in the country. My parents were in New Zealand visiting my brother Charlie, a travel writer. My other brother,

Jack, a merchant marine, was at sea. I knew I had to be her last choice since I'm not the most organized person in my family.

The marina is in the quaint seaside community of Cozy Harbor, Rhode Island. When I was a kid, my family would visit Gram every summer for several weeks. I can't believe I hadn't been up to Gram's in six years.

As soon as I got over the shock of Gram's phone call, I called my friends to inform them of my unexpected change in plans. They insisted we go out for a good-bye dinner the following evening. We met at one of our favorite hangouts, Maggie McFee's. Since I'd been packing all day and running late, I threw on a pair of beige capris and a white shirt, dusted my cheeks with some blush, put on a little mascara and some lipstick, and jumped in the car.

I walked in the door to find the bar packed. I looked at the large TV screen behind the bar and instantly knew why—the Phillies were playing. I looked around and spotted Laura and Helen sitting at a round table across from the bar. When I got to the table, Helen whined, "I can't believe you're leaving us for the summer."

I threw up my hands and said, "I don't really have a choice. I couldn't say no to Gram. I'm going to hit the highway early tomorrow morning."

Laura, always the positive one, said, "I think it will be good for you, Meggie. You've been in a rut since Jimmy the Rat Bastard did the unthinkable."

Yeah, a rut after the rat, I thought to myself. You'd think after three years of dating, he'd be ready to make a commitment, but instead he wanted a break. While I've spent the last six months wallowing in misery, I heard he's happily dating a girl named Barbie he met at a bachelor party. She probably jumped out of the cake. Thanks to Helen and Laura, who ran into them at the mall, I learned Barbie had a big nose, big hair, a big mouth, and a really huge ass.

I just can't picture Jimmy with someone like that. I'm not beauty queen material, but people have told me I'm pretty. I have blue eyes and straight, thick, copper-red hair that sits just below my shoulders. My parents said that when I was born, my hair stood straight up in spikes as if I came out scared to death. The doctor swore he never saw so much hair on an infant. My mother claims it was sticking up because she had read a couple of Stephen King novels when she was pregnant. I'm 5'4" tall, and a size 6 or 8, depending on how many potato chips I ate last week. I wish I could say I was tall and willowy with large voluptuous breasts, but I'm just an average height and weight, with small to medium boobs. I thank God every day for the Miracle Bra.

The waitress came to take our orders. When she left, I said, "I think getting away will be good for me, too. I've been feeling a little lost lately. Not just the Jimmy thing either. I'm not too crazy about my job anymore, and I'm disgusted with the dating scene."

Laura said, "It can't be that bad. There are plenty of good guys out there."

"Easy for you to say; you met your Mr. Wonderful in fifth grade," I said.

Laura was the homebody of the group. She and Danny dated for years, then got married right after college. She immediately spit out two adorable boys one after the other.

Helen chimed in. "The last date I was on, I was so bored I

felt like I was going to slip into a coma. He just never shut up. It took him forever to get to the point of what he was trying to say. I just wanted to scream at him and say, 'SHUT UP AND GIVE ME THE CLIFF NOTES!' I decided he was toast halfway through our date."

Beautiful, super-smart, and more self-confident than most, Helen was a force to be reckoned with. She says she doesn't have balls; she has something better—breasticles. At 28, she was one of the top engineers at her civil engineering firm. For the past two years, she'd been working on a new sports complex being built in Philly. Unfortunately, as smart as she is at work, her personal life, mainly her love life, was always high drama. She plowed through boyfriends like Sherman went through Georgia. Helen always says the world is full of old boyfriends. What she doesn't say is most of them are hers. Men don't know what to make of Helen because she intimidates the shit out of them. The guys at work call her Hell-n-Back, because by the time she's done with them, they feel like they went to guess where and back.

Laura asked her, "Any new prospects on the horizon?"

Helen laughed and said, "No. I've been so busy with this project at work; I've barely had time to do my laundry. When it's over, though, I'm going on a manhunt. I want a McDreamy or McSteamy like on that show 'Grey's Anatomy'. I want him just for a weekend of hot, sweaty, uninterrupted sex."

We all laughed. I said, "If you find him, see if he has a McBrother or a McCousin for me. I'm taking a break from men, but I would make an exception for a McAnything. While in Rhode Island, I'm going to run the marina, take walks on the beach and do some soul-searching and figure out what I really want to do with my life."

Laura said to Helen, "You should fix her up with that Mr. McBoring you just dumped."

The waitress delivered our meal and I was enjoying my delicious, messy buffalo chicken sandwich when I noticed Laura's eyes grow wide. I turned around to see what caught her attention. I almost choked when I saw Jimmy the Rat Bastard walking through the bar with a beautiful strawberry blonde. I haven't seen him since we broke up. My hand shook as I took a drink of beer to wash down the chicken that had stuck in my throat. I felt a presence beside me and looked up to find Jimmy standing next to me. He had a smug smile and I wanted to reach up and slap it right off his face. Of course, I would never do anything like that, but, boy, it was tempting. Sometimes being a nice girl is a bitch.

He glanced around the table and said, "Hi, girls." He then looked back at me and said, "Meggie, you have some kind of sauce on your face." Barbie started to giggle and he draped his arm around her and said, "See you around, ladies," and strolled off toward the restaurant section.

Mortified, I picked up a napkin from the center of the table and wiped my face. I then turned my anger toward my friends. "Why didn't you tell me I had sauce on my face?"

Laura said, "We didn't get a chance. He made a beeline for our table the minute he saw you. What an asshole!"

I put my hands over my face, wishing the floor would open up and swallow me. "I knew I should've ordered a salad," I moaned.

Helen said, "Yeah, but then with your luck, you would have had lettuce in your teeth."

That's when I got mad. "You both lied to me. You said Barbie had a long nose, big hair, and a huge ass. The only thing big about her was her boobs."

Helen said defensively, "Her ass is too big." She turned to Laura. "Don't you think she has a big ass?"

Laura nodded and said, "*Huge* is the word I would use. No, humongous. I actually feel sorry for her. She has a JLo butt times three."

Helen nodded in agreement. "You need to get another look at her, Meggie."

I muttered, "No wonder he dumped me. He went to boob heaven."

Helen looked over her shoulder and said, "At least he and the Barbette are sitting in the other room. Also, did you notice he didn't even introduce her? If I were Barbie, I'd think that was really rude. Meggie, you're always selling yourself short. You are ten times hotter than her. You don't need a ton of makeup or flashy clothes. Barbie had about five pounds of makeup on and her clothes were two sizes too small. You're a natural beauty. You've got it all over her."

I rolled my eyes. "Yeah, right."

Laura said, "Personally, I've always been really jealous of you, Meggie."

I tried not to laugh, but I couldn't help it. I may not have a boyfriend at the moment, but I sure had great friends who support me through thick and thin and rat bastards.

Helen flagged down the waitress and ordered another round.

* * * * *

Connecticut has to be the road construction capital of the world. My old Volvo wagon valiantly battled the trucks for position on I-95, but the drive from Philly to Rhode Island is not for the squeamish. I'm glad I had a CD player installed in old Susie so my new favorite band, Three Legged Fox, could keep me company.

Between the traffic, all the coffee I drank, and a slight hangover, my nerves were shot. Not to mention the fact that I'm terrified I'll destroy Gram's marina within the first few minutes of my arrival. I just know some catastrophe will happen on my watch. A hurricane, an earthquake, or the fuel dock will blow up, and all the boats and docks will burn in a big ball of fire. I thought I was just a loser magnet, but my brothers say I'm a disaster magnet.

I guess I've given them some good-enough reasons to think that over the years. Like the time in high school when I volunteered to feed the neighbors' fish while they were on vacation. They had a large aquarium with all kinds of rare tropical fish. The neighbors had only been gone three days when I went over to feed the fish. I looked at the tank and couldn't see so much as one swimming around. Did someone break into the house and take the fish? Who the heck would steal fish? Then I noticed the top of the tank and saw the once-colorful, lively fish all floating belly up. I ran home crying, devastated that I'd done something wrong. My dad went over, scooped them all out of the tank, and flushed them down the toilet. He assured me repeatedly that it wasn't my fault. It was a problem with the air hose. The neighbors weren't too upset with me, although they did say they were glad they put their dogs in a kennel. To this day, I still feel terrible. At the young age of fifteen, I was a murderer.

My second big disaster happened in college while I was house-sitting for a professor and his wife. I started a load of wash and went to class. The machine overflowed and caused about $500 worth of water damage. Just my luck their appliances were on the second floor.

I don't even have to be around for disasters to occur. My poor car has been hit three times, always in parking lots. Every time it happened, I was nowhere near the car. I could go on and on but what's the point? I guess my brothers are right; I am a disaster magnet.

Nevertheless, I'm glad to get out of Philly. After last night's humiliation with Jimmy, I couldn't wait to see the City of Brotherly Love disappear in my rearview mirror. A change of scenery is just what I need. It'll help me keep my mind off the male species for a while. Who knows, I might learn some management skills and maybe start a new career.

I was nervous about running the marina but also excited to get back to Rhode Island. Some of my best childhood memories come from visits there with my family. It's a little-known vacationer's paradise.

Not long after seeing the WELCOME TO RHODE ISLAND sign, I got off I-95 and meandered my way east to Route 1, then headed north to Cozy Harbor. I could feel the tension in my body fading away as I soaked up the peaceful scenery of the ponds and the rural beauty of the South County area. A few more miles down the road, I took the exit for Cozy Harbor and came to the end of this Nightmare from Hell drive. Even though it'd been several years since I'd been there, I knew it would be just as I remembered it. I pulled into the marina parking lot, which was pretty full for a Monday. Most of the vehicles were trucks or SUVs necessary for transporting boating and fishing supplies. The big building at the end of the parking lot was the marina office and store. On the left was Gram's cottage, and on the right, the big parts and repair shop. Beyond the buildings were the boat docks, the fuel dock, the Snack Shack, and the fish store.

Although there were a lot of cars in the parking lot, no one was around. Considering the beautiful day, I surmised that everyone must be out on the water. After my six-hour drive, I decided I really needed to unpack the car and get moved into Gram's cottage as quick as possible. A hot shower and a nap sounded good, too.

Out of the corner of my eye as I stepped out of the car, I saw a guy walking across the parking lot. He was tall and lean with broad shoulders. God, I love a guy with broad shoulders. He wore tan cargo shorts, a white T-shirt and a navy-blue baseball cap. My gaze followed him up the steps to the store. As he opened the door, he must have sensed my stare because he turned to look at me. The bill of his cap shadowed his face, but I saw his smile and my heart stopped. Just as fast, he proceeded into the store, leaving me gaping. I didn't even get a good look at him, yet I felt an instant attraction. I'll be in big trouble if all the guys around here were that good-looking. Here I said I was off men for the summer. I haven't been here two minutes and I'm hot for the first guy I see.

With a shake, I dragged myself back to business. I opened the door to the small cottage and looked around. It was the same as always, warm and welcoming with its shiny hardwood floors, chintz curtains, overstuffed chairs and sofa. The two bedrooms, living room, and kitchen with a table and six chairs reflected Gram's simple lifestyle perfectly. In the kitchen was a hutch displaying Gram's collection of locally made pottery.

A lifelong over-packer, it took me a few trips before I hauled everything out of the car and into the guest room. I wasn't giving up hope that Gram would change her mind and come back early before I totally screwed up her livelihood.

When Gram had called, she was sketchy about her plans. She said she'd be out west and would call when she could. What had me worried was that this whole trip was so out of character for her. Mom was going to have a canary when she found out. I'd left a message on my brother, Charlie's cell to call me when he had a chance, figuring I'd let him deal with telling Mom. In the meantime, maybe some of the people around the marina could shed some light on Gram's recent state of mind.

At 72, my grandmother, Betty, was a beautiful lady and sharp as a tack. She was a strong, loving, fun person whom everyone couldn't help but love. She grew up at the marina and when her parents passed away, she kept it going. She raised her only child, my mother, Eileen, by herself. My grandfather died in a car crash before Mom was born and Gram never remarried. Come to think of it, I can't remember her ever having a boyfriend.

My stomach started to growl. No wonder, since I only stopped once on my drive up for some much-needed coffee and a potty break, I was famished. I took inventory of the kitchen and fridge and found them well stocked. I threw together a turkey and cheese sandwich with a healthy dose of chips. Gram knew her chip girl was coming and she had loaded up the cupboard with potato chips, tortilla chips, barbeque chips, and sun chips. Chips are definitely my drug of choice. I was in chip heaven. After stuffing my face and unbuttoning my shorts, I laid down on the sofa for a quick twenty-minute nap. Twenty minutes turned into six hours. By the time I woke up, it was 9:00 P.M., so I decided to call it a night and start fresh early in the morning.

The alarm went off at 4:00 A.M., and it took me a few minutes to remember where I was. It all came back in a flash and I knew I had to get moving. Gram always said life at the marina started when the day was in diapers. I threw on some clothes and put my hair up in a ponytail. Dressed and nervous, I went over to the Main Building, which housed the marina store and Gram's office.

Gram said the two key people who would be helping me run the marina were Mo, who ran the Snack Shack, and Greg, who ran the parts and repair shop. Gram said hiring Greg was the best thing she ever did for the marina. Her parts and repair business had tripled since he arrived. He was the "go to guy" if you had boat or engine problems.

Since the store lights were on, I figured Greg had already opened up for the day. Gram said Greg would be filling in, doing his job *and* Gram's, until I got there. I heard a male voice say, "Hi, you must be Meggie." I looked around, and in the doorway to Gram's office stood a friendly-looking bald guy, about 45 years old, wearing jeans and a Harbor Marina T-shirt.

I waved. "You're right. You must be Greg."

He gave me a big smile, shook my hand, and said, "It's nice to meet you, Meggie. Your grandmother has told me all about you."

I groaned. "Ugh, well, I hope she told you that I don't know anything about running a marina. I'm more than a bit nervous."

He gave me a big reassuring smile and said, "No need to worry. You'll do just fine. If you have any questions, just ask me or Mo. Betty left you notes in the office. Everything is on the computer. Also, Betty hired a college student to help out in the store for the summer. Her name is Journey. She dresses a little funky, but she's a nice girl and smart as a whip. She's a nutrition major at the University of Rhode Island. She doesn't come in until 9:00 and works until 6:00. That way, since you start early, you can take a break in the afternoon."

"That sounds like a great plan."

He said, "Hey, I hope you don't mind but I hung a sign in the window. My daughters decided to go into the dog-walking business this summer so they made up a flyer to drum up some business. We live a few blocks up the road."

"Oh, that's fine. How old are they?"

He rolled his eyes. "Twelve and fourteen, going on thirty. They're giving me and my wife a run for our money."

I laughed and said, "I teach teenage girls; I can just imagine."

Greg nodded, turned, and started walking toward the back door. Over his shoulder he said, "Well, I'm going over to the repair shop. Don't forget; if you need anything or have any questions, don't hesitate to ask. I'll be back after Journey gets here and I'll give you a tour around. I can introduce you to the fuel boys and anyone else we run into."

"Thanks, Greg, I really appreciate that."

I went into the office and read through Gram's notes. Thoughts of Gram kept popping up in my head as I looked around the office. I wondered where she went. I wished I could've seen her before she left.

The office looked out into the store, so I was able to keep an eye out if someone came in. After about half an hour, the door opened and in walked my old friend Mac. He had on a pair of old gray pants and a black sweatshirt that read "I don't give a clam." He sported a Red Sox baseball cap and a big smile on his weathered face.

"Mac, is that you?" I shouted as I ran over to give him a big hug. He hugged me back and then stepped back to take a good look at me.

"Meggie, you're so cute I could just put you in my pocket."

"Oh, Mac, you always say that," I beamed.

"Your grandmother said you'd be here for the summer. I hope you'll take a couple hours off sometime and go clamming with me."

I grabbed his hand, squeezed it, and said, "It's a date."

When I was little, my favorite thing to do was to go clamming with Mac. His full name is Alex MacTavish, but everyone calls him Mac. Mac and Gram have been friends for years. He's kept his twenty-foot Boston Whaler at the marina for as long as I can remember. The name of his boat is *My Marie* after his wife who passed away twelve years ago. Mac has got to be in his late eighties now. Gram told me he was doing great and still went clamming every day, weather permitting. As kids, my brothers and I would play on the docks until they hooked up with some of the local boys and ditched me. The joke was on them though. They'd fish off the dock and just catch a couple of ugly green crabs. I, on the other hand, went clamming with Mac and came back with a bucket full of fresh clams.

Mac took off his cap, scratched his head, and said, "I was really surprised Betty took off. In all the years I've known her, I don't remember her going away in the summer."

This brought on that ill feeling I kept getting in my stomach whenever I worried about Gram.

"Do you think she's okay?" I asked.

"She seemed fine. Maybe she just needed an adventure."

"I hope so. This is turning out to be *my* adventure, since I don't really know how to run this place."

"You'll do just fine, Meggie. Betty has this place so organized it practically runs itself."

"I hope you're right."

At that point, three guys came walking into the store and Mac introduced them as Big Howard, Medium Howard, and Just Howard. Howard must be a popular New England name. Big Howard towered over everyone in the store. Medium Howard was next in height, and Just Howard was the smallest. I guessed he was Just Howard because he didn't want to be called Little Howard. Men don't like that word *little* associated with them in any way. After studying them a moment, I'd say they were all in their late forties or fifties. Mac said they were recreational fishermen who do the occasional charter. Big Howard bought some fishing line, and Just Howard bought some hooks. I wrote up their purchase slips, since they all had accounts, and they left to go fluke fishing. Fluke is summer flounder and they said the fishing had been pretty good. Gram always kept up with these reports because people were always calling the marina asking how the fishing is. I guess I'd better stay on top of what our clients are catching.

Mac said goodbye, too, and went clamming. Over the next several hours, I met a few more marina patrons. Journey walked in around 9:00. I knew at once who she was from Greg's description. She had multi-colored hair with shades of burgundy, blond, and red all spiked out in different directions. She was very thin with a pixie face and wore an orange shirt, red pants, and black high-top sneakers. She had five piercings on her left ear, three on her right, and a piercing on her left nostril with a small diamond inserted. Greg was right when he said she dressed a little funky. Some people can pull off funky, and Journey was one of them. Despite the outfit, she was a pretty girl.

"Are you Meggie?" she asked.

"Yes, it's nice to meet you, Journey," I said, holding out my hand with a smile.

We shook hands and she said, "I don't know if Betty told you, but this is my second summer working here, so if I can be of any help, let me know."

"I'm sure I'll be taking you up on the offer."

Journey put her backpack behind the counter and said, "Betty is really cool. I hope she has a good time on her trip."

I couldn't help myself; I had to ask. "Did my grandmother seem okay to you before she left?"

"Yeah, she seemed fine. She was kind of mysterious about the trip though. I tried to pin her down about where she was going, but she just said out west."

"That's what she told me too. I'm a little worried about her."

"Betty is a tough lady. She has all these fishermen wrapped around her little finger. I'm sure she'll be fine."

Not wanting my concern to freak people out, I changed the subject and said, "Journey is a pretty name. Unusual."

"Yeah, well, my parents were hippies. I guess they still are in a lot of ways. My brother's name is Quest."

"Wow."

"At least we never had to worry about someone else in school having the same name as us. There were five Heathers and six Tiffanys in my grade alone."

I laughed thinking, how true, as I had four Emmas in one of my classes last semester. I said, "I bet that was confusing."

"It was. Well, I'll take over out here if you want."

"That sounds good. Greg is coming over in a little while to introduce me around. I do know a couple of people who have been around a long time, but I haven't been here in years, so I'm sure there are a lot of new faces."

"Oh, yeah! Lots of characters, but they're all nice people," she said.

Coming from Journey, I thought that was pretty funny.

I went back in the office and skimmed through some paperwork. When Greg showed up a little while later, we proceeded out to the docks. Greg refreshed my memory, pointing out the different sizes and types of boats moored to each dock. There were four docks at Harbor Marina, labeled A, B, C, and D.

A dock had twelve cabin cruisers, thirty- to forty-five-footers. Half of them never leave the dock but are used as summer homes. I met Kathy and Mike who were sitting on the deck of their cabin cruiser, the *Dancing Queen*.

B Dock had 12 sport-fishing boats, ranging in sizes from thirty-two to forty-five feet. Greg pointed to the right side of the dock and said, "This section is called Divorce Row. All the guys are divorced and half of them live on their boats. Things can get pretty entertaining down here."

I giggled and said, "I can imagine. Do they live on their boats in the winter, too?"

"Just a few. Betty keeps the electricity running for them and they help her out during the winter shoveling and taking care of other small maintenance jobs that need attention."

Greg introduced me to a fisherman named Randy on the *Blood, Sweat and Beers,* tied up on the left side of the dock.

C dock, the smallest, had four small sailboats and four small motor boats such as Mac's Boston Whaler.

D dock, on the end, was the largest. In front of it was the Snack Shack with some tables outside, and next to that the Fish and Bait store, which sold bait, fresh fish, lobsters, and clams. Beyond that was where the big lobster boats dock. There are four sixty-foot and two forty-foot boats. The lobster boats were usually out every day, today being no exception.

I breathed deeply, taking in the beautiful day and the smell of the fresh salt air. As we walked around the marina, I couldn't help but laugh at some of the boat names: *Breaking Wind, Cod Father, Costa Lotta,* and *Atsa My Boat* were some of my favorites. Boat names usually say a lot about the owners. I can't wait to meet them.

Greg introduced me to Matt and Brian, who work the fuel dock and tend the fish and bait store. Matt's a cute kid, tall with blond hair and big blue eyes. He's Mo's nephew and, from what Greg said, a good worker. Brian is really tall with long, brown, shaggy, surfer-type hair. Greg said the kid always has his head in the clouds and his iPod in his ears.

When we reached the Snack Shack, Greg and I parted ways, since I told him I already knew Mo, and he had things to do in the repair shop.

Mo was running the Shack the last time I visited, and I remembered her as a warm, funny person. I'd been looking forward to seeing her again. Mo was in her late fifties, a retired Marine Corps cook born and raised in the South. She not only cooks up good food, but juicy marina gossip. If Mo didn't know, no one knew. She'd dated a few guys around town over the years, but when nothing jelled, she moved on to cyberspace. Gram told me she was dating up a storm on the Internet and having a ball. Some of the guys say she reminds them of a tugboat—strong, powerful, and broad in the beam.

I walked into the Snack Shack and wasn't surprised that it looked the same, except for the new white curtains and the robin's-egg blue walls. Mo manned the grill with her back to me. I took a seat at one of the six counter stools and glanced over at a guy a few stools over. He was looking me up and down as if I were on the menu, so I decided to take a little inventory myself. He had very dark, brown-black hair and big, chocolate-brown eyes with eyelashes that most women would die for. A little scar just below the outer edge of his left eye added to his subtle sex appeal. His skin was that great tan-olive color that Latin men have. His tight, black T-shirt accentuated his toned arms and broad shoulders. I didn't get a chance to check out his bottom half, but if it was anything like the top, WHOA. Good thing I was off men right now because he looked like trouble.

Mo turned around and when she spotted me, her friendly blue eyes went wide and she said, "Hey, girl, welcome back." Mo looked great. Her blond hair was cut in a short bob that complimented the shape of her round face. She looked like a chubby Doris Day.

I smiled and said, "I'm glad to be here, Mo. How are you?"

She put her hands on her hips, wiggled, and said, "Fit as a fiddle and ready for love."

The hunk at the counter piped up and asked, "Mo, aren't you going to introduce me?"

"Sorry," she said. "Tony Maroni, meet Meggie Quinn, Betty's granddaughter."

He gave me a slow, sexy smile that showed off his perfect white teeth. "Meggie, it's nice to meet you."

I could feel the blood rushing to my face as I said, "Nice to meet you, too."

Tony put his coffee cup down, gave us a dazzling smile and said, "Well, ladies, I've got to get back to work." He stood and I got a look at six feet of hunk-o-rama. From head to toe, the view just got better and better. As he walked out the door, he turned around, winked at me, and said, "Meggie, I have visions."

Mo and I laughed together.

Mo warned, "Watch out for that one. The name of his boat is *The Stallion*. What's that tell yah?"

"You're kidding, right?"

"No, I'm not. It would be tough keepin' that horse in the barn, if you know what I mean. Tony always has a girl on his boat and you never see the same girl twice. He's a real Casanova. He should put a big sign on his boat, IF THE

BOAT IS SWAYIN', THE CAPTAIN'S PLAYIN.

"Well, he sure is gorgeous. I could see him on a billboard somewhere, possibly modeling Calvin Klein underwear. He's six feet of solid muscle."

Mo sighed and said, "Yeah. He could wear one of those things. You know. One of those banana hammocks."

I laughed and said, "You mean a thong?"

"Yeah, but I like to call them banana hammocks."

I couldn't help my curiosity. "Is he a fisherman?"

"No. The only thing he fishes for is bootie. He has an auto body shop in town. The rumor around the marina is that he's connected. Probably because he grew up on Federal Hill, a.k.a., the Rhode Island residence of the Mafia. I guess that, and the fact that his uncle is Carmine "the Cannoli" Maroni, doesn't hurt the rumor either. Don't get me wrong; Tony is a good guy, but nobody you'd want to play hide the salami with."

"Don't worry, Mo, Tony really isn't my type. He's too beautiful for me. I like guys with a bit more character to their looks. I guess a bit more rugged-looking. I don't like to date anyone prettier than I am. Besides, I've sworn off men right now."

She reached over and patted my hand sympathetically. "Oh yeah, Betty told me all about that devil dog boyfriend of yours dumpin' you. He must be some kind of idiot."

I told her, "I was really upset at first. Now, I think it was all for the best. He probably wasn't Mr. Right. He was just Mr. Okay for Now."

I smiled and thought to myself, Wow, I can talk about Jimmy now without that hurt feeling washing over me.

Mo said, "You'll have a good summer up here, and if you

want to get back on the datin' circuit, I can teach you how to meet guys online. I've met a couple of nice men. No big love connections yet, but I've had some fun times and I just know my right man is out there lookin' for some huggin' and lovin'. I've decided I'm gettin' married this year. I think it's time I settle down with one guy. I'm an ex-marine on a mission for love."

"Well, Mo, I wish you all the luck. Keep me posted and I can live vicariously through you."

"You got it, girl."

"Hey, Mo, do you know anything about my Gram and her trip?"

Mo leaned closer to the counter. "I wish I did, Meggie. She was pretty close-mouthed about it. She said she was going out west to visit some friends. I never heard her talk about any friends out west. Maybe she's just havin' a late midlife crisis."

Her half-smile told me she was worried, too.

I said, "I hope so. If you hear anything, let me know."

"I'll keep my ear to the counter as always. Now how about me makin' you a nice sandwich or wrap for lunch? Or, I've got some great chowder I just made."

"A bowl of chowder would be great, thanks."

It was better than great—it was out of this world. My taste buds were singing.

The rest of the afternoon went by with Journey stocking shelves and taking care of customers. I spent some time getting familiar with Gram's computer, taking extra time studying the inventory and payroll programs.

After Journey went home at 6:00 and I closed up the store, I decided to e-mail Helen and Laura:

Hey, Girls:

I survived my first day on the job and no disasters yet. I met a lot of new marina customers and saw a few old friends. I think I'm going to enjoy being here, but miss you guys. Keep me posted on everything.

Meggie

P.S.: I've given it some thought and I think you're both right—BARBIE DOES HAVE A HUGE ASS!

I made myself a salad for dinner, then took a glass of wine out to Gram's deck. There's nothing better than watching a sunset over the water. This was always my favorite time of day at the marina. Seeing all the beautiful colors of the sky would steal my breath away while I waited for the great big ball of orange to descend. I love watching sunrises and sunsets on vacation, and though I'm not on vacation now, I'll certainly be up at sunrise.

The bugs by the water are ferocious. When I felt a mosquito take a huge bite out of my right arm, I retreated to the cottage. I'm allergic to mosquitoes so, of course, they love me. When I do get bit, I get a big welt. I'll have to remember to put bug cream on. I bought this great bug cream when I was on vacation in Mexico. They told me it worked a lot better than spray. I've used it for a couple of years, and when I put it on, I never get bitten. I was a little afraid of it at first, expecting my arm to fall off or something, but I've never had a bad reaction. Whenever anyone I know goes to Mexico, I get them to bring some back for me.

Leaving Philly on short notice, I forgot to bring some books to read, so I decided to see what Gram had. Her three favorite authors were Elizabeth Adler, Maeve Binchy, and Rosamunde Pilcher. I decided to work my way through them all and start with Elizabeth Adler's *Hotel Riviera*. Since my evenings will probably be spent alone, I'd have plenty of time to make it through the whole collection.

CHAPTER TWO

My brother Charlie finally called last night from New Zealand and I dropped the bomb about Gram. He wasn't too thrilled about having to break the news to our parents, but he said he'd do the dirty deed and have Mom call me back.

Mom's usually even-tempered and rarely loses it. The only time she would was when she was worried about one of us.

A half-hour later, my phone rang. I cringed and picked up the phone.

Mom shrieked into the phone, "What do mean your grandmother took off to go out west for the summer? She doesn't know anyone out west. I think she must be losing it. She was fine when I talked to her before I left. She never leaves the marina in the summer. I should come home and track her down."

I tried to calm her down and said, "Gram said she needed a vacation. She sounded fine on the phone. I've asked people around the marina how she was before she left, and they all said she was her usual self."

"Well, I don't believe it."

"You know how strong she is, Mom. I'm sure she'll be

fine. Try not to worry. I promise I'll call you the minute I hear from her again."

"Well, Meggie, I'll give it a couple of weeks, but if you don't hear from her, I'm coming home."

"Okay, Mom, try and enjoy your trip." I thought I'd better change the subject so I cheerfully asked, "How's the trip going?"

"It was going great until I heard your grandmother flew the coop. New Zealand is beautiful and we've met the nicest people. You would love it here. This country is overflowing with handsome young men. You and your girlfriends should try and plan a trip down here soon."

I said, "I'll definitely do that. Well, try not to worry and have fun. I'll talk to you soon."

I knew what was going through her mind—*grandchildren, lots of them.*

"Okay, honey, love you."

"Love you too, Mom."

I wasn't entirely convinced myself that Gram was okay, but hey, I didn't want to upset my mother anymore than she already was. I can't believe Gram didn't leave me a number where I could reach her. I was so surprised when she called; I forgot to get one from her. Well, when she does phone in, I'm going to get the full skinny on what's she's up to.

It's Friday morning and I have almost made it through my first week without any disasters. I think I have things under control. There were a few things I had to ask Mo and Greg about, but for the most part, Gram's notes were pretty good. If I can just make it through the weekend, I'll breathe easier. I keep waiting for all hell to break loose.

The weather's been great, sunny days with not much wind. The only boats that go out in the wind and rain are the lobster boats, unless, of course, there's a major nor'easter. This weekend's forecast calls for light winds, which means a lot of boats will be going fishing, cruising up the bay, or going over to Block Island. People would be buying supplies, bait, and fuel, so I geared myself up for a busy day.

Today I dressed in a pair of black shorts, my beige Three Legged Fox T-shirt and my old Nikes. Gram always made us wear sneakers around the marina because she was afraid we'd step on a fishhook. I twisted my mass of red hair in a clip, put on my age-defying moisturizer, and headed for the office. I'd been dreading getting up at 4:00 every morning, but since I've had nothing to do in the evenings, it hasn't been too bad.

A couple of the fishermen had charters booked. They were going out fluking and some of their customers came in to buy T-shirts and some fishing items. Gram kept a good supply of Harbor Marina T-shirts and sweatshirts on hand, along with some Guy Harvey T-shirts, which sport colorful pictures of marlin, mahi mahi, and sailfish.

The morning was flying by and I was glad to see Journey walk in at 9:00 in one of her very original outfits. I actually looked forward to seeing her fashion statement for the day. Today she was sporting a green headband, a tight-fitting, black, long-sleeved T-shirt, a pink tutu-like skirt, and under that, she wore black leggings. On her feet she had a pair of black combat boots that laced up the front. I'd be sweating like a pig in that outfit but I've never seen so much as a glisten on the girl.

"Hey, Meggie, how's it going?" she asked.

"It's been busy this morning."

"Fridays usually are. Hey, my boyfriend, Dash, and I are going to a party tonight down in Misquamicut. I know you don't know many people up here. You're welcome to come with us if you want. It'll be a crush and a lot of college kids, but it's a night out."

"Oh, Journey, that's really sweet of you, but I think I'll pass on tonight. Maybe some other time."

"Sure," she said.

"I'm going to go over to the Snack Shack for some coffee. Do you want some?"

She shook her head in disgust and said, "Never touch the stuff, but thanks."

"Okay, be right back."

Before I even got to the Shack I could smell the aroma of bacon, coffee, and onions. As I walked in the door, Mo was flipping pancakes on the grill. Seated at the counter were Kathy and Mike from the *Dancing Queen* and another couple. Kathy introduced them to me. The woman's name was Marion and her husband's was Pierce. They have the cabin cruiser, *The Lady Marion,* which I had seen down on A dock.

I said hello to everyone and took a seat at the counter.

Mo looked over at me and asked, "Coffee?"

"That would be terrific and some blueberry pancakes. They look good "

"Comin' right up, sweetie," Mo said.

I sat on the end stool next to Kathy. Mike, Pierce, and Marion were on Kathy's other side. Pierce and Marion were eating omelets that made my mouth water, and Kathy and Mike were waiting on the pancakes. They all looked to me to be around the same age, mid-forties.

I turned toward them and asked, "How are things going?"

Kathy turned to me, sighed, and said, "Well, I hate to bother you with this, Meggie, but we have a little problem on A dock."

"I'm sorry to hear that. What's up?"

Kathy turned around and shot a look to the rest of them. Marion and Pierce put their faces lower in their plates, and Mike looked out the window.

Kathy threw up her hands and said, "Well, somebody has to tell her." She took a deep breath and said, "The thing is, that new couple Cathy and Kenny on *The Grain Man* make a lot of noise. They've been keeping everyone up at night."

I asked, "Do they have loud parties or is it music?"

"It's more like a party of two. They have really loud sex all night. She's a screamer. 'OH, OH, OH KENNY. YES, YES, YES. YOU BAD BOY. DO IT, DO IT, DO IT HARDER, MORE, MORE, MORE BABY,' and it goes on and on and on. She makes Meg Ryan in *When Harry Met Sally* seem like a mute. The first time we heard them it was funny, but this goes on every night they're down here and that's usually on the weekends when the rest of us are here, too."

"When the three Howards were in here the other day for lunch, they were complainin' about them, too. They said they could hear them all the way over on B dock, and they weren't gettin' any sleep either," Mo said.

Kathy said, "I know it's kind of embarrassing for you to deal with, Meggie, but if any of us say anything to them, it'll cause a lot of tension on our dock."

Mo suggested, "Hey, Meggie, maybe you could suggest

Kenny put some duct tape on her mouth. Maybe they're into that H&M stuff."

I laughed and said, "You mean S&M."

Mo chuckled, "Yeah, that's what I meant."

I tried to sound confident. "Well, don't worry about it. I'll have a talk with them today."

The conversation moved onto other things until the four of them left. I was finishing up my pancakes and coffee, which weren't going down too good because I was freaking out. What was I going to say to our local porn stars?

"So, Meggie, what are your plans for the weekend?" Mo asked.

"Well, other than working here, not much. I guess I'll do what I've done every other night since I've been here: take a shower, make dinner, and read. Just relax."

"You're welcome to go the Pinewood Inn with me and my friends. They're all married, but once in a while we have a girls' night out. The Pinewood has a live band and a good crowd on Friday nights. Most of the people are old farts like me, but you'd have fun. We kid around and try and guess which guys are takin' Viagra."

"Oh, thanks, Mo, maybe next time."

Mo leaned on the counter and looked me in the eye. "You know, Meggie, you're too young to be sittin' around. You've gotta get over that son of a bitch Jimmy and start datin'. You've gotta climb up on that horse again." She looked up and then said, "Speakin' of horses, here comes the Stallion."

I turned to see Tony Maroni and all six feet of his handsomeness walk through the door. He had on a Hooters baseball cap, a white T-shirt that fit like a glove, and olive-green cargo shorts. I couldn't help but notice his well-muscled calves.

"Hey, Mo, Hey, Red Hot," he said as he sat down on the stool next to mine.

I giggled and Mo said, "What can I getcha, Tony?"

"I'll have an everything bagel with smear and a large coffee to go."

Tony looked over at me, wiggled his eyebrows, and said, "So, Meggie, are you going out with me tonight? I can show you sights you've never seen before."

I could just imagine the sights he would show me. In fact, I'll probably fantasize about them all night.

"Sorry, Tony, I'm not dating right now," I said.

His eyes widened and he asked, "Do you bat for the other team?"

"No, just taking a break from dating."

He wrapped his arm around me and put his face a few inches from mine. God, he smelled so good. I wondered what aftershave he used.

He said, "In other words, some guy dumped you. In that case, I'm your man, Meggie. I'll make you forget him and every other guy who ever broke your heart. I'll erase them all from your memory. Just call me Eraserman."

I laughed and said, "That's a really nice offer, Tony, but I think I'll pass."

He turned to look at Mo. "How about you, Mo? You wanta go out with the Tone tonight?"

Mo put her hands on her hips and said, "Baby boy, you wouldn't know what to do with a real woman like me. But I will say, you made my day, handsome."

We all laughed.

Mo handed Tony his bagel and coffee and he got up to go. As he walked out the door, he said, "Hey, Red Hot, I still have visions. That beautiful hair of yours would look really pretty on my pillow. Let me know if you change your mind."

When he was gone, I turned to Mo and said "Mo, I don't think I've ever been called Red Hot. I think I kind of like it."

"Enjoy it while you can, Meggie. Next thing you know you're my age and invisible. When I was your age and in the Corps, the guys called me Sizzle. When I walked by, they stood in line and saluted, and I'm not talkin' with their arms. Those were the good old days."

"Well, Mo, I think you look great."

"Yeah, well, I got a little more meat on my bones, but how's that old song go? 'It ain't the meat, it's the motion, that makes that Mama want to rock.' Well, maybe I'll meet someone at the Pinewood tonight who wants to do some rockin'."

"Have fun, Mo. I guess I'd better get my talk with Cathy and Kenny over with."

"Good luck, honey. I'd volunteer to do it for yah, but I can't piss anyone off. It's not good for business. They won't give you a hard time because there are more boats than boat slips in this area, and they were lucky to get one here. In my case, there are a lot of restaurants they can eat at, and I need to keep my customers."

"No problem, Mo. I'll let you know how it goes."

Like a prisoner being sent to the gallows, I slowly walked over to A dock and, with dread, proceeded on down to *The Grain Man,* which was in the middle on the right-hand side. As I approached, I saw Cathy sitting in a chair wearing a hot pink bathing suit top and beige shorts, sunning herself on the deck. She was a beautiful woman, very sexy-looking with just enough curves. I'm going to put curves on my letter to Santa this year. I didn't see Kenny, and I was hoping he wasn't below because it would be easier to talk to her alone.

I took a deep breath and said, " Hey, Cathy, can I come aboard?"

She looked up at me and waved me on. "Sure, come have a seat."

"Is Kenny here?"

"No, he went to the liquor store. What's up?"

I breathed a sigh of relief and went down the ladder and sat in the other deck chair.

I cleared my throat and said, "Cathy, I'm really embarrassed about what I have to say to you, but I've had some complaints from the other customers about the noise coming from your boat at night."

She looked surprised and said, "Oh. Is our radio too loud? Kenny loves his music."

"Well, not really the radio. The thing is, people have been complaining they can't sleep because they can hear you having sex all night."

Cathy started laughing. I nervously laughed with her. I'm sure my face was as red as my hair at this point.

She said, "Well, Meggie, there are some frigid people around here, you know. Maybe some of these women should be thanking me instead of complaining about me. I bet I've gotten them laid. Their guys have probably gotten hot listening to me and jumped their bones."

"Well, that may be the case, Cathy, but even some of the

fisherman over on B dock have been complaining they aren't getting any sleep, and they have to get up early to catch the morning bite."

She shook her head and said, "What's up with those guys anyway? You would think they were monks. I've hardly ever seen a woman on that dock."

"I don't know anything about that. All I know is they've been having trouble sleeping, too."

She smiled at me and said, "To be perfectly honest with you, Meggie, I just do it because it gets Kenny excited. He likes things sexy."

"Well, Cathy, maybe you could think up something else that would work as well. You could do some fantasy stuff."

"Like what?"

Oh boy, now I really stepped in it. Why did I open my big mouth? Sometimes I'm verbally incontinent.

I said, "I don't know. I'm not that experienced. Maybe you could pretend Kenny is in prison, you're having a conjugal visit, and if you make noise, he has to do more time. Or maybe he could be a pirate who kidnaps you and tapes your mouth shut while he has his way with you."

"I like that idea. It's just like Claire in *The Pirate and the Tavern Wench* except they didn't have tape back then. You must read romance novels, too."

"Every chance I get. I'll pass along any good ones I come across this summer."

"Thanks, Meggie. We'll try and keep it down. Sorry about the complaints."

"No big deal. Just keep it down and they'll forget all about it. I'm so glad Kenny wasn't here and I could talk to you alone.

I would've been so embarrassed if he were here. Have a great weekend," I said.

I climbed up the ladder and onto the dock. One fire put out, and I can only hope I won't hear any more complaints. I guess I'll have to go to the bookstore in town and buy some romance novels to pass on to Sexy Cathy. I've gotta 'fess up though. I like a good steamy romance novel myself once in a while, but don't usually admit it.

I high-tailed it back to the office to do some paperwork, which seems endless. I also needed some time to recover from my encounter with Sexy Cathy. I thought dealing with teenagers was bad. Scolding adults was twice as stressful.

After Journey left and I locked up the store, I decided I needed some fresh air. I noticed the lobster boats were in and I thought I'd say hello and introduce myself to some of the guys. They leave early in the morning when I'm opening up the store, and I hadn't had a chance in the afternoon to catch them when they come in. Perhaps someone will be around.

There were four large lobster boats on D dock and two smaller ones. Three of the large ones were owned by Mr. Brady, who was always nice to me when I was a kid. They are the *Intrepid*, the *Miss Kay*, and *The Stalwart*. The other large one, the *Allie E*, was owned by Harry Randall. The four large ones were the farthest down on the dock. I walked past the two smaller boats, the *Wake Maker* and the *Shell Seeker*, and didn't see anyone around. Further down, I spotted a man on *The Stalwart* hosing down the deck. It didn't look like Mr. Brady, so I figured it was one of the guys who worked for him. I hurried past a couple of bait barrels on the right side of the dock. Nothing smells worse than lobster bait, which is made up of dead fish parts such as heads and guts. After they fillet their catch, the other fishermen toss the remaining carcasses in the barrels for the lobstermen to use as bait.

From what I could see of the guy on *The Stalwart,* he was tall, lean, and muscular, with broad shoulders and light brown hair. I thought he resembled the guy I saw in the parking lot when I arrived. At least I'd be able to get a better look at him. He had on black rubber boots, jeans, and a navy blue T-shirt. He didn't notice me until I was right in front of his boat. He looked up and gave me a smile that screamed *sexy*. I felt the bottom drop out of my stomach. Now this was my type of guy, ruggedly handsome and scorching hot. He had a tanned, handsome face with a straight nose, strong jaw, and lips that I could make a meal out of.

I finally found my voice and said, "Hi, I'm Meggie Quinn, Betty's granddaughter. I just wanted to introduce myself."

His big green bedroom eyes looked me up and down a few times, and then he gave me that killer smile again. I felt naked and had to look down to check if I still had clothes on. A rush of heat coursed through my body and my heart started to thump in my chest.

When he finally finished taking inventory of my body, he said, "So, this is Meggie all grown-up. I guess you don't remember me. I used to terrorize you with your brothers."

It suddenly dawned on me who this mysterious hunk was who had the ability to turn me into a puddle with one look. It was Ian Brady, my first crush when I was about twelve and he was sixteen. I hesitantly asked, "Ian?"

Ian grinned, "Yep. I thought that was you the other day, but since I haven't seen you since you were about twelve, I wasn't sure."

"Well, that was quite a while ago. I hope I've changed a little since then. Are you working for your father now?"

He said, "I guess no one told you. My dad retired, and he and my mom moved to Florida. I bought the business from him."

"I remember my brother Jack telling me you went to Massachusetts Maritime with him."

"Yeah, when I graduated I worked up in Maine at a shipyard for several years, until I bought the business from my dad. How is Jack?"

"He's working on container ships. He loves it, but we don't get to see him too much."

"How about Charlie?"

"Charlie's a travel writer and at the moment is touring New Zealand with my parents for the summer. I was the only one left at home who could fill in for Gram. I'm a teacher and had the summer off."

"Well, I'm sure you'll enjoy yourself. I hope the old salts around here don't give you too hard a time."

"Everyone has been really nice and it's good to be back."

He looked around the deck of his boat and said, "Guess I'd better finish up here. I'll count on seeing you around."

I probably sounded a little too eager when I said, "I'll look forward to it."

I turned around and started back up the dock. All of the sudden my world was a happy place. If I could sing, I would've burst out in song. I walked a couple of yards and couldn't resist another peek at him. I turned my head as I was walking and slammed into one of the bait barrels. The lid popped off and half of the contents fell on the dock, the other half in the water. I wound up sprawled on the dock with the barrel next to me. My whole body was covered in fish guts. The stench was unbelievable.

I quickly sat up and wiped the back of my hand across my mouth and spit. "Oh my God. Oh geez. How disgusting. Yuck," I cried out in horror. I waved my arms hoping to shake some of the slime off my body.

Ian jumped up on the dock. He had a big smile on his face, and I could tell he was trying not to laugh.

He put his hands on his hips. "You falling for me, Meggie?"

"Ha," I said.

Since I wasn't laughing, he took on a more serious tone and asked, "Are you okay?"

"I think so, but I hope this stench doesn't seep into my skin."

He held out his hand to help me up. I reached up and took his strong hand in mine. He pulled me up and set the barrel upright.

He looked me over and said, "You'd better get cleaned up, and throw your shoes and clothes away because you'll never get the smell out of them. I'll hose down the dock."

Mortified, I said, "Thanks."

I hurried up the dock and over to Gram's cottage as fast I could, hoping nobody would see me looking like Swamp Thing. I'm sure I was a sight to behold with fish guts in my hair, on my face, and all down my body. I hosed myself down, trying to remove as much as I could before I went into the house, since I couldn't take my clothes off outside. I threw my trainers in the trash can, opened the door, and ran into the kitchen for a trash bag. In the bathroom, I tore off my clothes and dumped them in the bag. Then I got into the shower and scrubbed myself raw until I ran out of hot water.

After the shower, I put on some shorts and a T-shirt, and took the trash bag out. I still smelled like fish, but it wasn't as bad as it had been. I'll just have to get up early and take another shower in the morning.

Once I was clean, the humiliation of what happened started sinking in. I knew exactly what I did. I was so attracted to Ian that I wasn't paying attention, and my make-an-ass-out-of-yourself gene took over. Well, I guess he won't be in a hurry to see me again anytime soon. He probably had a live-in girlfriend, or with my luck, he's dating a Victoria's Secret model. It's probably just as well, since I'm not dating right now, but if I had to pick only one word to describe him, it would be *yum*.

I decided to e-mail Helen and Laura.

Hey, Friends:

What's up with you girls? Haven't heard from you. Made an ass out of myself today in front of the best-looking guy around here. I fell, got covered in fish guts, and even spit in front of him. Great first impression, wouldn't you say? I'm sure he's at home lusting after me at this moment. I think he was supposed to be the father of my unborn children, but I blew it. I think I'm doomed to being a spinster with lots of four-legged friends to keep me company. If my brothers ever get around to procreating, I'll be the eccentric aunt who spoils the kids rotten and serves pie and whipped cream for breakfast. Other than that, things are fine. E-mail me or I'll get royally pissed.

Love, Meggie

P.S.: I'm actually enjoying myself and I love being in RI, except for the fish guts.

CHAPTER THREE

Could I have been lucky enough to make it to the cottage without anyone seeing me in my fish guts outfit? No. As it turned out, one of the fishermen was on his boat, *Bite Me,* on C dock when I had my run-in with the bait barrel. He snapped pictures of me on his cell-phone camera and then proceeded to show them to anyone and everyone. Someone had the bright idea to print out the pictures and nail them to the pilings around the marina. I noticed them when I was on my way to the Snack Shack for coffee Sunday morning. Nobody has any secrets in Cozy Harbor. Gram always said she thought men were worse gossips than women. I'm starting to think she's right.

I was relieved to find Mo alone when I entered the shack.

"Meggie, I didn't see you yesterday," Mo commented.

"Well, I was kinda hiding," I said sheepishly.

Mo shook her head and said, "Can't hide from anyone around here."

I laughed and said, "You can say that again. I can't believe they put those pictures of me up on the pilings; I'm so embarrassed."

"Yeah, the boys can be brutal. Don't worry, Meggie, you'll be able to get them back by the end of summer. I've gotta tell ya, I laughed like hell when I saw those pictures."

"If it didn't happen to me, I would've laughed too, Mo. The worst part about the whole thing was that it happened in front of Ian. He must think I'm a clumsy idiot."

"So, you finally ran into Ian. I wondered how long that would take. He's a handsome devil, that Ian, and nice to boot."

"What's the scoop on him, Mo?"

"Well, he bought the business from his dad."

"Yeah, he told me all that. I was wondering what you know about his marital status."

Mo raised her eyebrows at me and smiled. "Well, I know he's single, lives alone. He inherited his grandparents' house on Sand Hill Cove and has been renovatin' it the last couple of years. Rumor has it he dates now and then, but when somebody starts to get serious, he pulls out the old dump truck. A real heartbreaker. What do you care, I thought you were off men?"

"Oh, just curious, that's all. I do have to 'fess up though. He's pretty cute. My kinda cute."

"Well, if you're gonna date one of them, you should set your cap for Ian. Tony is even more of a heartbreaker."

"I doubt Ian will give me a second thought after seeing me dancing with his bait barrel."

"You never know, hon."

"Mo, do you have any plans for tonight? How is the online dating going?"

"Well, it just so happens that I have a big date tonight. I've been chattin' it up with this guy from Warwick who works at a car dealership. I thought after e-mailin' for a month, it was time to take him out for a test drive. We're goin' to meet tonight at Foxwoods Casino. He's gonna buy me a steak at that fancy big steakhouse down there. I've never been to Foxwoods."

"I hope you have a great time."

"He gave me directions and told me to chalet park."

I laughed and said, "You mean valet park."

"Yeah, valet park. I got a new outfit and everythin'. I'm a little nervous though."

"He'll be crazy about you, Mo. What's not to like?"

"I'm not worried about him likin' me. Guys all love the Mo. I just hope I won't be disappointed. It's all about me, Meggie."

I gave her a big smile and decided I've got to be more like Mo.

The door to the shack opened and in walked Mac. He tipped his cap and said, "Hello, beautiful ladies."

Mo said, "You old flatterer. Want a cup of coffee?"

"Make it to go, Mo. I've gotta go home and get some things done at the house. I just came in here looking for Meggie. I wanted to ask her when she's going clamming with me."

I suggested, "How about Tuesday afternoon, Mac? Journey has off today and Monday, but she'll be back on Tuesday, and I can take the afternoon off."

He winked at me and said, "Meet me on my boat at 1:00, and we'll do some digging."

"Can't wait," I told him.

* * * * *

Later that afternoon, Kathy from the *Dancing Queen* dropped by the office.

"Meggie, I just had to tell you that we all got a good night's sleep Friday and Saturday. I don't know what you said to Cathy, but it worked. We didn't hear a peep out of them all weekend, and every time I saw Kenny, he had a big smile on his face."

"I'm glad, Kathy. At least something went right this weekend."

"Yeah, I saw the pictures of you with the lobster bait all over you. Are you okay?"

"Just a little smelly. Nothing that ten showers won't cure."

"You're doing a good job. Betty would be proud of you."

I reminded her, "Well, there's a long way to go until the end of August."

"You hang in there, and yell if you need anything. I owe you one."

"Thanks, Kathy. Have a good week."

After closing up, I decided to go into town and hit the grocery store for some much-needed supplies. I thought I'd better swing by the bookstore, too, and pick up some romance novels for Sexy Cathy. Gram left a note saying that she wanted me to drive her Buick at least once a week while she was gone. She said the salt air is tough on cars and it's good to start them up once in a while. Gram owned a big Buick LeSabre. I got in the car, and because it was such a nice evening, I put down the windows. I don't really like air conditioning and only turn it on when it's absolutely unbearable out and I'm ready to have heat stroke.

My first stop was the local bookstore. After looking over

the romance section, I picked out five books. If you bought four, you got the fifth free. I picked up *The Master and the Mistress, The Prince and the Parlor Maid, The Sword and the Honey Pot, The Captain and the Countess,* and, last but not least, *The Maiden and the Monk.*

When I got back to the car, I noticed the gas gauge was almost on empty, so I pulled into the gas station across the street. I couldn't believe it was a full service station. I hadn't seen one of those in years. I pulled up to the pump. A teenage boy in a uniform came over and looked at the car, then looked at me. He did this a few more times before he said, "I like your furry friend."

I looked in the backseat, thinking a cat or a squirrel must have climbed into the car while I was in the bookstore.

He said, "Not back there."

I quickly jumped out of the car and looked it over. There was a mouse running around on the trunk of Gram's car.

I'm sure he could tell I was a little freaked out. "Can you get it off?" I asked.

"That'll be an extra five dollars for mouse removal, ma'am."

I didn't know which pissed me off more, being called ma'am or the fact that he was going to charge me five dollars to get rid of the mouse.

He laughed and said, "Only kidding. I'll get it off the car."

"Well, wait until I get back in the car," I said in a panic as I threw my body back in the front seat and slammed the door.

I watched him knock the mouse off the car and herd it into the woods behind the station. When he got back, he popped the hood and found a nest near the engine. I guess when cars sit for a while, they're fair game to mice looking for a home. He finished pumping the gas and I gave him a five-dollar tip. I guess he earned it. Could this day get any worse?

The grocery store, thank God, was uneventful. I drove home and put the groceries away. By this time, the sun had gone down and it was dark. I decided to take a nonchalant stroll around the marina and remove all the pictures of me in my fish guts outfit. I was hoping no one would see me.

I walked down A dock, but all the pictures were down. As I was walking back up, Tony stepped off his boat. As usual, he looked gorgeous as ever. The man was definitely eye candy.

He spotted me and gave me a big smile. "Hey, Meggie. I saw your picture on the piling. Very photogenic, Red Hot."

"Yeah, Tony, I'm a real cover girl. You're down here late."

"I just stopped by to pick up my wallet. I left it on the boat. I'm just going to give my sister a ride home."

"Gee, that's funny. Mo told me you were an only child."

He laughed and said, "See you later, Red Hot. I'm still having those visions."

I proceeded on my mission. Nothing on B or C docks. I had just started down D dock when a beautiful black dog came running up the dock to say hello. I could tell from the way he was wagging his tail that he had Lab written all over him. Being a dog person, I got down on my knees to greet him. He licked my face, sat, and gave me a paw. We politely shook hands. He was a sweetheart.

I glanced up the dock and saw Ian walking toward me. My heart almost stopped. Tony was nice to look at but Ian has the power to turn me into a complete idiot. I can't believe the effect he's had on me. Why does he make me so nervous?

"I see you've met my best friend," he said.

I stood up and said, "So you're the lucky owner of this beautiful beast."

Ian nodded. "His name's Sam."

I petted the gorgeous creature a few more times and said, "He's beautiful. We had a black Lab female named Cassie when I was growing up. She was great at tricks. I would put a cookie on her nose and tell her to stay. She'd hold that cookie for five minutes if I wanted her to and then when I snapped my fingers, her nose would jerk up, the cookie would fly up in the air, and she'd snatch it every time. I loved that."

"Well, Sam knows some tricks, too. He shakes hands, does hi-fives, and gets the newspaper for me, but he doesn't know the cookie trick. Right now we're working on a trick where he opens the refrigerator door with a strap and brings me a beer."

I petted Sam and said, "I'm sure he'll master it in no time." I gave Sam a scratch on his ear and said to him, "Won't you, good boy?" Then I looked up at Ian and asked, "How old is he?"

"He just turned four. I got him when I came down here to take over the business."

I sighed. "I would love to get another dog, but I've been waiting until I get my own house. What are you doing down here so late?"

"I needed to drop some notes off to the other guys for tomorrow. How about you?"

"I was just looking around making sure everything was okay," I lied.

"I think maybe you were looking for these."

He gave me the papers in his hand. I took a quick look and saw they were the glamour shots of me.

Surprised, I said, "You took them down? I've been going up and down the docks looking for them. That was really nice of you." I thought, how sweet of him, and started to melt again.

He shrugged his shoulders and said, "I figured it was the least I could do since it was my bait barrel you fell into."

"Thanks Ian, I was really mortified. Not a good first impression to make with the customers. Now they all know how uncoordinated I am."

"It probably endeared you to them, Meggie."

I hoped it worked a little on him, too.

Ian cleared his throat and said, "I know it isn't any of my business, but I saw you with Tony. I just wanted to warn you; he really isn't the kind of guy you should be getting involved with. He has a bit of a reputation."

Who was he to tell me who not to get involved with? What a nerve. He sounded like one of my brothers. I hope he doesn't think of me in a sisterly fashion. Or maybe he's jealous. Wouldn't that be too good to be true?

I shot back, "You're one to talk, Ian. I've heard you have a bit of a reputation yourself."

He raised his eyebrows in surprise, laughed, and said, "I'm not in his league, honey. Tony will break your heart for sure."

"Well, maybe I'll just have to see."

He warned me, "Be careful, Meggie. I really care for your grandmother, so I felt I should say something. I would hate to see you get into any trouble this summer or have your heart broken."

Now I was really pissed. I said, "I'm a Quinn, tough as

nails. No need to worry."

He gave me a smirk and said, "I hope so. Well, I'd better get going. Goodnight."

When I first started talking to him I wanted to say, "Please take me home with you and have your way with me." After the little lecture, I just said, "Goodnight Ian. Goodnight Sam." Those romance novels were getting to me.

I watched them stride off into the parking lot, and then I walked home to the cottage, mortifying pictures in hand. I was looking at a long night ahead of me. I knew I'd replay that little scene with Ian twenty times in my head. I'd be lucky if I got a wink of sleep. When I got into the cottage, my first priority was to rip up the pictures and destroy all the evidence. After that I decided to check my e-mail. Finally, I received one from Helen.

Subject: I need a VACATION!!!

Hey, Girl:

Sorry I haven't gotten back to you. I've been so busy at work. I'm having total job burnout. This project is killing me, and the assholes who work for me have to be babysat 24/7. I was supposed to go out to The Bulls Eye and have a few beers Friday night with some of the girls but didn't get home from work until 11:00 and I was beat. All work and no play makes Helen a pissed-off girl. Anyway, this project is finishing up and I put in for a week off. I was thinking of coming up and visiting. You up for company? Let me know. By the way, Laura took the boys down the shore to her mother-in-law's, so that's why you haven't heard from her. Danny's been going down on weekends.

Oh, and don't give up the ship. We're still young and have plenty of time to find a Prince Charming. Have you seen the hunk again? If he's a real man, he'll get past the fish guts. Any real men up there for me?

Love, Hel

I replied:

Subject: Love to see you

Hey, Hel:

Let me know when you're coming. I'm so excited. Yes, I did see the hunk again and I got the impression he isn't interested. I thought he was going to pat me on the head and tell me to run along and play with my dolls. So, needless to say, I'm bummed and back to my "no men for the summer plan." I do like running the marina and so far things have been going good on that score. I'll keep my eye out for someone for you to play with while you're up here.

Love, Meggie

Now, if I would just hear from my grandmother, my world would be a lot better. I'm starting to get really worried. I can't believe she hasn't called to see how things are going with the marina. I'm expecting another call from my mom soon. If I don't have any info for her, she's going to blow.

I thought to myself, it's funny how life works. You can plug along for years and nothing changes. All of a sudden your world turns upside down. I guess you have to be prepared for anything. I wish I were.

*****

Tuesday morning the alarm went off at 4:00 and I jumped right in the shower. I'm still trying to get the fish stench off me. It's probably all gone by now, but being the paranoid person I am, I feel like I still reek.

Since it was going to be a hot one today and I was going clamming with Mac later, I put on a pink tank top and my gray swim shorts. I put my hair up in a clip, pulled on my only pair of sneakers left, and headed to the office. The morning was a little busy, but not too bad. I decided to sneak over to the Snack Shack for an early lunch.

I was glad no one was in the Shack when I got there because I wanted to ask Mo how her date went on Sunday night.

Mo turned and saw me when I walked in. She said, "Hey, girl. What can I getcha?"

"Any lunch specials today?"

"Yep. I have a roast beef wrap with lettuce, tomato, red onion, and horseradish sauce."

"You're making my stomach growl. I'll have that and an iced tea."

"Comin' right up."

"Hey, Mo, how was your date Sunday night?"

She leaned on the counter and said, "Between you and me, it was a disaster. The only thing good about it was the food. That steakhouse at Foxwoods was great, one of the best meals I've ever had."

"What happened?"

"Well, I knew right away when I saw that car salesman, he wasn't goin' to start my motor runnin' anytime soon. First of all, he was really short. I coulda' put my cocktail on his head.

But I thought, don't judge a book by the cover, so I decided to stick out the dinner. We chatted okay durin' the meal, but I could tell he was a big bullshitter. One lie after another. You know how I could tell he was lyin'? His mouth was movin'. He must have thought I fell off a turnip truck or somethin'. I didn't try to argue with him because I knew I was never gonna see him again, so why put forth the energy. The worst part of the night, though, was when we finished eatin'. He slid right next to me in the booth and turned into an octopus. Then he suggested we get a room. The clincher was when he started talkin' about how he wanted to give me all his man juice."

"Oh my God. That's disgusting."

She nodded her head. "You're tellin' me. I was off like a dirty shirt. I was bookin' through the casino to the valet parkin' area so fast that my high-heel mules were shootin' off sparks. I didn't even say goodnight."

Mo shook her head in wonder. "My perv radar must be malfunctionin'. I've been chattin' with him for about a month on the 'Net. I guess you never know."

I sympathized, "That's too bad. Are you going to keep dating online?"

"I'm not givin' up yet. I know a few gals who have met really nice people online. Besides, it's entertainin'."

"You're a brave woman, Mo."

By the time she served me my wrap, the Shack was starting to fill up with the lunchtime crowd.

After I finished every bite, I returned to the office. I wanted to finish up a little paperwork before I went clamming with Mac. Afternoons always seem a little calmer at the marina. I felt comfortable leaving Journey by herself since she was quite capable of handling things. I went to tell her I was leaving.

Journey was in another original outfit. Today she had on a tight black T-shirt and a green-and-blue plaid, short, kilt-type mini-skirt. She had pink knee socks on with black high-top sneakers.

"Hey, Journey, I'm taking a few hours off to go clamming with Mac."

"No problem, Meggie. I've got things covered here."

"I'll be back before you leave," I said, and walked out the back door toward C dock.

Mac was already sitting in his boat waiting for me, and I climbed aboard the *My Marie*. It was a beautiful sunny day, not a cloud in the sky. The water was flat calm. We headed out of the marina and crossed the deepwater channel to the tidal flat. Beyond the tidal flat sat a salt marsh, then a barrier beach, and then the Atlantic Ocean. Lucky for us, we hit the tide just right. During low tide on the flat, you can get out of the boat, and the water will only be up to your knees, perfect for clamming.

"Well, young lady, would you like a rake or are you going to do it the old-fashioned way?"

Excited, I said, "The old-fashioned way.

The old-fashioned way was when you use your feet to dig down in the sand and feel for the clams with your toes.

Mac picked up one of the rakes. "I can't do it with my feet anymore; it's too hard on my arthritis," he said.

We worked in harmony for about an hour. Between the two of us, we filled up a bucket. Since the tide was coming in, we decided to get in the boat and go for a little ride up Point Judith Pond, a large salt pond with South Kingstown on the west side and Narragansett on the east. It starts up in Wakefield and goes all the way down to Galilee Harbor, which opens up to the Atlantic Ocean. There are several small islands in the middle of the pond, and two larger islands, Harbor Island and Great Island, on the east side of the pond.

We headed up the pond, passing several boats and some enormous, beautiful homes on the shoreline. I was glad to see, though, that some of the small original beach cottages still remained.

Mac shook his head in dismay, "I can't believe some of these homes. It used to be all small summer cottages along here. In the last twenty years, people have snatched them up, torn them down, and built these large year-round monstrosities."

"I noticed that, too, Mac. It's more built-up since I was last here."

He said, "Well, I guess some people would call it progress, but I liked it the way it used to be."

"It's still beautiful, Mac. I see there are a lot of osprey nests on the poles."

"Oh yes, in fact, some people deliberately put poles up in their yards hoping that osprey will build nests in them."

As we continued up the pond, we saw a lot of other beautiful birds including egrets, cormorants, mallard ducks, mute swans, and, of course, sea gulls. We passed by a few of the summer camps for kids located on the pond. We went around six small sailboats and watched instructors teaching campers how to sail.

"Meggie, did you know that ospreys mate for life?"

"No. That's romantic," I said. I thought to myself, I'm such a loser. I'm twenty-eight with no boyfriend. Now I find out even all the birds have mates.

As if reading my mind, Mac asked, "Did you leave a boyfriend at home?"

"No. I had a boyfriend, but he broke up with me and is dating someone else."

"Well, honey, his loss is some lucky guy's gain. You're a beautiful, sweet girl, Meggie; I'm sure there is a great fella out there for you."

"I hope so. How did you meet Marie?"

He looked at me with a twinkle in his eye and said, "Well, the day I met Marie was the luckiest day of my life. It was just after I got home at the end of the war. I was a Seabee in the Navy during World War II."

"What's a Seabee?"

"Well, the Seabees was a nickname given to our battalion of construction engineers. We built airfields on islands all over the Pacific, among other things. Anyway, a buddy of mine's sister worked at the Veterans Hospital, and she wanted him to come to a benefit they were having for the disabled vets. He bought a couple of tickets, and I went along with him. It was a dance. They had a big band and a buffet, with every kind of food you can imagine. I was still trying to gain back the weight that I had lost overseas, so I headed right for the buffet. All the people working the benefit were volunteers."

"As I approached the table, I saw this beautiful girl serving food. She stopped me in my tracks. I just had to look at her for a while and appreciate her beauty. She had shoulder-length, shiny dark hair, and lovely, big blue eyes. I always told her she had blueberry eyes. She was a petite little thing with a big warm smile. I had dated different girls before the war, and a few since I got back, but I never had the kind of reaction I had when I saw Marie. A feeling of warmth and happiness came over me. I had been home from the war a few months, but when I looked at Marie, I finally felt that I was *really* home. I knew instantly that she would be my anchor. I let her fill my plate up with food, and then I asked her out for a date. We were happily married forty-eight years when she died. Oh, we had some tough times after our Billy was killed in Vietnam, but we always had each other to hang on to."

Sadly I said, "That must have been so hard for you both."

"It broke our hearts. We both loved that boy so much. We wanted to have lots of children, but God only blessed us with one. He was such a good boy. Marie loved children."

"I remember her well. She was so nice to us when we came up here to visit. She would come down to the marina with a tin of cookies and hand them out to all the kids. She made the best chocolate chip cookies. My brothers used to rave about them."

"How did you feel about your old boyfriend? Did you love him?"

"I thought I did at the time. After we broke up, I realized I cared about him, but I probably didn't love him. I think if I really loved him, I would miss him, and I don't. I never felt the way you did about Marie. I was comfortable with him, but I never got butterflies in my stomach when I saw him. When he would walk in my house, my only thought was would he want to watch hockey or basketball. He did me a favor breaking up with me. You were lucky. You had the real deal, Mac. My parents have the real deal. I won't settle for anything but that."

"Good girl. Maybe you'll meet someone up here. You

should find yourself a nice Rhode Island boy."

I gave him a wink and said, "I'm with the best guy in Rhode Island right now."

He laughed and said, "You sure know how to make an old man feel young again. There are a few nice boys at the marina. Have you met any of them?"

"I've met Tony Maroni and I ran into Ian Brady. I remembered Ian from when I was a kid."

"Tony's a nice guy. Ian I've known since the day he was born. Now there is a boy worthy of you, Meggie. He comes from a good family, and he's a stand-up guy. He's very well thought of around here. You two would be great with each other. You're both good people with big hearts."

"Well, don't get your hopes up. He probably isn't interested. He probably still thinks of me as twelve years old and klutzy. I bet he thinks of me as a sister."

"I'm an old man, Meggie, but not a blind man. I can guarantee you that Ian Brady doesn't see you as a twelve-year-old. Ian's not stupid. He's probably just biding his time and waiting for the right moment to ask you out."

As we pulled into the marina, we saw Ian on *The Stalwart* getting fuel. He looked over at us and waved. Mac and I waved back. I glanced at Mac who had a big smile on his face, and I could feel the blood rush up to mine. It doesn't take much to make me blush. I hate that about myself.

He nodded his head and with a twinkle in his eyes said, "I have a good feeling about you two."

I blushed again and changed the subject. "Mac, you know I still haven't heard from my Gram. I know my mother will call again this weekend, and she'll have a fit if I don't have some news."

"I'm sure your Gram will call soon, honey. Try not to worry."

"Thanks for a great afternoon. It helped take my mind off Gram. I hope you'll ask me again."

"I'd cook the clams for you tonight, but it's my poker night with the guys. You take some, though."

I took some clams to steam for dinner, and Mac took the rest.

"Meggie, how about we go again next Tuesday afternoon?"

"I'd love to. You know people will begin to talk Mac," I said jokingly.

"Maybe it will make the young fellas jealous," he said.

We both laughed, and I took the clams up to the cottage to put in the fridge for later.

I then made my way over to the store to check on things, do some paperwork, and call some suppliers. I caught onto things faster and more easily than I thought. Maybe I inherited some marina gene. After all, I'm the fourth generation in my family to work at the marina. After I closed up shop, I decided to go for a walk down to the beach. I needed to start getting more exercise. I've been eating all of Mo's good food for breakfast and lunch. I didn't want to gain a lot of weight this summer. My mom always said, "A moment on the lips, ten years on the hips."

This is one of my favorite times of day, especially at the beach. All the daytime beachgoers were gone, and there were just a few people walking their dogs or just taking a stroll. I walked to the left and continued all the way to the rocks. This side of the channel was called Jerusalem, and the other side was Galilee. Galilee was a fishing village and home to not only large fishing vessels, but to the Block Island ferries. It was a popular spot for tourists. People stop and buy fried clams or chowder from the restaurants, then sit on the rocks and watch the boats come in and out of the channel. I sat on the rocks for a while enjoying the passing boats and the view, which included the Point Judith lighthouse. The sun was getting ready to set, so I headed back home.

The phone was ringing when I opened the door. I ran to answer it, dreading the likelihood that it was my mother.

"Meggie, it's Gram. How are you? How are things going?"

Thank God. Just in the nick of time.

"Oh, Gram, I've been so worried about you. Where are you?"

"Oh honey, I'm fine. I'm in San Diego visiting an old friend of mine. I haven't called because we took a cruise to the Channel Islands and I just got back today."

"Mom's really worried. I thought it would be her calling from New Zealand. She threatened to come home and track you down."

"Well, I'm sorry to have caused such a fuss."

"You were just so sketchy about your plans, and it was so unlike you to take off like that."

"I didn't want to say too much about the trip and make a big deal about it, just in case I changed my mind and came home early. But, that isn't going to happen; I'm having the time of my life."

I asked her, "Who's this friend you're visiting?"

"Well, it's a very old friend of mine I knew before I got married. We ran into each other in Newport last winter and got reacquainted. My friend lives in San Diego and invited me for a visit. I needed a change, and here I am having more fun than I've had in years. So, you can tell your mother not to worry. I promise I'll call more often. How are things at the marina?"

"Going surprisingly well, to my amazement. There were a few problems among the customers, but I sorted them out. Greg is pretty busy in the shop, and Journey and I are handling the store and office. She's a nice girl. I love her outfits."

"She's definitely an original. She's a good kid. Have you been having any fun? I don't want you to work too hard. Go out sometime. Go down to Kelly's Bar on Friday or Saturday night. They have good music, and people of all ages go there. I even go once in a while when they have a good Irish band."

"I'll do that, Gram. I hope you don't mind, but my friend Helen is coming to visit for a week in July?"

"Not at all. I'm glad she's coming. You girls have fun."

"Thanks, and I can't tell you how relieved I am to finally hear from you. Keep me posted on your vacation. Can you give me a number where I can reach you?"

She rattled off some numbers and said, "If I don't get right back to you, it means we've gone off to Palm Springs or Santa Barbara for a few days. We may even hit the Napa wine country at some point."

"You really should think about getting a cell phone."

She chuckled. "Maybe one of these days. Well, take care, honey, and thank you so much for taking over for me. I love you."

"Love you too, Gram, bye."

"Bye, sweetie," she said.

I knew worrying about Gram was probably ruining my parents' trip, so I wanted them to know as soon as possible that I'd heard from her. I called my brother Charlie's cell and left a message saying Gram called and she was in San Diego with an old friend having a blast.

I was so relieved, I felt like celebrating. I opened a bottle of Chardonnay and poured myself a glass. I cooked my clams, tossed them over some pasta with a little garlic and olive oil, and made a salad. A girl has to be good to herself, right?

CHAPTER FOUR

Days fly by here because there's so much to do. Orders need to be placed, shelves stocked, and bills paid. So many people stop by to chat and though I enjoy talking to them, then I have to hustle to get all my other work done. Talking to them is always a riot because they're a cast of characters. My favorite part of the day is when I pop into the Snack Shack.

As soon as Journey showed up on Friday morning, I went over to the Shack to grab a cup of coffee. There was a woman sitting at the counter. Mo introduced us. Her name was Deb. She had short brown hair and a friendly smile. She had on gray shorts, a yellow T-shirt and a baseball cap that proclaimed "I'd rather be sailing." Mo had told me about Deb and her partner, Terry. They have the sailboat *You Go Girl* over on C dock. Known to locals as "the girls," they've been a couple for about fifteen years. Deb is a retired police officer, and Terry is a successful divorce lawyer. They'd bought their boat last year and it was their second season at the marina.

I asked Mo for a cup of coffee and sat down at the counter.

Deb asked, "How's it going, Meggie?"

"It's going great. I finally heard from my grandmother.

She's in San Diego having a wonderful time with an old friend."

"I'm so glad she's enjoying herself. Your grandmother is one of my favorite people. When Terry and I came here to talk to her about getting a slip, she was so nice. She made us feel really welcome," Deb said.

"My grandmother has the knack of making everyone feel at home."

"She's a sweetheart all right," Mo said.

Big Howard walked into the Shack.

He looked around and zeroed in on Deb. "I'm glad I found you here. I've been looking for you."

Deb asked, "What's up?"

"Well, I need to get Terry's number at work. I want her to represent my sister in her divorce," he said.

Mo looked shocked. She said, "Oh no. Tell me you're not talkin' about Sue?"

"Oh yes, I'm talking about Sue. That no-good Dave decided to trade her in after twenty years of marriage and two kids," he said in disgust.

Mo asked, "Why? Sue is the sweetest girl I've ever met."

"Well, he traded her in for some twenty-four-year-old salesgirl he picked up at a mall in Georgia. He was on a business trip."

Mo shook her head and said, "That dirty dog. You let a man out of eyeball range, forget it."

Big H said, "Deb, Sue needs a good lawyer. I want Terry to rip Dave to shreds and bleed him dry. When that girl realizes he's an asshole and broke, she'll leave old Dave high and dry. Let him see how it feels."

Deb got a pen and piece of paper from Mo and wrote down Terry's number and handed it to Big H.

"Terry's at the office today, so you should have no trouble reaching her. I'm sure she would be happy to take Sue's case. Terry isn't a good sailor, but she's a dynamite lawyer. She always goes out of her way for her clients. Sue and the kids will be in good hands," Deb assured him.

"Thanks, Deb, I'll go give her a call. Mornin', ladies," he said and left the Shack.

Mo shook her head and said, "I don't think I've ever seen Big H so worked up. I guess this business with Sue is bringing back memories of his girlfriend Ginger."

Deb asked, "What happened with Ginger?"

Mo said, "Big H and Ginger lived together for fifteen years. About five years ago, Ginger started foolin' around with a much younger guy she was workin' with. Big H found out about it and tossed her out on her rump. I haven't seen him with anyone since. Of course, that doesn't mean he isn't seein' someone, maybe he just hasn't brought her down the marina."

"I guess under those circumstances it can be a big blow to a person's ego, whether you're male or female," Deb said.

I asked Mo, "Have you ever thought about dating Big H? He seems like a good guy and you would look cute together."

Mo arched her brow and said, "Believe me, that thought has crossed my mind a thousand times. I'd go out with that big hunk of love in a New York minute, but I think," she raised her hands and made quotation marks, "he's just not that into me. He's certainly had plenty of opportunities to ask me on a date. He'll come and sit at the counter and talk to me for hours. Sometimes I pick up a lusty vibe from him, but nothin' ever happens. Sometimes it's hard to control myself. I just want to leap over the counter, grab him by his fish-blood-stained T-shirt, push him against the wall, and… Oh, sorry, girls, I got carried away."

Deb and I looked at each other and laughed. "That's okay," I reassured her.

Mo said, "I got so much passion stored up in my body, sometimes I feel like my head's gonna blow off. I've gotta get me a man soon. This isn't good for my blood pressure."

Deb asked, "Does Big H know you're dating online?"

Mo threw up her hands and said, "You'd have to be deaf, dumb, and blind not to know that around here. One time I was tellin' Dancing Kathy and Marion about a guy I just met. Big H was sittin' at the counter and got a real grouchy look on his face, slammed a dollar down on the counter for his coffee, and stormed out. Marion and Kathy think he has the hots for me and got jealous. He could very well like me, but what's a girl to do?"

I said, "I feel sorry for his sister."

Mo agreed. "Yeah, it's a shame about Sue. Why can't people just stick with their own age group? You got old geezers takin' Viagra wantin' young girls. You got middle-aged women wantin' boy toys. If someone really wants to get laid, it isn't that hard to find someone your own age to do it with. I bet I could get laid five times on the way home if I wanted to. Okay, I would probably have to stop off at the VFW and the American Legion Hall, but I could find willin' partners my own age."

Deb and I started laughing.

"Mo, you're a riot," Deb said.

"Well, I'd better get back to work. I'll see you later," I said. I went back to the office and settled down to do the payroll.

Just as I was finishing up, Journey popped her head in my office.

"Meggie, I'm leaving now. Just thought I'd let you know," she said.

"Thanks. I guess I'll close up and call it a day, too."

"Hey, Dash and I are going to Kelly's tonight if you'd like to join us."

I thought about it for a few seconds and answered, "You know, I think I'll take you up on that. I haven't been out since I got here, and I could use a night out."

"Dash and I like to go a little early before it gets too crowded. How about we swing by and pick you up around eight?"

"That would be great. Thanks for asking me."

"No problem. See you later."

After she left, I closed up the store and went to the cottage to hunt through my closet. I was hoping I would run into Ian around the marina, but I haven't seen him since Tuesday when Mac and I came back from clamming. I can't seem to stop thinking about him. Maybe a night out will get him out of my head.

I ate some leftover stir-fry I had made last night, took a shower, and got dressed. I decided to wear my favorite white skirt with a pink tank top and my shell belt. I put on some white sandals and finished my outfit off with a silver necklace, earrings, and bracelet. Since it wasn't that humid today and my hair looked great after I dried it, I decided to wear it down. I put on a little blush, some mascara and lipstick, and I was ready to go.

I'm looking forward to tonight. Maybe I'll meet some cute guy and tomorrow I won't remember who Ian is or why I thought he was so great. I can't imagine that happening, but I'll try my best. No sense torturing myself about something that will never happen. Time to move on.

Journey and Dash picked me up in Dash's old Ford Explorer, and we headed to Kelly's Pub. I'd been to Kelly's with my parents a couple of times for dinner years ago when we were up here on vacation. Kelly's is your typical local tavern. It's nothing fancy, but they have good pub food and great music. It's right on the beach, and it's frequented mostly by locals, although in the summer it gets its share of tourists as well.

When we got out of the car, I had a good look at Journey's outfit for the evening. Her hair was spiked out and she sported the usual variety of jewelry. She was in total black tonight with a T-shirt that said "Why Not?" in big white letters, and big baggy black pants that hung low on her waist, exposing yet another piercing on her belly button, where a silver peace sign dangled. I couldn't even make out what was on her feet, her pants were so long. Dash had on a pair of baggy jeans also, and an army green T-shirt. Dash was a cute guy, but he also was into the piercing thing. He had them in his ears, eyebrows, and nose. Next to them, I looked like Sandy in the movie *Grease* before the Pink Ladies did her makeover.

As soon as we opened the door, the smell of beer-battered onion rings, chicken wings, fried shrimp, burgers, and fries hit me. Even though it was early, the pub was pretty full. All the tables were taken, but we did manage to get the last three stools at the bar. I was on the end, then Journey, then Dash. I bought the first round, since they were nice enough to invite me. I got my usual Coors Light, Journey had a Newport Storm, and Dash ordered a Bud.

I turned to Journey and asked, "Do you know who's playing tonight?"

She pointed to the flyer on the bar and said, "It's a local band called Midnight Express. They're really good. They play a combination of things. A little reggae, some top forties stuff, and some classic rock and roll for the older crowd."

"Sounds great. Do you guys come here often?" I asked.

"Every now and then, not too often. Dash's cousin actually plays in the band. He's the drummer, so we usually show up when they do a gig here."

Just then Dash turned around and with genuine dismay, and said, "I was going to introduce you to my cousin Tommy, but I found out today he got back with his old girlfriend."

I rolled my eyes. "That's the story of my life, Dash, but I appreciate the thought. Do you go to the University of Rhode Island, too?"

"No, New England Tech. I'm a media major. I hope to eventually get into documentary film making," he said in a surprisingly serious tone.

Curious, I asked, "What kind of films do you want to make?"

"Well, I'm an environmentalist, so I think that will be my focus," he said.

Just then we heard two loud blasts of a horn and half the guys in the bar ran outside.

I jumped halfway off my stool. I turned to Journey and

asked, "What's going on?"

She answered, "There must be a fire somewhere. Most of the local volunteer firemen hang out here."

A minute later, they all came back in the bar and one of them shouted, "False alarm."

Just after that, the band started. For only three musicians, they had a great sound. We listened to the first set and when they took a break, Journey turned to me and asked, "Would you mind if Dash and I left for a little while? We want to take a little walk on the beach."

I said, "Sure, go right ahead. I'll try and save your seats."

I ordered myself another beer and as I was doing so, I felt a large presence behind me. I turned around and saw two huge guys. They were both about six-four and looked as if they could've been linebackers. I blinked my eyes; I thought I was seeing double until I realized they were identical twins. They ordered a couple of beers. They were cute guys with dirty blond hair, baby faces, and they looked to be about my age. They were wearing shorts; one had on a black T-shirt, while the other one had on a yellow Hawaiian shirt.

The guy in the black shirt smiled at me and asked, "Is anyone sitting here?"

"My friends are, but they went for a walk. You can sit until they get back," I said.

Mr. Black Shirt sat next to me, and his brother next to him.

Black Shirt smiled and introduced them, "Hi, my name is Dick Van Dyke and this is my brother Dave. What's your name?"

I thought, you've gotta be kidding me. I chuckled and

said, "Mary Poppins."

"Sure it is. You think I'm kidding about my name being Dick Van Dyke. I go through this all the time. Here, let me show you my license," he said.

He pulled out his wallet from the back pocket of his shorts and showed me his license. Sure enough, it said Dick Van Dyke. He looked at me with one eyebrow raised.

I said, "Okay, I believe you now. My name is Meggie."

"Nice to meet you, Meggie. My mother was a big Dick Van Dyke fan, and since our last name is Van Dyke, she named me Dick. Dave got off easy and I've been making him pay for it his whole life."

Dave agreed. "Yeah, you wouldn't believe the guilt trip I get. I think it would've been easier if I got the Dick name. We know almost all the locals around here, so you must be here on vacation."

"I'm here for the summer. I live outside of Philly. I'm working at my grandmother's place, Harbor Marina," I said.

Dave said, "Oh, we know Harbor Marina. Are you enjoying yourself?"

"Absolutely. I'm having a great time. I love Rhode Island."

"Well, here's to Rhode Island," said Dave, holding up his beer in a toast.

By this time, the bar was getting really crowded and the band started their second set. A guy came up to the twins. He was as tall as the twins but a little stockier. He had a shaved head, a pug nose, and a brown mustache. He shouted over the band, "Hey, Dick, Dave, how you doin'?"

"Great, Buddy, how are things with you?" Dick asked.

Buddy said, "I'm working too hard. I need a whore and a

vacation."

At that point, Buddy turned and looked at me.

Dick laughed. "Don't look at her. She's a nice girl. Besides, Dave and I saw her first."

They introduced me, ordered another round, and handed me a beer. I'm not much of a drinker and I was already feeling my first two beers, but I figured what the hell. I wasn't driving and I hadn't been out in weeks.

I glanced around looking for Journey and Dash and spotted them in the back of the bar talking to some people. Journey gave me a wave and I waved back. I took a look toward the front where the band was, and just as I was turning back to talk to Dick, the front door opened and in walked Ian with a girl. She was petite with a great figure; all her curves were in the right places. She had long, shiny, chestnut-brown hair, and a cover girl face. My heart dropped down to my toes and my great mood vanished into oblivion. Now I had my proof. He really is dating a Victoria Secret model. No way could I compete with her. No wonder Ian hadn't stopped by to say hi. Why waste his time with me. I was having a pretty good night until they walked in. I tried to keep myself from looking in their direction again. I didn't want him to notice me. Since I was surrounded by linebackers, there was a good chance he wouldn't.

The boys decided to order some shots.

Dick handed me a shot and I asked, "What's this?"

Dick gave me a big smile and said, "We thought because you're a redhead we'd get Red- Headed Sluts."

Amused, I asked, "What's in it?"

Dick said, "One shot of Jagermeister, one shot of peach

schnapps, and it's topped off with cranberry juice."

I needed something to ease my pain and drown my sorrows, so I downed it. The boys were commenting on all the women in the bar. Three women walked in. They were in their forties, attractive and dressed as if they were on the prowl.

Buddy said, "Look, 'Sex and the City' plus twenty years."

The twins laughed.

I was horrified. I looked at Buddy and said, "You're awful."

I was thinking to myself, that will probably be me in another fifteen years.

The band was really playing some great dance music, so I took turns dancing with Buddy and the twins. The Philly girl came out in me and I became a dancing fool. I'm a pretty good dancer, if I do say so myself. Of course, the alcohol probably helped a lot. A little liquid courage never hurt anyone. The band was in the middle of their last set, and I had just sat down for a break. Somebody tapped me on the shoulder and I turned around to find Ian behind me.

He smiled and said, "Having fun?"

I guess he saw me after all. I smiled back and said, "Oh yeah. I'm having a great time."

"Journey told me you came with them, and I told her I'd give you a ride home since they're going in the other direction."

I looked up at him and said haughtily, "That's okay, Ian; I can get a ride, and I wouldn't want to interrupt your date."

"I'm not on a date."

Why was he so cheerful and lying to my face?

"I saw you come in with a date," I fired back.

"That's my cousin Christine. She came down from Boston for the weekend. She left with some friends of hers a little while ago."

Now I felt like a moron.

I told him, "Well, I appreciate the offer, but I can get a ride."

"Meggie, do you know these guys you've been dancing with all night?"

"I just met them, but they're my new best friends," I answered meekly.

He gave me a steely-eyed look and said, "I don't think it's a good idea to get a ride from them. They look pretty wasted to me."

"I could just call a cab."

"No, Meggie. I think you should let me take you home, and I'm not taking no for an answer."

I asked, "Are you leaving now?"

"Yep, I've had enough and so have you."

"Who are you, the party police? You're acting like my brothers. I'm twenty-eight, Ian. I can look after myself."

"I'm sure you can, sweetheart, but tonight I'm looking after you and you're coming with me."

"All right, all right, just let me say goodbye to the boys."

I gave big hugs to all the boys and left the bar with Ian. As soon as I got outside, the fresh air hit me, and I realized I was drunker than I thought. I tripped on the curb and Ian caught my arm. I then felt a stone in my sandal and started to limp.

Ian asked, "What's wrong? Did you hurt your foot?"

"No. I have a stone in my sandal."

Ian stooped down and gently undid the strap on my sandal, removed it from my foot, shook the stone out, put it back on, and buckled the strap. How sweet was that? Jimmy the Rat Bastard would have never done that.

Still in amazement of his gallant gesture, I said, "Thank you."

He looked into my eyes and said, "My pleasure."

We walked down the block, and he helped me into his truck.

As we drove away, he asked, "Meggie, do you always party like this?"

Embarrassed, I said, "No, I'm not really a big drinker. I haven't been out in weeks, so I just wanted to have some fun tonight."

"Well, you sure looked like you were having some."

"Did you have a good time?"

"Yeah, I like to go to Kelly's once in awhile and listen to music. I always run into people I know."

I'll just bet he does. Probably all blond, hot, big-boobed sluts.

Being brave, I said, "I'm surprised you didn't have a date tonight. Don't you have a girlfriend?"

He turned to me, smiled, and said, "I have lots of girlfriends."

"Oh, lucky you."

"How about you? Any boyfriends back home?"

"Nope. Had one, but we broke up about six months ago. He dumped me for a bimbo."

He laughed and said, "Well, you sure attracted a crowd tonight."

I smiled. "Yeah, I did, didn't I? You should have come over and danced with me."

He gave me a smirk and said, "I'm not much of a dancer. I have other talents."

"I'm sure you do."

He pulled up to the cottage, got out, and came around to help me out of the truck. I was okay, just a bit wobbly. I gave him the keys and he opened the door for me.

He said, "Drink a lot of water before you go to bed. You'll be glad you did in the morning."

I turned around and he was inches from me. It could have been the alcohol, but I couldn't help myself. I leaned in and kissed him on the lips. He seemed surprised at first, but then he started to kiss me back. I opened my mouth and he dove in, deepening the kiss even more. His arms came around me and he held me close while he kissed the life out of me. Our tongues mingled and explored as our bodies meshed perfectly together. I put my arms around his neck and held on. He was turning me into a wet noodle. I don't know how long we kissed, but it wasn't long enough. I was hoping we would still be at it in the morning. I was so turned on, I wanted to rip my clothes off. He eventually broke the kiss, and we looked at each other. He looked as surprised as I felt.

He took a step back and abruptly said, "Goodnight, Cinderella," turned around, and practically ran out the door.

I shut the door and had to sit down on the couch to catch my breath. I put my hand in front of my mouth and exhaled. Yep, just as I thought, beer breath. My first kiss with the man of my dreams and I had beer breath.

Well, I did find out what two of Ian's other talents are. One is kissing, and the other is the hundred-yard dash.

I sat there and relived the night—the kiss, the music,

the kiss, the dancing, the twins, the kiss. Finally I got sick of myself and got up and went to bed. I guess I couldn't have been too drunk, because I set the alarm and it went off at four in the morning. I dragged myself out of bed and got in the shower. I wasn't feeling so good. There were cloudy skies in my head, but I knew I had to rally. I opened up the store and went into the office to make some coffee. Saturday mornings are the busiest, and both Journey and I were struggling. She was as hung-over as I was. I let her take lunch first. When she got back, I went over to the Snack Shack for something to eat.

With the lunch rush over, I found Mo all alone. She took one look at me and said, "Meggie, you look like a hurtin' cowgirl."

"Yeah, Mo, I had a little too much fun last night at Kelly's."

"I heard you were the life of the party, dancin' up a storm."

Surprised, I said, "Did Journey tell you that?"

"No, Don and Mikey Murphy on the *Tuna Kahuna* came in for coffee this morning and said they saw you at Kelly's."

I moaned. "Boy, I guess there are no secrets around here."

"Well, honey, I'll fix you my hangover cure. How about a cheeseburger, fries, and a big coke?"

"Sounds great. I feel like I've been run over by a truck and I'm suffering from party remorse."

"Why? There's nothin' wrong with havin' a good time."

"Well, I agree with you there, but I really blew it with Ian. He was there and saw my performance. The thing is, I saw him come in with this gorgeous girl, the every-man's-fantasy type. I was crushed and got a little bummed out and had a few too many cocktails."

"Oh yeah, I heard he took you home."

My jaw dropped and I said, "You're kidding?"

"Afraid not."

"Well, it turns out it wasn't his girlfriend but his cousin Christine."

"I've met her. She comes down once in a while from Boston for the weekend."

I confessed, "I'm going to be so embarrassed next time I see him. He walked me to my door and I kissed him."

Mo leaned on the counter. "Now *that* I didn't hear. This is gettin' better and better. Did he kiss you back?"

"Yes, I've never been so thoroughly kissed in my life. Then he said 'Goodnight, Cinderella,' and ran out the door. He couldn't get away from me fast enough. It was probably my beer breath."

"Oh, honey, I think he might just be your Prince Charmin'," she said, laughing and shaking her head.

"I wish. He probably thinks I'm a big party girl now. If he wasn't interested before, I probably ruined any chance I had with him. Besides, he told me he has lots of girlfriends."

Mo, trying to make me feel better, said, "Keep the faith, honey, you never know. Guys are slow-movin'. They might love you to death, but they fight it every step of the way. I don't know why. I guess they're all born with the stupid idea that quantity is better than quality. Eventually, they do smarten up, and then they're happier than a bear with a picnic basket."

She served up my lunch and I ate every bite.

"Mo, you're a lifesaver. I feel so much better now. I'm going to bed early tonight and I'll be a new woman tomorrow."

"You're welcome, honey."

I got through the day and went home. I checked my

e-mail and had one from Laura.

Subject: Miss you

Hey, Meggie:

Just got back from the shore. The boys had a great time and Danny came down on the weekends. My mother-in-law babysat a couple of nights so Danny and I could go out for a few cocktails. Went to the Windrose and ran into Jimmy the Rat Bastard. He isn't dating Barbie, the Bimbo anymore. He didn't say who dumped whom but I hope he was the dumpee. He asked about you and I told him you were up in RI for the summer having a wild time. He looked really sad when I shared that news. Of course, I enjoyed every minute of it. Talked to Helen, and she is really looking forward to coming up. I miss you. How are you? Have you seen that cute guy again?

Love, Laura

I answered her back.

Hi, Laura:

I'm so glad to hear from you. Too bad about Jimmy and Barbie. Do I feel sorry for him? NO! I'm having a good time and I don't really think about him anymore. Getting away has been good for my mental health. The marina keeps me busy and I did go out last night to a local pub. I drank too much, danced a lot, and am totally hung-over today. I've made an ass out of myself a few times since I've been here, but what else is new. You know me. Anyway, I did run into that cute guy again last night. His name is Ian. I knew him as a kid up here. He's a lobsterman who keeps his boats at the marina. He is hot, hot, hot. I'm totally infatuated with him, but unfortunately, I don't think he's interested. I'll let you know if anything changes. Any advice for the lovelorn? Give the kids a hug.

Love, Meggie

I hit Send and shut my computer off. I made myself some dinner and got in bed with *The Maiden and the Monk.*

CHAPTER FIVE

I can't believe next weekend is the Fourth of July already. Independence Day is a big deal in Cozy Harbor. People decorate their homes and yards in preparation for the traditional Cozy Harbor Fourth of July Parade. It's usually pretty hilarious. I've been here for a few of the parades and I wouldn't miss it for the world.

Greg came by yesterday. He told me he would haul out the decorations for the marina that are stored in the shop and enlist Matt and Brian to put them up. This is the busiest weekend of the summer at the marina. Everyone who has a boat will be down for the festivities. I'm predicting that Journey and I will have a pretty hectic week. We'll have to make sure the shelves are well stocked, which means I'll have to do inventory and order more supplies.

I had a busy morning, then I left Journey on her own so I could keep my date with Mac. It was another beautiful day with blue skies and low humidity. We haven't had a lot of rain this summer. Luckily, when it has rained, it's usually been in the evenings or in the middle of the night. So far, it's been a great summer weather-wise for boaters and beachgoers. I met Mac on his boat, and we headed over to the tidal flat, our favorite spot. We clammed for about an hour and did pretty well today, getting almost a bucket full. After we were done, we took a little boat ride over to Potter's Pond.

I asked Mac, "Are you playing poker tonight?"

He laughed and said, "Yeah, I'd better show up, too. I won the pot the last two weeks in a row, and the guys will be out for blood tonight."

"Is it a high stakes game?"

"Just a nickel a hand, but the guys take it serious. You'd think we were playing for big bucks."

"Sounds fun."

He nodded and said, "Oh, it is. We've known each other for years, and we reminisce a lot and tease each other unmercifully. Hang on to your old friends, Meggie. There is nothing better than having lifelong friends you share a history with. You laugh at the same things and have the same values. Our opinions differ sometimes, but that makes life interesting."

I told him, "I've had the same two best friends since grammar school. After high school, we went to different colleges, but we've never drifted apart. My friend Helen is coming to visit next week."

"She's invited to go clamming with us any time. I'll look forward to meeting her."

"She'd like that, Mac. I just have to warn you; she's a character."

"You girls should have a good time then."

"Oh, we will."

"Have you seen Ian lately? Any progress?"

I blushed and told him about Friday night and that I

haven't seen Ian since.

"Well, I think Ian's starting to come around. First he insisted on taking you home. That's a good sign. I don't think he liked you dancing with those other fellas. Second thing is, if he kissed you back, then he is definitely interested. It's not like you're some girl he just met. Ian's known you and your family for years. If he kissed you, he meant it."

Doubtfully I said, "I don't know, Mac. I hope you're right. To be perfectly honest with you, when I saw him for the first time after all these years, I felt like you did when you met Marie, all warm inside. Every time I see him, it's like there's this magnetic force field pulling me toward him. I never felt that way before about a guy. I can't get him out of my head. He's on my mind constantly. People always say you'll know when you meet the right one. I never believed in any of that. Now I wonder if there isn't something to it."

"Always go with your gut, Meggie."

We headed back to the marina and saw Ian coming in on *The Stalwart*. He looked over at us and gave us a wave. My heart started to pound and my hands began to sweat. I've been anxious but nervous about seeing him again. Mac and I got the boat tied up. We each took some clams, and I went back to the office.

I just got settled in at my desk paying some bills when Randy from the *Blood, Sweat and Beer*s knocked on my door jam.

He said, "Hey, Meggie, sorry to bother you."

I turned toward him. "No problem. What can I do for you?"

"Well, I had a pair of really nice Maui Jim sunglasses on

the boat, and they're missing. I could have misplaced them, but I always keep them in the exact same place, and they're gone. I just wanted to let you know in case somebody turns them in."

"Sure. I'll put a notice up on the bulletin board and let you know if I hear anything."

"They were expensive," he informed me. "My wife bought them for me for my birthday and she doesn't part with a buck easily. She told me she found them on sale. She's the consummate bargain shopper. She cruises a sale rack like a shark going through a chum slick."

I laughed and said, "I hope you find them."

"Me too," he said and left the office.

I made up a notice about his missing glasses and put it on the bulletin board out in the store. By the time I finished the bills, it was time to close up. Journey took off for the day, and I closed up the store. After sitting for most of the afternoon, I needed a little exercise, so I thought I'd take a walk on the docks with the ulterior motive of maybe running into Ian. To my disappointment, he was gone. There were a few fishermen cleaning their catch on B dock, however, and I went over to say hi. Medium Howard was there, along with Dino from *Atsa My Boat* and Jim from the *Bonnie Blue.*

Medium Howard said, "Hi, Meggie. We had a good day today. We caught a lot of good-sized fluke."

"That's great," I said. I looked over some of the fish they were cleaning. I told Dino, "Boy, that one is as big as a doormat."

Dino asked me, "Would you like a piece? It doesn't get fresher than this."

"Gee, thanks, I'd love some." I started to think about how I would cook it.

Dino put a big portion in a zip lock bag for me. I thanked him and continued my stroll around the marina. As I wandered down A dock, I saw Tony cleaning his boat. He looked up and gave me a smile. He looks great with a shirt on, but without a shirt, he is downright mouth-watering.

"Well, if it isn't Red Hot, the great hoofer, standing right in front of me," he teased.

I laughed. "I bet everyone around here knows what I had for breakfast, too."

He looked up at me and said, "A waffle?"

"Close, I had a pancake."

"Meggie, you look beautiful today. I want to skinny dip in those gorgeous baby blues of yours. When are you going out with me? You're doing real damage to my fragile ego."

"Tony, the only thing that's fragile around here are the planks on A dock. They're worn out from the parade of women traipsing down to your boat."

He winked at me. "They're all cousins. I have a big family."

"Tony, speaking of parades, are you going to be in the Cozy Harbor Parade on the Fourth? Maybe you could go as a sultan and bring your harem."

Excited, he said, "That's a great idea. I always have room for one more if you're interested."

I told him, "I'll keep that in mind. Well, I'd better put this fluke Dino gave me in the fridge. Have a good evening."

"You too, gorgeous. I'm still having those visions. I'm not giving up."

I laughed and headed back to the cottage.

After a hot shower, I put on a pair of old gray drawstring shorts and a black tank top. Since it was too hot to dry my hair, I let the air do it. I then made myself a great dinner. I've always loved to cook. I was so excited three years ago when I found out this great restaurant in Philly was offering cooking classes on Saturdays. I think I've taken every one they offered. First I had the clams, which I sautéed with a little olive oil, some white wine, garlic, hot pepper rings, and cherry tomatoes. After that, I had the main course, which, of course, was the fluke. I cooked it in parchment paper with asparagus, shallots, lemon juice, and some Old Bay Seasoning. I washed it down with a glass of Chardonnay. I'm getting spoiled by all this great fresh seafood. I can't wait until the tuna start showing up.

I settled on the sofa to finish off *The Master and The Mistress*. I'm whipping through these romances. I'll drop the ones I've finished off to Sexy Cathy tomorrow. I dozed off while I was reading and woke up when someone knocked loudly on my screen door. I got up and peeked and was shocked to see it was Ian at the door. My heart went in my mouth. I must look like hell. My hair was probably a mess, not a touch of makeup graced by face, and I was braless. Not being all that well endowed in the boob department, a girl like me needs a bra. Oh well, there is nothing I can do, he's already seen me.

I walked to the door and said, "Hi, Ian."

"Meggie, I'm sorry to bother you," he said.

"Come in," I said.

He walked through the door and ran his fingers through his hair. He seemed upset. He finally said, "Meggie, I just wanted to be the one to tell you, because stories get exaggerated.

It's probably just nothing."

I sensed by the way he was acting that something was seriously wrong. "What is it? You're scaring me."

Ian hesitated, then said, "I just went down to the boat to drop off some supplies, and on my way home, I passed by Mac's house. There was an ambulance and a fire truck there, so I stopped. They were just putting Mac in the ambulance. I know some of the firemen, and they told me Mac had some chest pains and called 911. They took him to the hospital in Wakefield."

I put my hand over my mouth and sat down on the couch. I started to cry. "Oh my God. I hope he's okay. Maybe we shouldn't have gone clamming. Maybe it's too much for him and he was just going because of me. It's probably my fault."

My Catholic guilt was overwhelming me and I became hysterical. I don't cry too often, but when I'm upset and get started, it's hard to stop. I'm not a quiet crier either. I get loud and then my nose starts to run, and then I get the hiccups.

Ian came over and sat down next to me. He put his arm around my shoulder, kissed the top of my head, and said, "Meggie, don't be so upset. It's not your fault. Maybe it will turn out to be nothing and he'll be fine. Why don't you get dressed and I'll take you to the hospital."

I snorted a couple of times and said, "I love Mac."

"I know, sweetheart. That's why I wanted you to know right away. Now go get dressed, and we'll go see how he's doing."

I went to my bedroom and threw on some clothes. By the time Ian and I got to the hospital, the ER nurse said they had Mac resting comfortably, and they were doing some tests on him. An hour went by; I paced while Ian read a magazine. He then went to the cafeteria and got us both some coffee.

When he got back, I said, "Ian, I know you get up really early. You don't have to stay. I can call a cab later. I'd like to stay until they know something."

"It would be hard for you to get a cab this time of night. I want to stay and find out how he is, too. I've known Mac my whole life. He and my grandfather were good friends. I know Mac has a nephew in Warwick. I think his name is Mike. I would imagine Mac gave the hospital that information but I'll go ask the nurse."

Ian came back a few minutes later. He told me, "Mac *did* give them Mike's number, and he's on his way."

"That's good. I'm glad he has some family close by."

Another half-hour passed and Mac's nephew, Mike, showed up. A little while later, the doctor came to talk to us. He said Mac did not have a heart attack but just suffered a little angina. They were going to keep him in the hospital overnight for observation and they'd evaluate him in the morning. If he feels better then and all the tests results are good, they'll let him come home.

I gave Mike my number and asked him to call me if anything changed.

I turned to Ian on the way home and said, "Ian, God really screwed up when he decided people should die. I don't know what he was thinking."

He tried to reassure me, saying, "Don't worry. Mac's going to be fine."

"I haven't lost anyone close to me. I guess I've been pretty lucky. When my dog, Cassie, died it broke my heart. It took me a long time to get over it."

He said, "I was very close to my grandparents, my father's parents. I was a senior at Mass Maritime when they died. My grandfather got pneumonia and within a week, he was gone and then my grandmother died three months later. My grandfather had a few problems, but my grandmother was in good shape. She went downhill fast after he died. My mother swears she died of a broken heart. They were both in their late seventies. When people are older, you kind of expect it and think you're ready. The reality of it is, you're never ready to lose someone you love. It's a kick in the stomach."

"I'm so sorry, Ian. It must have been a hard time for you."

He swallowed hard and said, "Yes, it was."

I asked him, "How did you get through it?"

"I just kept reminding myself of how lucky I was to have had them in my life as long as I did. They were a big influence on me. If I ever meet the right girl and get married, that's what I want. I want a marriage that will last forever with a person I can't live without."

I was going to raise my hand and say, "How about me?" but it wasn't the time or the place for that statement.

We pulled up to the cottage and I turned to Ian.

"Ian, thanks so much for coming to tell me and for taking me to the hospital. I'll go in the morning and see how he is."

He gave me a warm smile, took my left hand in his, and squeezed it.

He said, "He'll be fine, Meggie. I'll stop by the office to see you after work tomorrow. I'm sure by then you'll have some good news for me." He released my hand and I got out of the truck.

I shut the door and leaned back in the window and said, "Goodnight."

He smiled and said, "Try and get some sleep. Goodnight."

I went into the cottage and got ready for bed. It took me a long time to fall asleep.

*****

The next morning when Journey got in, I headed off for the hospital. The information desk told me Mac was on the second floor in room 211. I got off the elevator and ran into Mac's nephew, Mike, in the hallway.

"How's he doing?" I asked.

"The doctor was just in to see him. He said Mac's doing great and he can go home around 11:00."

Relieved, I said, "Oh, I'm so glad."

"I'm sure he would love a visitor if you want to say hi."

When I went into Mac's room, he was sitting up in bed watching TV. He saw me, smiled, and clicked off the remote.

I went over to his bed and grabbed his hand. "Oh, Mac, you gave me quite a scare last night."

He squeezed my hand and said, "Mike told me you and Ian were here. Don't you worry, sweetie, I still have a lot of time left. When the inevitable happens, I'm ready. I'll get to be with Marie and Billy, so don't you worry about old Mac."

"Well, it's so nice to see you feeling better. I can't stay long, but I'll come by tonight and check on you after work."

Mac smiled and said, "I'm always up to seeing a pretty face."

I gave him a kiss on the cheek and drove back to the

marina.

Before I went to the office, I stopped by the Snack Shack. I wanted to tell Mo about Mac.

Big H was sitting at the counter having a cup of coffee with Mo. They looked up when I walked in and I said, "Hi, you guys. I've got some bad news."

Mo told me, "We already heard about Mac. A couple of the firemen were in for breakfast and filled me in. How is he?"

I said, "I just went to the hospital. It turns out he just had some angina. They're going to release him today."

Mo sighed, "Well, thank the good Lord for that. I'm gonna make him up a couple of heart-healthy meals this afternoon. I'm pretty fond of that old coot."

"That would be great. He's being discharged around 11:00. I'm planning on going to see him after work. If you want, you can put the meals in my fridge, and I'll take them to him. His nephew, Mike, is going to stay with him for a few days just to make sure he's okay."

"Well, in that case, I'll make enough for two," she said.

I sat at the counter next to Big H. "Could I get a cup of coffee, Mo?" I asked.

"Sure, honey. I guess you had a rough night."

"Well, I felt really bad because you know how I care about him, and he took me clamming yesterday. Maybe it was too much for him."

Big H turned to me and said, "Meggie, that old man goes clamming every day in the summer and has for years. He would have been out there whether you were with him or not, so don't think for a minute that it was your fault. I guarantee you, Willard Scott will be putting his picture up on the *'TODAY Show'* when he turns 100."

I knew he was probably right, but I couldn't help feeling a little responsible.

Mo put a cup of coffee and a slice of her apple coffee cake on the counter in front of me. I wasn't going to turn down a piece of Mo's specialty, so I dug in.

On purpose, since Big H was sitting there, I looked up at Mo and asked, "Mo, didn't you have a date the other night with a new guy?"

She smiled and said, "I sure did. He was a sweet talker, too. He took me to dinner and then to a show at the Granite Theatre in Westerly."

I asked, "What was the show?"

"It was *Gypsy*. It's one of my favorites so he got special points for that. I had a great time. He's a really nice guy. I think we'll go out again soon."

I took a quick peek at Big H's face, and he didn't look too happy. He put his coffee cup down and stood.

He said, "Well, ladies, I've gotta go change the oil in my boat. Meggie, give my regards to Mac."

"I will, Big H," I said.

As soon as he left, I said to Mo, "Well, he didn't look too happy about your date. Maybe Big H will come around. It's pretty obvious he likes you."

"Yeah, but the Mo is gettin' old. I'm not gonna be this gorgeous forever. Father Time is an asshole and he's sneakin' up on me."

We both laughed.

I said, "Well, I'd better get back to the salt mines. See you later."

"Sure thing, honey."

I went back to work and around 5:00, Ian stopped by the office. I was filing some paperwork when he appeared at my office door. I looked up at his frame, which filled the doorway, the sun behind him outlining all his yummy features. As my eyes adjusted, I saw he had on a dirty T-shirt, dirty work pants, and he smelled like lobster bait. I'd never been more turned on in my life.

"How's Mac?" he asked. His level of concern was written all over his face.

I updated him. "I went to see him this morning at the hospital and he looked good. They were going to release him around 11:00. Mo whipped him up a few meals, so I'm going to take them over after work."

He suggested, "How about I run home and get cleaned up? Then, I'll stop back, get you, and we'll go together? I should be back here by 6:30?"

Trying not to sound too eager, I agreed. "That would be nice."

He smiled. "Okay, see you then."

He left and I plopped down in my chair. I thought to myself, Oh boy, I've got it bad. I hope I don't make a fool of myself.

I ran home after I closed up the store and jumped in the shower. I was just finishing putting on some lip gloss when Ian knocked on the screen door. God, does he clean up good.

He asked, "Are you ready to go?"

I waved him in. "Let me just grab the food out of the fridge."

I went into the kitchen to get the meals Mo made and

put them in a bag. Ian followed me into the kitchen, took the bag from me, and we left. It only takes about three minutes to get to Mac's house. When we arrived, we could see Mac through the screen door, sitting in a recliner. Ian knocked and Mac looked up and said, "Come in, you two."

We went in and I went over and planted a kiss on his cheek.

Mac said, "Meggie, if you keep kissing me, all the young fellas are gonna be mad at me."

We all laughed, and I blushed.

Ian held up the bag of food. "Mo made some meals for you and Mike."

Mac grinned. "Oh, that was really nice of her. Mike and I had something to eat a little while ago, but we can have Mo's good cooking tomorrow. Ian, can you just put it in the fridge?"

Ian went into the kitchen.

I asked Mac, "Where's Mike?"

He said, "He went home to get some clothes and should be back in a little while. I feel bad taking him away from his family."

"Well, I'm sure he's glad to be here for you," I said.

Ian walked back in the room and inquired, "How are you feeling, Mac? What did the doctors say today?"

Mac told us, "They gave me some medication and told me I had to get plenty of rest and lay low for a while. I'm feeling better already. I probably do too much sometimes. Once in a while, I guess I have to remind myself I'm eighty-eight years old."

Mac looked at me and said, "Meggie, I want you to use my boat anytime you have a chance. You know where I hide the key. You can run that boat as well as I can. You should take your friend out clamming when she gets here."

"I'll take you up on it, Mac. When you feel better, maybe you can come down and I'll take you both for a ride up the pond."

Mac smiled and said, "That will give me something to look forward to."

Mac asked Ian how the lobstering had been, and they talked about that in detail. After a while, Ian stood up and said, "Well, you should probably get some rest. We don't want to wear you out."

Mac asked, "Are you two going out to dinner?"

To my surprise, Ian immediately said, "Yes."

Mac waved cheerfully. "Enjoy your dinner."

When I bent down to give him a kiss goodbye, Mac winked at me. I knew exactly what my old friend was up to. I told him I would come by sometime tomorrow to check on him.

As we walked to the truck, Ian asked, "Where would you like to go, Meggie?"

I said, "Ian, Mac put you on the spot back there. If you have other plans, don't worry about me."

He said, "I would like to go to dinner and we both have to eat. Now where would you like to go?"

"This is your neck of the woods. You know more places than I do."

"I know a great place. Are you sick of fish by now?"

"Are you kidding? I could eat fish every day of the week."

"My kind of girl."

The restaurant was pretty crowded, but they had a table

for us. We ordered an appetizer of fried calamari to share, and we both ordered the seared sesame tuna with soy and wasabi for our entrées. The waitress opened the bottle of wine that Ian ordered and poured us both a glass.

We each took a sip.

Ian asked, "Do you like teaching?"

"I basically decided to be a teacher because I really didn't have any idea of what I wanted to do. I'm not passionate about it like some of the other teachers I work with. I work with some amazing people. I'm not a bad teacher. I try and make the classes fun and informative for the girls, but my heart just really isn't in it. The main draw to teaching for me was having the summers off. I thought a lot about changing careers this past year. To be perfectly honest, I've enjoyed working at the marina this past month more than I've enjoyed teaching these past few years. I love being by the water and not being stuck in a classroom all day."

He said, "I know what you mean. When I got out of college, I went to work in a shipyard as an engineer. It was a good experience and I learned a lot, but I love being out on the water, and I like working for myself. When my dad decided to retire, I jumped at the chance to buy the business. I think it was always in the back of my mind that I wanted to do that, but I felt I should have another work experience just to make sure. I also missed Rhode Island. Maine is beautiful, but it's just not home."

"You were very lucky to grow up here. I know my mother misses Rhode Island."

"They say when you're trying to figure out a career path, you should try and think of where you want to be in your life ten years down the road. I knew this is where I really want to be. What do you see yourself doing in ten years?"

I thought about it for a minute and said, "As far as a career, I don't have a clue. I do hope that by that time, though, I'll have a family of my own. I definitely want to have kids."

"I was an only child. If I ever have kids, I'd want more than one. I would want them to have each other."

"When I was a kid, I sometimes wished I were an only child. My brothers could drive me crazy; it was always two against one. I could bore you all night with tales of how they terrorized me. They were very creative and I never knew when they would strike. Those two were pretty slick."

He laughed and said, "If you remember, I got in on a few of those when you were up here on vacation."

"That's right, you were. You should be extra nice to me to make up for it."

He gave me that killer smile of his and said, "I'll see what I can do."

The waitress served the calamari, and we settled in to enjoy our meal. The calamari was tender and cooked to perfection. The tuna was even better. We talked about friends, our families, and places we've traveled to and would like to go. Ian told me he tries to take a couple of trips every winter.

I made a mental note to renew my passport, just in case.

Ian cleaned his plate and finished off my tuna for me. I was stuffed.

While we waited for the check, I said, "That was just too good. I'm definitely going to have to walk more at night. The food up here is unbelievable."

"Would you like to go for a walk?"

"I'd love that."

I offered to buy dinner, but he insisted on paying. We got back in his truck and drove over to Narragansett. We found a place to park up by the Wishing Well and crossed Ocean Road to the sea wall, which is a popular place year round to stroll and enjoy the views of Narragansett Bay. Before we crossed the street, Ian took my hand. My hand felt so small compared to his. He had a working man's hands— strong, rough, sexy. As we walked along, I could smell the ocean and hear the surf pounding on the rocks. It was a beautiful evening with just a gentle breeze. We walked toward the Towers, two stone structures at either end of an enclosed bridge that crosses Ocean Road. The Towers were all that's left of the Narragansett Casino, which burned down in a fire in 1900. Further down past the towers was the Narragansett Town Beach. It's a nice walk with stunning scenery.

By the time we headed back toward Ian's truck, it was starting to get dark. We walked along in companionable silence. I didn't want to just babble and I didn't feel I needed to. I was just enjoying being with him.

On the drive home, I said, "Ian, this was a nice evening. I'm so glad Mac is feeling better."

"Me, too. I'll be honest, when I saw that ambulance last night I thought the worst. I thought his color was good tonight though. I think he's on the mend."

At the cottage, he walked me to my door. He took my hand and pulled me close. My heart started to pound, and I got that warm feeling I always get when I'm close to him.

He lean down and kissed me, warmly and gently. I put my arms around his neck and kissed him back. He removed my hair clip and ran his fingers through my hair. We finally came up for air, he nibbled on my neck, worked his way up to my cheek and gave me a quick peck on the lips.

Ian then drew back and handed me my hair clip. He looked at me with sultry eyes and said in a husky voice, "You have the most beautiful hair I've ever seen. I just had to get my hands on it. It's like silky fire."

I blushed and whispered, "Would you like to come in?"

He smiled and said, "I think I'd better go."

Disappointed, I said, "Thanks again for dinner."

"My, pleasure."

He turned and did his hundred-yard dash through the parking lot.

I went into the cottage a little sad but happy at the same time. I didn't want the evening to end. It was a magic night. Mac is feeling better and I think Ian and I just had an unofficial date. I probably shouldn't have asked him in, but I couldn't help myself. The words just came out of my mouth. I hope he doesn't think I'm easy now. He is so nice and handsome and sexy and sweet. I know I shouldn't, but I'm falling fast.

I checked my e-mail before I went to bed. There was one from Helen, and one from my parents in New Zealand. I decided to read Helen's first.

Hi, Meggie:

I'm planning on driving up on Sunday. Can't wait. I got directions on the Net. I'm planning on getting up at 4:00 A.M. and hitting the road to beat the traffic. Do you want anything from Philly? If so, let me know. I need this vacation bad. Have you found anyone for me to play with?

Love, Hel

I answered back.

Hi Helen:

I can't wait to see you. I just had an unofficial date with the perfect man and I'm in total like and lust. I only hope I'm not setting my self up for another heartbreak. My fragile heart can't take another crack. I'll fill you in when you get here. I'm sure you won't have a hard time finding someone to play with while you're here. You were the queen of the playground since first grade. See you Sunday.

Love, Meggie

I then read my mom's e-mail.

Hi, Meggie:

We're having a great time. Charlie keeps us really busy. Have you heard from your grandmother again? Hope things are going well at the marina.

Love, Mom

I guess it's time to bite the bullet and call Gram. Because California is three hours behind, I figured it wasn't too late to call.

I dialed the number she gave me. It rang a few times and a man answered in a cheerful voice, "Cal O'Callaghan."

Did I have the wrong number? I tentatively asked, "Is Betty there?"

He said, "Is this Meggie?"

Surprised, I said, "Yes, it is."

He said, "I'm Betty's friend Cal O'Callaghan. I've heard

all about you."

I didn't know quite what to think, let alone what to say. I finally said, "Is my Gram there?"

"Yes, my dear, I'll go get her for you."

Gram came on the line and said, "Hi, Meggie. Is everything okay?"

I told her, "Yes everything is fine here. Mac had a little angina and was in the hospital overnight, but he seems to be bouncing back."

"Oh, honey, I'm sorry to hear that. You give Mac my love. How's the marina?"

"The marina is fine, Gram. I just called to see how you were. What have you been doing? Most of all, who's Cal?"

She laughed and said, "Are we sure I'm the grandmother and you're the granddaughter? I thought I was supposed to ask all the questions. Well, Cal is my old friend, Meggie. We've been having a lovely time. Last week we went to Santa Barbara for a few days and we visited Hearst Castle. I thought the mansions in Newport were spectacular, but Hearst Castle is something else."

"Mom e-mailed and asked about you, so I thought I'd call and check on you."

"I'm fine, darling. Couldn't be better."

I smiled to myself and said, "Well, Gram, you keep having fun, and I'll let Mom know you're okay."

"Please do that, honey, and again, give Mac my love."

"I will, Gram. Love you."

"Love you too. Goodbye."

I hung up in shock. I wanted to ask her more about Cal, but how do you ask your grandmother if she has a boyfriend.

Hey, Gram, are you sleeping with Cal? Are you doing the rumba between the sheets? I just couldn't do it. I've never heard her sound so happy. Whoever Cal is, if he can make my Gram sound that happy, he's okay in my book.

I quickly e-mailed my mother back.

Hi Mom:

Just talked to Gram and she's doing well and having a great time. I miss you and I'll keep you posted on Gram.

Love, Meggie

CHAPTER SIX

The next morning after Journey arrived, I went over to the Snack Shack for a late breakfast. Mo stood behind the counter, hands on hips, looking at the four large tubs of chicken wings in front of her.

I asked her, "What's with the chicken wings?"

She leaned on the counter and said, "Oh, my God. I've got a gazillion orders for these wings. Every fisherman in Cozy Harbor wants at least two orders for the weekend."

"They must be really good. I don't think I've ever had them."

"Well, most of them haven't either. I'm gonna put them in the fridge and I'll be cookin' them tomorrow afternoon. I'll be lucky if I get out of here by midnight."

I asked, "Why the run on chicken wings all of a sudden?"

"Well, the warm water has moved into the canyon. It's about eighty miles offshore and a prime fishing area for tuna and mahi. The Murphy brothers went out to the canyon fishin' the other day on the *Tuna Kahuna*. I guess there were quite a few boats out there and no one was catchin' a thing. The boys bought some wings from me before they went out fishing.

Don was chompin' down some wings and tossing them in the water. Next thing you know, all their rods were bent over and they caught six yellowfin tuna and a couple mahi. None of the other boats got so much as a nibble. When they filleted the fish, guess what was inside?"

"Your chicken wings?"

"You got it. Now every fisherman around thinks my wings are the best bait goin'. I'm thinkin' of raisin' my prices."

I laughed and said, "That's unbelievable."

Mo shook her head and said, "Believe me, it was just a fluky thing. These fishermen will try anythin' to catch a fish. They'd throw their own mother overboard if they thought she'd make good bait."

"If you want, Mo, I'll be happy to help you after work tomorrow."

"Oh, Meggie, you're a lifesaver."

"No problem. Can I get a cup of coffee and a bagel?"

"Sure, just let me get these wings in the fridge."

Mo put the wings away and made my bagel for me.

She asked, "What's the latest on Mac?"

"Ian and I went over to see him last night and he's doing much better. He said to thank you for the meals."

"Good. So, you and Ian went together?"

"Yes, and afterward we went for dinner and a walk at the sea wall."

"A walk at the sea wall sounds pretty romantic to me. I'm so happy for you, honey." She raised her eyebrows and asked, "Any action afterward?"

"He kissed me goodnight and left. I invited him in, but he said he had to go."

"He must think you're special. I know a couple of local girls who went out with Ian, and I never heard nothin' about him bein' a slow mover."

"Well, I hope that's a good sign, but he needs to speed things up. I'm only here for the summer. Gram will be back before you know it. By the way, I talked to her last night. I called her at the number she gave me and a man answered the phone."

Mo looked shocked and said, "Get out of town!"

"Nope. The friend she went to visit is a guy named Cal."

"Well, I'll be damned. Good for her."

"Yeah. She told me they just got back from Santa Barbara and had a lovely time. I couldn't believe it. I wanted to ask her so many questions about Cal, but I felt uncomfortable."

"Well, sure. I can see why."

"I'll tell you, Mo, she sounded so happy."

"Well, honey, that little bit of info made my day. Maybe there's hope for the rest of us lonely hearts. Who would have ever thunk it, though. Betty has a boyfriend."

"Well, keep this info under your hat, or I guess I should say under your counter, Mo. Gram wouldn't want everyone knowing her business."

"My lips are sealed, sugar."

"Thanks and thanks for breakfast."

"Anytime."

"See you later," I said and left the Shack with Mo smiling and shaking her head.

I went back to work and the rest of the day went by fast. I decided that before I went home, I would check on Mac's boat. I walked down the dock and saw Tony on Mac's boat giving it a good cleaning.

He looked up at me and gave my body the once-over. "You look gorgeous as usual, Meggie."

I looked down at myself. I had on a pair of old white shorts and a navy blue Harbor Marina T-shirt.

"Tony, you must have had a slow week with the ladies if you think I look good."

"Are you kidding, Meggie? You always look smokin' hot."

"You always have a line, Tony. It's so nice of you to clean Mac's boat. You're just a teddy bear under that macho veneer."

"Well, the Tone has a soft spot for the old Clam Man. I'll let you in on a little secret. When I bought my boat, I didn't know a thing about them. I was a city kid. I'd been out on a few boats, but I basically hadn't a clue about boating. I figured, hey, I have a business down here, I live near the water, I should have a boat." He gave me a leer, wiggled his eyebrows, and said, "Besides, I figured the ladies would love a boat ride. So, I bought a boat and didn't know what to do with it. I was nervous as hell to take it out. Well, Mac had my number from the get go. That old man spent that whole first summer with me. He taught me the rules of the road out there and taught me about engines and electronics. I owe him big time and I'll never forget it."

"That's Mac."

"Well, I heard you check up on him. You tell him I'm taking care of his boat and I hope to see him soon."

"I will."

"Hey, you want to go out this weekend?"

"I can't. I've got to help Mo tomorrow night and Saturday night I have to clean the cottage. My friend is coming to visit for a week, so I have to get ready for company."

"Is she of the female persuasion?"

"Yes."

"Well, since my charms haven't worked on you, maybe you could introduce me?"

"I'll think about it. You might just meet your match. She's a man-eater."

He smiled, licked his lips, and said, "Well, sweetheart, I'm a tasty morsel."

I chuckled "See you later, lover boy."

"Night, hot stuff."

I went home, took a quick shower, ate some dinner, and went to check up on Mac. Mike was still there and Mac was doing a lot better. I visited for a while and headed home.

* * * * *

The next morning I was in my office e-mailing some supply orders when I heard a knock. I turned around and smiled at my Gram's best friend, Dossie Woods. They've been friends since they were young girls.

I stood up and said, "Mrs. Woods, what a nice surprise."

She gave me a warm smile back and said, "You're all grown up, Meggie. Let me have a good look at you." She lifted up my chin to look at my face and exclaimed, "Pretty as a picture."

I blushed and asked, "How are you?"

"Good, honey. I came by to see if you've heard anything from your grandmother?"

"I just talked to her. She's with her friend in San Diego having a great time."

"Oh, I'm so glad to hear that. I miss her, but if anybody deserved a vacation, it's Betty."

"Mrs. Woods, do you know an old friend of Gram's named Cal O'Callaghan?"

She looked nervously around the room and answered, "No, don't think I can recall anyone with that name."

I pressed on, "Are you sure? Gram said she knew him years ago."

She shook her head, "No, I don't remember him. Well, I hate to run, Meggie, but I'm playing in a little nine-hole tournament at the country club. If you can believe it, I'm the ringer in my foursome."

"Do you still play a lot of golf?"

"Every chance I get. Tell your grandmother to call me when she has a minute."

"I will. It was nice seeing you."

"You too, dear."

She hightailed it out of the store. There's no doubt in my mind that Dossie knows exactly who Cal O'Callaghan is. I can't imagine my grandmother not telling Dossie every little detail about this big adventure of hers. I should have thought of Dossie a few weeks ago when I was up to my ears with worry. I guess I'll have to wait a little while longer to find out more about the mysterious Mr. O'Callaghan.

Later, it got crowded in the store, so I went out to give Journey a hand. Don and Geri on the *She's the Boss* told me they were missing a big flashlight. Since they never take it off the boat, they couldn't imagine where it had gone. They asked around if anyone had borrowed it, but everyone said no. I told them I'd put a notice on the bulletin board and let them know if someone turned it in.

People here have never had to worry about leaving their boats open. I can't imagine who would be stealing things. For now, I'm going to assume that the glasses and flashlight are just misplaced and will turn up eventually.

I was hoping to catch a glimpse of Ian today, but no such luck. I closed up the store and went over to the Snack Shack to help Mo with the wings. Since she starts work as early as I do, she usually closes at 2:30 after she takes care of the lunch crowd. The Shack had a Closed sign on the door, but I could see her behind the counter. She waved me in.

"How are things going?" I asked.

"I've been busier than a rooster in a henhouse today. Everyone is down for the weekend, so I extended lunch until 3:00, and then I had to prep for tomorrow. So, my friend, I'm just startin' on the wings."

"What can I do?"

"Well, the first thing we need is mood music. Why don't you go put that oldies station on the radio. When I'm runnin' on fumes, I need good tunes to pick me up."

I went over and turned on the radio. According to the DJ, it was sixties night.

Mo rubbed her hands together. "Boy, we hit the jackpot. I love sixties music. It brings back good memories for me."

We sang, danced, and worked on the wings. Mostly though, we talked. Curious, I asked, "Mo, where are you from originally?"

"I'm from the great state of Alabama," she proclaimed with pride.

"How did you end up in Rhode Island?"

"My brother Tom got transferred up here with his job about twenty years ago. Whenever I got leave, I would come up and visit him, his wife, Mary, and the kids. The kids are grown up now. The eldest one is Amy; she's a beautiful girl. She and her husband, Neil, live here, and they're expectin' their first. The next in line is Becky. She followed in Aunt Mo's footsteps. She's a pastry chef at one of those ritzy, glitzy restaurants up in Providence. Matt's the baby of the family, the apple of my eye. I don't know how much you've talked to him since you've been here, but that boy is funny as hell. Well, by the time I got out of the Corps, our parents had passed on. I wanted to live near family, so I moved up here, bought my little house, and started workin' here."

"Do you miss the South?"

"Sure, especially in the middle of winter. I still have friends and cousins down in Mobile that I visit every January."

"Any more Internet dates?"

"Yeah, I went out with a good-lookin' tall drink of water the other night. He lives in Providence so we met at a restaurant in Warwick for dinner. He was a nice guy, very mannerly, and I didn't pick up any perv vibes, which is always a good sign. He's a widower with two grown girls."

"Sounds promising."

"Yep. I'll definitely go out with him again."

"What happened with the other guy who took you to the theater?"

"He's out of town. To be truthful, though, I had a great date with him but the sparks weren't flyin'."

"Oh, that's too bad."

She shook her head and said, "My big problem is I gotta

get that big galoot out of my head."

"You mean Big H?"

"Yeah. I think I'm being picky because I want every guy I meet to be him. Just when I think I'm over him, he stops by and chats with me for an hour, and then I'm all mushy about him again."

"Guys will do that to you."

"Any progress with Ian?"

"Nope, I haven't seen him since the other night. I was hoping he would stop by and ask me out, but no go."

"Hey, I've got a bottle of wine in the fridge here. Since we're halfway done, let's open it and have a few glasses. Girls have to have some fun on a Friday night."

"Sounds good to me, Mo."

She poured us each a big glass of wine. We were drinking and singing along with Aretha Franklin when there was a knock at the door.

I opened the door and in walked Big H.

"Evenin', Meggie, Mo." He looked at Mo and said, "Mo, I'm sorry I didn't get to ask earlier, but I was wondering if I could get a couple orders of wings. I'm going fishing tomorrow along with every other boat around. I don't believe in the chicken wing theory, but if all the boats catch fish with the wings and I don't catch a thing without them, I'll never hear the end of it."

Mo said, "No problem. I planned on makin' extra just for this reason. I figured tomorrow mornin' a couple of extra people would show up wantin' some."

"Thanks, Mo. Hey, I don't know if you girls have plans to see the fireworks on Monday night, but if you don't, you're welcome to come with me. I'm taking the boat out to watch the town beach fireworks. It's fun watching them from the water. I've invited my sister Sue and her kids, plus I invited Terry and Deb."

I said, "Oh, thanks, Big H, but I've got my friend Helen coming up for a week, and she gets here on Sunday."

He said, "She's welcome too, Meggie."

I said, "Thanks. I'll let you know."

Big H looked at Mo and asked, "How about you?"

"Sounds good to me. What time you leavin'?"

"Come around seven, after the parade. We're having a potluck dinner first."

Mo told him, "I'll bring somethin' tasty."

He tipped his cap. "Well, goodnight, ladies. Mo, I'll see you in the morning for the wings."

After Mo made sure he was halfway down the dock, she turned and said, "I can't believe he invited me. That's a first. See, it's just like I said. I almost have him out of my head, and he pops right back in. He's like a friggin' jack-in-the-box."

I threw my hands up. "Men! Who knows what they're thinking."

"You got that right, girlfriend."

We finished off the wings and the bottle of wine. I helped Mo put everything away, said goodnight, and went home. It was 11:00; I had just put on my pajamas when there was a knock at my door. Since it was late and dark, I peeked out the door. I was hoping to see Ian, but to my shock, it was Jimmy the Rat Bastard—in the flesh.

I yanked opened the door. "What in the world are you doing here?"

He said, "Meggie, I need to talk to you."

He sounded desperate.

I was confused. "Why? I don't really know what we'd have to say to each other. You pretty much said everything six months ago."

"Please, Meggie, let me come in and hear me out."

"I'll let you in, but you're wasting your time. How did you find me?"

I ushered him in. I sat on a chair so he wouldn't sit next to me, and he took the sofa.

He said, "I ran into Laura and she told me you were up here. I remembered you talking about the marina and I remembered the name. I got directions on the Internet and drove up."

Curious, I asked, "So, what is it you have to say to me?"

He took a deep breath. "Meggie, I was a fool. I felt that we were getting serious, so I panicked and told you I wanted to take a break. I've dated a few people since we broke up, and I finally realized that I would never find anyone like you. I know I blew it, and you don't have any reason to trust me, but I'd really like you to give me another chance."

"What happened with Barbie?"

"Oh, she was just too high maintenance. She always wanted me to take her somewhere. It was either a concert, a party, a new restaurant, or to a bar to hear some band. She was costing me a fortune. You were so easy to be with. You just liked to hang out and watch TV."

Boy, he doesn't have a clue.

I said, "That's not true. I love to do things. Look, I was really hurt when you broke up with me. In the end, though, it was the best thing you ever did for me. I've thought about this a lot, and we were never right for each other. We have different interests. We wouldn't have worked in the long haul."

He looked bewildered and said, "We had things in common."

"Not the important things. At least, not the things that matter to me."

"I can change."

"Jimmy, people don't change, and I wouldn't want someone to change for me. I want to love someone just the way he is, and I want someone to love me the same way. We were comfortable with each other, but that's not enough, at least not for me. Besides, after the way you treated me, I don't think I could ever forgive you. You killed any feelings I might have had for you."

"I'm sorry you feel that way and I never meant to hurt you. I came up here ready to ask you to marry me."

I was floored. I couldn't believe what just came out of his mouth.

"Jimmy, I'm sure there is a right person out there for you; it just isn't me."

What I really wanted to say was, "Are you out of your freakin' mind?"

He shrugged his shoulders. "You can't blame a guy for trying. We did have some good times, though. I hope you remember those."

"Of course I will."

He narrowed his eyes and said, "Is it because you've met someone else?"

"No. That's not it at all."

He asked hopefully, "Is there anything I can do or say that would make you change your mind?"

Sadly, I said, "No."

He stood and said quietly, "Well, I guess I better go. Is there a motel around here? I've just drove six hours and I'm beat."

I couldn't believe it, but I felt sorry for him. I said, "You can sleep on the couch. I get up at 4:00. I'll wake you up and you can head back and beat the traffic."

"Thanks. I'll get my bag from the car."

I went and got him a blanket and pillow. He came back into the cottage, I showed him where the bathroom was, and said goodnight. I shut the door to my room and sat on the bed, my mind constantly flashing back over the three years Jimmy and I were together. I heard him use the bathroom and get settled on the couch.

It was a pretty restless night for me. I dragged myself out of bed when the alarm went off, dressed, and walked into the living room. Jimmy was already up folding the blanket I'd given him.

I asked cheerfully, "Did you sleep okay on the couch?"

"It was comfortable, but I didn't get much sleep. Are you sure about us, Meggie? Maybe you just need a little time to think about us being together again."

My response left no doubt. "I'm sure. I won't be changing my mind. I'm sorry, but we're over. Come on, I'll walk you out on my way to the store."

I may have been imagining it, but I actually thought I saw tears in his eyes. He was probably welling up thinking about all the money he would have to spend dating. He grabbed his bag and we walked out to his car in the marina parking lot.

He turned to me and said, "I hope you're happy, Meggie."

I gave him a hug and said, "I hope you are too, Jimmy."

I watched him drive away. I thought to myself, I gave that guy probably three of the skinniest years of my life. Since he dumped me, I'd daydreamed that he would come crawling back, begging for my forgiveness. Of course, I would turn him down and enjoy every minute of it. Now that it's actually happened, I just feel sad. As I turned toward the store, I saw Ian standing next to his truck watching me with a cold stare. He slammed his truck door and stormed off toward the dock. I knew right away what he thought he saw. I ran after him to clear up the misunderstanding.

I yelled, "Ian, wait!"

He ignored me and kept walking.

I ran after him. Finally catching up to him, I said breathlessly, "Ian, that wasn't what you think it was."

He said stiffly, "It doesn't matter what I think. We had a couple of kisses, no big deal. You can sleep with anyone you want. It's none of my business."

I pleaded with him. "Please, let me explain."

He wouldn't even look at me. He shouted, "I've gotta go, I'm running late." He jumped on his boat, started the engines, and pulled away from the dock.

I watched the boat until it was out of sight. I felt sick to my stomach and tears streamed down my face. I hadn't even realized I started to cry. Why can't I get a break? Why does everything always have to be so hard for me? He just assumed I went out last night, picked up a stranger, and brought him home for a wild night. That is *so* not who I am. He must have a very low opinion of me. It hurt that he didn't care enough to give me a chance to explain. When will I ever learn? Well, I'm done making a fool out of myself. No more mooning over Ian. Obviously, he wasn't interested in me anyway. If he cared at all, he wouldn't have been so quick to jump to the wrong conclusion.

Well, back to plan A: no more men this summer. I'm going to keep my nose to the grindstone, have fun with Helen, and keep this marina running to the best of my abilities. I'm doing it for Gram. I just wish my heart didn't hurt so much.

* * * * *

This was the busiest Saturday since I've been here, which was a good thing because it took my mind off my nonexistent love life. A lot of the fishermen were out fishing with their chicken wings, but we had a steady stream of tourists come through. I don't know what I'd do without Journey. She's great with the customers and knows the area so well. She's always giving someone directions, recommending restaurants, or helping people decide which local beach they might prefer. We both breathed a sigh of relief when we locked up at 6:00.

Before I went home to clean the night away, I decided a walk out on the docks might cheer me up. I noticed most of the fishing boats on B dock were still out, so I took a stroll down A dock where the cabin cruisers sat. All of A dock was in Fourth of July party mode. People sat on their deck chairs having cocktails, blenders buzzed, and music blared. I walked up to the *Dancing Queen*. Sitting on the boat were Kathy and Mike, Marion and Pierce, and to my surprise, Sexy Cathy and

Kenny. They were drinking martinis. I guess all's forgiven and peace reigns on A dock.

Dancing Kathy looked up. "Meggie, come have a martini with us. Mike makes the best dirty martini you'll ever taste."

I smiled, "Kathy, I'm a lightweight, but I'll have a beer if you have one."

Mike said, "Coming right up." He reached into a cooler and handed me a Coors Light.

Since the boat was full, I sat on the dock in front of it and dangled my legs over the water.

Marion asked, "Hey, Meggie. Have you heard from Betty?"

"Yeah, I just talked to her the other night. She's in San Diego visiting an old friend of hers and having a great time."

Dancing Kathy held up her martini and said, "Good for her."

I glanced down the dock and noticed Joe Turner on his boat, the *Summa Home*. He was in the middle of laying a big kiss on a blond with really big hair. I commented, "Gee, I met Joe and his wife the other day, and that isn't the same woman I met."

They all looked at each other and started laughing.

Marion informed me in a whisper, "That's because it isn't his wife."

I raised my eyebrows.

Dancing Kathy explained, "That's Number Two."

I was confused, "Number Two?"

She nodded, "Yep. He calls his wife Number One and that's his girlfriend Rosie. She's Number Two."

I probably had a shocked look on my face because they

all laughed.

Sexy Cathy sang, "He's hopelessly devoted to two." Then she continued, "I guess it isn't funny, especially for Number One or Two for that matter, but we all get a kick out of watching the hanky-panky.

Dancing Kathy said, "I always tell Mike, if he ever pulls something like that, I'll make Lorena Bobbitt look like a surgeon."

At that remark, all the guys adjusted their shorts.

I shook my head and said, "Boy, I guess you never know."

Marion said, "When you get a little older, Meggie, things like that won't shock you as much. Men can be dogs."

Kenny got his back up. "Hey, women can be just as brutal. I work with a guy whose wife is screwing around with their dentist."

Mike said, "That's giving getting a filling a whole new meaning."

We all laughed at that one.

I said, "I don't think I'm ever getting married."

Marion said, "They're not all assholes, Meggie. You just have to weed through the crap, and then you'll find the right one to be in the trenches with."

I told them, "Well, I haven't had much luck lately with men, so I'm taking a break."

Dancing Kathy said, "That's exactly what I was doing when I met Mike. I was taking a hiatus from dating and wham. I looked across that funeral parlor and there he was."

Marion and I said at the same time, "You met at a funeral?"

Kathy said, "Yeah, my Great-aunt Sophie's death was the best thing that ever happened to me. Not so good for Aunt

Sophie, but she was eighty-seven. Mike grew up next door to her. Mike and his parents came to the funeral, I took one look at him, and that was it."

Mike said, "I tried to shake her off, but she got her teeth into me, and I've been her lap dog ever since."

Kathy smiled and said, "His tail is still wagging after all these years."

I love to know how people met, so I asked Marion how she and Pierce found each other.

She said, "Well, Pierce and I met at an orphans' dance. We were in separate orphanages in Massachusetts. He was in an all-boys, and I was in an all-girls. The two homes would take turns hosting dances throughout the year. Well, this particular one was hosted by the boys. I was incredibly shy back then and I was sitting with a bunch of my friends with my head down staring at the floor. I was terrified someone would ask me to dance. A pair of huge feet appeared in front of me and I looked up to see this dorky guy with this huge grin on his face. He put his hand out, I took it, and we went to dance. Pierce is the worst dancer in the world. His arms and legs were all over the place, gawky as hell. I figured, hey, I can dance better than he does, and all of a sudden my fear vanished. We danced all night. I realized that night after dancing and talking with him that he was the nicest guy in the world. I fell in love with the goofiest guy I'd ever met. Pierce was a year ahead of me in school and won a scholarship to Penn State. When I graduated high school, he convinced me to move there. We married when he graduated, and the rest is history."

Sexy Cathy said, "That's so sweet."

Dancing Kathy said to Kenny and Sexy Cathy, "How

about you guys?"

Kenny cleared his throat and said, "Well, I'd been out of college a couple of years. I was a grain broker. I got a little bored living in St. Louis, so I connected with a headhunter who got me a good lead on a job in Rhode Island. I jumped on a plane and went out for an interview. Cathy was a flight attendant on the plane. I was seated in the back of the plane, she kept coming back to talk to me, and when we landed, slipped me her number. Of course, that kind of thing happens to me all the time."

Sexy Cathy rolled her eyes said sarcastically, "Sure it does."

Kenny said, "She never believes me when I say that. Anyway, I called her the following week, and shc invited me to go to a wedding with her. She has a huge family. I don't know who I fell in love with first, her or her family. I got the job in Rhode Island, and we started to get serious. Eventually, I convinced her to give up flying and marry me."

Sexy Cathy said, "Sometime I'll tell you guys my version of the story."

Dancing Kathy changed the subject. "Meggie, I heard a rumor you and Ian were dating."

"No," I said, "just a rumor. Ian isn't really interested."

Mike said, "Well, he's a fool. If I were younger, you'd be just the kind of girl I'd go out with."

I smiled at him and said, "Thanks, Mike, I appreciate that."

I had finished my beer and decided I'd better get back to the cottage and get ready for Helen's arrival tomorrow. I thanked them for the beer and left. I turned into a cleaning demon and by 9:30 the cottage was sparkling. I was exhausted and hit the hay early.

CHAPTER SEVEN

Even though I'm devastated about Ian, I woke up in a good mood. Helen was coming today and I knew she'd cheer me up. The store had a lot of traffic with the fishermen dropping by to brag about their trip to the canyon. Everyone did exceptionally well, bagging a couple of nice-sized tuna, and some good-sized mahi mahi. Only one chicken wing was found in the bunch, so I guess Mo was off the hook in the future. At 10:00 I had a little lull. I was alone in the store when Helen walked in. She's one of my best friends, but secretly, sometimes I hate her. After a six-hour drive, she looked like she just stepped out of a beauty salon.

If Helen wanted another career besides engineering, she could have been a *Sports Illustrated* swimsuit model. She is tall, five-eleven, with long, blond hair, and a beautiful face with enormous blue eyes. Along with all that, she's slim with big boobs, a tiny waist, and legs that go on forever. One of the advantages of hanging out with her was that you can always count on meeting a lot of men. She's always been a man magnet.

She spotted me and we both screamed.

I said, "Oh my God, you're a sight for sore eyes."

She gave me a big hug, took a look around, and said, "So, this is the marina?"

"Yep. I'm so glad you're here."

"Me too. I need this vacation so much. I'm glad I left early; the traffic wasn't bad at all."

"Let me help you with your luggage, and I'll get you settled in the cottage."

I hung a Be Right Back sign on the door, picked up one of Helen's two bags, and took her over to the cottage.

She looked around the house and glanced out the window. "Wow, Meggie, it's beautiful, what a view! I've never seen so many boats."

"It's one of the biggest marinas in the area."

She stretched and said, "I can't wait to just lie out in the sun and relax. I'm going to be a lazy bum and enjoy every minute of it."

I told her, "Well, I'm going to try to take a little time off, but unfortunately, I'll be working most of the time. You can lie out on the deck, though, and I can tell you how to get to the beach. We'll be able to do stuff together in the evenings."

"That would be great. I'm just here to spend time with you and veg."

I put her in Gram's bedroom.

I asked, "Are you hungry?"

"Not really, but I'd kill for a cup of coffee."

"Hel, why don't you get settled. I'll run over to the Snack Shack and get you a cup of joe."

"You're a lifesaver."

"Be right back"

When I got to the Shack, Mo was sitting at the counter having a cup of coffee with Dancing Kathy.

Mo said, "Hey, Meggie. Anything new with you and Ian?"

I quickly filled them in on Jimmy's visit and told them about Ian seeing us in the parking lot.

Mo told me, "I could make sure he finds out the truth. This here's gossip central."

"Frankly, Mo, I give up. He can think whatever he wants. I don't understand men, and I'm tired of trying to. Can I get a cup of coffee to go? My friend Helen just arrived, and she's in desperate need of some caffeine."

"Sure." She got up to get the coffee and said, "You'll have to bring her over and introduce her."

"Oh, I will. She's a little burnt out from the drive."

Kathy got up and was looking out the window. Puzzled, she said, "I wonder what those guys are looking at?"

Mo said, "What do you mean?"

Kathy said, "Well, I can see at least four guys with binoculars. Oh, I see what they're looking at. I think that must be your friend, Meggie."

Mo and I went to the window and looked out. Helen was on Gram's deck in a very tiny black bikini, bent over putting a towel on a chaise lounge.

Mo shook her head and said, "Dang, that's the body I was supposed to have."

"Me too," said Kathy.

The door to the Shack opened and in walked Tony Maroni.

He looked at me and smiled. "Okay, Meggie. Who's the goddess?"

I laughed and said, "That's my friend I told you about, Helen Jakowski."

Dreamy-faced, Tony announced, "My Polish Princess has arrived. I think I'll go introduce myself."

I handed him the cup of coffee and said, "Here, she might be nicer to you if you show up with this."

He took the coffee and said, "Thanks. Have a good day, ladies. I know I will." He winked at us and swaggered toward the cottage.

We all watched from the window. Tony walked up on the deck and started talking to Helen. We couldn't tell what they were saying, but Helen picked up her towel, wrapped it around her waist like a sarong, and then they proceeded hand in hand down to Tony's boat.

Mo whistled. "That took about two minutes. People shouldn't be allowed to be that good lookin'. It's not fair to the rest of us mere mortals."

I said, "Well, at least I know she'll be entertained while I'm working."

Mo said, "No doubt about it."

Dancing Kathy snickered, "Oh, I think we'll all be entertained."

I laughed, said goodbye, and went back to work. Things slowed down quite a bit in the late afternoon, so I closed the store up at 4:00, and went down to A dock to look for Helen. Helen and Tony were sitting on the deck of his boat like two peas in a pod, having a beer.

Helen asked me, "Are you done for the day?"

"Yeah, I closed up early."

Tony said, "Want a beer?"

"I'd love one. What have you two been up to this afternoon?"

Tony said, "Well, I took the Polish Princess here for a little boat ride and when we came back, she took a little nap down below."

Helen sighed, "It was heaven. I never get to nap."

I teased. "Are there mirrors on the ceiling down there?"

Tony snapped his fingers and said, "No, but that's a good idea. I should have thought of that myself."

I asked Helen, "What do you want to do tonight?"

She replied, "I'm up for anything."

Tony piped up and asked, "Are you girls hungry? I know where the best food in the state is."

I asked, "Where's that?"

He said, "My parents' house. It's Paisano Sunday."

Helen asked, "What's Paisano Sunday?"

Tony said, "Once a month, we have a big family get together. All my aunts, uncles, and cousins show up and bring a dish. The best food anywhere. I was thinking of making an appearance. Would you girls like to join me?"

I looked at Helen. "You decide."

She shrugged her shoulders and said, "I'm game. Won't your parents mind you showing up with two extra people?"

"No, they're used to it. When I show up with you two beauties, I'll reach legend status. Watch out for my uncle Guido, though; he's right off the boat and likes to pinch booties. Most of the people will be hanging in the backyard, but if you go in the house, don't sit on any chairs against the wall. Those are for the guys only. Guys in my family like to sit with their backs to the wall."

Helen and I looked at each other and then back at Tony.

He held up a hand and said, "Don't ask."

I said, "Okay. What time do you want to leave?"

Tony suggested, "How about I head home, change, and pick you girls up in about an hour?"

I said, "Sounds good."

Helen and I went back to the cottage to get changed.

Helen said, "You were holding out on me. You never mentioned Tony. I assume he isn't the guy you're interested in."

"No, that was Ian. But that's over."

"What happened?"

I told her all about Ian and then about Jimmy showing up.

Stunned, she said, "I can't believe Jimmy asked you to marry him. Thank God you said no."

I was a little taken aback. "What do you mean? Jimmy isn't all that bad."

"Oh, come on, Meggie. Jimmy is a couch potato with hardly any personality. The fun factor just isn't there. He's a slug. You would've spent your whole life waiting on him while he watched ESPN."

"Boy, I never knew you felt that way about him."

She explained. "I never said a word because I didn't want to hurt your feelings or our friendship. Laura and I were thrilled when you broke up. You're too good for him. You like to have fun, go out, and do things. If you recall, Jimmy never wanted to do anything. Every time Jimmy did something with us, he looked totally miserable. He was holding you back from enjoying yourself. He would have eventually bored you to death."

I agreed. "You're right. He would have."

"It sounds like you really have a thing for Ian."

"You can say that again. Not that it's going to do me any good."

"I wouldn't give up on him yet, Meggie. It seems he cares about you. Otherwise, he wouldn't have gotten jealous when he saw you with another guy, right?"

"I have a hard time believing that. We never really had an official date and he certainly didn't knock himself out to spend time with me even before the Jimmy incident."

"We'll go out and raise some hell while I'm here. It'll take your mind off him and maybe you'll meet someone else."

"I don't want to meet anyone. My heart is tired of getting stomped on. I'll go out and raise some hell, though."

"Good girl. Now, tell me about the hunk I spent the day with. What do you know about him?"

"Well, I'm sure he told you a little bit about himself. What did you talk about all day?"

"Oh, he told me about his auto body business and showed me all around the boat. He gave me a little tour on the boat ride and pointed out landmarks like the Point Judith Lighthouse. Mostly we just bullshitted about this and that. What I want to know is, what's up with his love life?"

I told her, "Ladies man with a capital L. You never see him with the same girl more than twice. Come to think of it, he's like the male version of you."

We laughed.

I continued. "When I first met him, I thought he was just a macho guy who thinks he's God's gift to the ladies. But, since I've gotten to know him, he's actually really sweet."

Helen said, "He sure is easy on the eyes. He has one of the best bodies I've ever seen on a straight guy."

"That's for sure."

I put on a blue sundress and a pair of white sandals. Helen looked as stunning as usual, with a black short skirt that showed off her long legs and a white haltertop. She wore her long blond hair down, and I put mine in a ponytail.

Tony showed up in a black BMW. He took a look at us, blinked a few times, and said, "Now *that* is a vision."

I looked at Helen and she rolled her eyes.

I commented, "Nice car."

He shrugged, "Well, the ladies like it better than driving around in my truck."

Helen matter-of-factly said, "I drive a truck. It comes in handy for work, and it's easier to drive on the construction sites."

Tony said, "Baby, you're turning me on."

We got in the car. Helen sat up front with Tony. I made him make a quick stop at the grocery store so we could pick up some flowers for his mother.

On the drive up, Helen asked him, "Do you always bring girls you've just met home to meet the family?"

He said, "Sure. I just never bring the same girl more than once. If I brought a girl back a second time for Paisano Sunday, my mother would be booking the church, and my aunts would be freezing meatballs and gravy for the reception."

I laughed, "You're kidding."

He said, "My mother's been hounding me for years to get married. I'm an only child, and she wants grandchildren in a bad way. She can't wait until I give her some little Maronis. She goes to church every day and lights candles."

I said, "What do you say to her?"

"I give her a kiss and tell her when I find someone as beautiful as she is, I'll get married."

Helen said, "What does she say to that?"

"She smacks me in the head and says a bunch of stuff in Italian that I don't understand."

I asked, "So, you grew up on Federal Hill?"

He said, "Only until I went to high school. Then we moved to Lincoln. I'll take you girls on a tour of Federal Hill before we go to my parents'. It's on the way."

Tony exited off I-95 onto Atwells Avenue. We passed under a huge arched gateway with a bronzed pinecone in the center. Tony told us this landmark is the entrance to Federal Hill, and the pinecone is an Italian symbol of abundance and quality. He then started pointing out all his favorite restaurants and bakeries, which lined both sides of the street. He also pointed out where some of the famous Mafia hits took place. At the end of the restaurant district, he hung a left and took us in a neighborhood that consisted mostly of old triple-decker homes. He pulled up in front of one of them and parked.

He said, "This is my old house. Most of my relatives still live on the Hill. I think I'm related to most of the people up here. When we lived here, we had the top two floors of this house; my grandparents, my mother's parents, lived on the bottom floor. My grandmother is still alive, but my grandfather died about fifteen years ago. My grandmother lives with my parents in Lincoln now. My mother is the youngest of nine. I have five aunts and three uncles, and that's just on my mother's side. My father has six brothers. We rent a hall for our family Christmas party."

He then drove us to Lincoln. We pulled up to a huge house that sat on about two acres of land. The driveway was full, and more cars were lined up on the street. We got out of the car and walked up to the house. Tony opened the front door and ushered us in. It was a hot day, and the first thing that hit us was the smell of garlic and sounds of Frank Sinatra. The house was comfortably air-conditioned, which was a nice change from the humidity we'd been experiencing. We entered a big two-story foyer. The living room was on the left, and off to the right was the biggest dining room I'd ever seen in a house. The dining room table was covered with food. The living room had three card tables surrounded by older men playing cards. When we walked in, they all looked up at once.

In unison they shouted, "Hey, Tony." Then all twelve of them slowly looked Helen and me up and down. Tony escorted us into the living room.

He introduced me. "Everyone, this is my friend, Meggie. Her grandmother owns the marina where I keep my boat." He then put his arm around Helen's shoulder and with great fanfare said, "And, this is Helen, my Polish Princess."

Tony then introduced us to his uncles. There was Leo, Marco, Louie, Joey, Paulie, Nando, two Uncle Tonys, Mario, Dominic, Nick, and the ass-pinching Uncle Guido.

At that point, Tony's dad, Al, came in, and Tony introduced us. He was a tall, barrel-chested man. He gave each of us girls a big bear hug and welcomed us to his home.

He said, "Tony, you've gotta fatten these skinny girls up." He turned toward the other guys, put up his hands, and said,

"Girls these days, they think men want skinny women. We like curves on our girls, don't we, guys?"

They all nodded. One said, "Love curves. Somethin' to hold on to when you're doin' the rumba."

Al told his son, "Tony, take these two beauties and get them something to eat and drink. You girls like cannolis? My wife makes the best." He lifted his right arm, kissed his fingers, and threw them in the air.

Helen and I nodded.

Tony said, "Okay, Dad, I'll take them out to meet Ma and get them something to eat."

Tony's dad told him, "Make sure they get some antipasto. Aunt Loretta made it special for today."

"Okay, Dad."

We walked into the kitchen, which was full of women. He stopped to introduce us to his cousins Jeanne, Mary, and Mary Lynn and then went off to find us some drinks.

Jeanne said to us, "It's always nice to meet Tony's friends. Is one of you dating him?"

Helen and I looked at each other and said at the same time, "We're just friends of his."

Jeanne said, "Well, our Tony's a good catch. He's the smart one in the family. He went to Brown, you know. The only one in the family that went Ivy League."

Helen and I had no idea that Tony had gone to Brown. This was going to be an interesting evening.

Mary Lynn asked, "What do you girls do?"

I told her, "I'm a teacher."

Helen said, "I'm an engineer."

Lynn said, "An engineer. Wow. I haven't met too many

women engineers."

Helen got her back up and said, "I know quite a few women engineers."

Jeanne said, "Well, this a first. Most of the women Tony brings around are a bit different from the two of you." The three cousins looked at each other conspiratorially.

A small, attractive, older woman came into the kitchen and immediately rushed up to us. "Are you the girls my Tony brought?" she asked.

We said, "Yes."

She folded her arms and asked, "So, which one of you girls is going to be the mother of my grandchildren?"

We both looked at her and shrugged our shoulders in unison.

She looked us over from head to toe and said, "Well, you are both beauties. Either one of you would make beautiful babies with my Tony."

I blushed and handed her the flowers. "Thank you for having us to your home Mrs. Maroni."

She looked at Jeanne, Mary, and Mary Lynn and said, "Classy girls, too."

They smiled and nodded their approval.

Helen and I were relieved when Tony walked in the kitchen carrying a glass of wine for each of us. "Ma, I brought my girls some of Uncle Mario's homemade wine."

She smiled at us and said, "My brother makes his own wine." She patted our cheeks. "You girls enjoy."

Tony laughed and gestured us toward the back door. "Let's go out back, and you can meet the rest of the family."

We walked out into the yard. It was big and full of people.

Three barbeques were going, and there were at least thirty kids of various ages running around. Everyone came to a complete stop when we walked out and looked at us. Tony announced, "Everyone, I would like you to meet my friend Meggie and my Polish Princess, Helen."

Everyone said, "Hello." Tony found us a couple of seats at a table near the back door. One of the guys beckoned Tony over. Helen and I sat enjoying our wine, taking in the festive atmosphere. A little girl about five, with curly dark hair and big brown eyes, shyly walked our way.

She came to a stop in front of Helen and sweetly asked, "Can I sit in your lap?"

Helen said, "Sure." She reached down, picked the girl up, and set her across her lap. The little girl looked up at her adoringly and asked reverently, "Are you really a princess?"

Helen said, "Sweetheart, all girls are princesses."

The little girl said, "My dad says I'm a princess and my mom's the Queen of All Things."

Helen looked at me, winked, and said, "Your daddy is a smart man."

The little girl introduced herself. "My name is Christina."

Helen said, "That's a beautiful name."

Christina asked, "Are you from the land of Polish?"

Helen laughed and said, "I'm from Pennsylvania."

Christina said, "My dad said most of Tony's girlfriends come from a town called Hooters."

Helen and I looked at each other and smiled.

Helen said, "I think there's a town called Hooters in every state."

"I think you should be the one to marry Tony," Christina

said.

Helen smiled at her and asked, "Why do you think that?"

She said, "Well, you're the prettiest girl I've ever seen him with."

Helen gave her a hug and said, "Well, I'll think about it, sweetheart."

We suddenly heard a voice yell, "Christina, you come here and finish your dinner."

Christina said, "I've gotta go. Bye, Princess Helen; bye, Meggie."

She hurried over on her little legs back to her mother.

Tony came back and escorted us in to get something to eat. The spread was unbelievable. There were four different kinds of pasta salads, squid salad, Aunt Loretta's antipasto, which looked delicious, four different kinds of sausage, meatballs, barbequed chicken, steak, and stuffed olives. I could go on and on. It was a feast. We all filled our plates and went out back again. I finished my plate, while Helen and Tony went back for a refill. Helen can eat like a horse and not gain a pound. They came back, sat, and shoveled in their food. Three older gentlemen were setting up to play music. Four more guys came around the corner from the side of house with a portable dance floor. It was starting to get dark, and a couple of women were lighting torches that surrounded the yard. The smell of citronella permeated the air.

One of the men announced on the microphone that dessert was being served in the dining room. I had no room left for dessert, but Helen and Tony jumped right up and went into the house. They each came back with three different desserts.

Tony bragged, "My cousin Jeanne makes the best lemon cake. What do you think, Hel?"

Helen swallowed and nodded yes.

At that point, an old woman dressed from head to toe in black came to our table. Tony introduced her as his grandmother, Josephine. She was even shorter than Tony's mother, who barely reached five feet.

After Tony did the introductions, she pointed her finger at Helen and said, "You eat good." She then gave me a scary look and walked away.

Tony looked flabbergasted.

Helen asked him, "What's wrong?"

He said, "I can't believe she spoke to you. I've been bringing people home for years, and she's never spoken to any of them."

Helen looked at me and shrugged her shoulders.

After dessert, the band started to play and the fun really started. Tony explained they always play two sets. The first one is Dean Martin hits and the second set, of course, is Old Blue Eyes. All the card players came out to the yard, and people started to dance. Tony got us more of Uncle Mario's homemade wine. I don't know what Uncle Mario put in it, but I was feeling no pain. Tony grabbed Helen to dance. Lucky me, I got to dance with Uncle Guido. He pinched my ass at least three times. The band struck up Dean's pizza pie song, and everyone in the yard sang. During the second set, Tony and Helen were dancing to Frank's "The Way You Look Tonight" and a drop-dead gorgeous guy came over to me.

He smiled and with a strong Italian accent said, "Hi, my name is Bond, James Bond. Make my day," and held out his hand. I thought, what the hell, and we hit the dance floor. He was a smooth dancer. When the song was over, he took me back to Helen and Tony.

Tony said, "I see you met my cousin Maurizio. He just came from Italy, and doesn't speak any English. The only English he knows is what he's learned from the movies."

Maurizio smiled at me and said "Hasta la vista, baby," and walked away.

By the end of the night, I had danced with Uncle Frank, Cousin Joey, Uncle Nick, Cousin Sonny, and a little old man named Harry the Hammer. After the band played their last song, I turned to Tony.

I said, "Tony, I hate to be a party pooper, but I've got to get up at 4:00."

He nodded, "We'll go. Let's just say goodbye to my parents."

We went and found the Maronis, who were sitting at a table with Tony's grandmother and some of his aunts.

I said, "Mr. and Mrs. Maroni, thank you for a wonderful evening."

Helen patted her stomach and said, "That was the best food I ever ate."

Mrs. Maroni said, "You girls come back anytime. My Tony is a good boy. He'd make a great father."

Tony said, "Okay, Ma, I think they got the message." He kissed his mother, and she smacked him on the head. He shook hands with his dad, and his dad gave us girls both a hug.

On the way home, I was half-asleep in the backseat when Helen told Tony, "I'm so full I have to unbutton my skirt."

Tony glanced at her and said, "Babe, don't say things like

that when I'm drivin' the Beamer."

I woke up when the car stopped outside Gram's cottage. I told them I would go open the door and turn on the lights. I wanted them to have a chance to say goodnight in private. Ten minutes later, Helen walked in.

She threw open her arms and said, "Was that fun or what?"

"I had a great time. Uncle Guido pinched my ass three times, and I didn't even care. Did he get you?"

"Oh, yeah. When I went to the bathroom, he got me in the hallway."

We both laughed and I said, "I've got to hit the hay. Come over to the store tomorrow when you wake up. Goodnight, Hel."

She said, "Nite, Meg, and thanks for having me up."

CHAPTER EIGHT

Today is the Fourth of July, one of the biggest summer events in Cozy Harbor. I rallied myself out of bed, jumped in the shower, and headed over to the store. Helen came over around noon. I sent her over to the Snack Shack to pick us up a couple of sandwiches, since Journey was off and I couldn't get away. She came back with two southwest chicken wraps and two iced teas. I asked her whom she met over at the Shack.

She said, "Well, of course, I met Mo. She is a riot, Meggie. I also met a woman named Linda and her daughter Allie. Linda's husband, Harry, owns the *Allie E.* Allie is a cute four-year-old-redhead. She looks like a mini-me of her mother. I also met an older guy named Joe Turner. He tried to hit on me. I looked over at Mo, Joe's back was to her, and she shook her head no. Not that I was interested anyway."

I informed her, "Well, he calls his wife Number One, and his girlfriend Number Two. You would've been Number Three."

Helen said, "You know me, Meggie, I'm the only star of my movie."

We laughed.

I asked, "Was anyone else there?"

She said, "Yeah, a couple named Jim and Bonnie.

"Bonnie's the only woman you ever see on B dock where the sport fishing boats are. She's always down with Jim working on the boat, and she's the only wife who goes fishing. She catches more fish than the guys. She's invited me to go tuna fishing anytime I want. I plan on taking her up on her offer before the end of the summer. I've always wanted to go offshore fishing and reel in a big tuna."

Helen said, "Well, she seemed really friendly. I'll tell you, Meggie, I can really understand why this marina's been in your family for years; the people are really nice up here."

I asked, "What do you think of Tony after last night?

She took a bite of her wrap and chewed for a while. Finally she said, "You know me. I usually meet guys who are dumb as a door nail. Either that or they're pompous asses. They're so full of themselves, I can't stand them for more than a minute. Remember that guy from the Main Line I dated a couple of times who was filthy rich. He was such a snob and rude as hell. After two dates, I knew I was smarter than he was, and he knew it, too.

When we went to a restaurant, he would be so obnoxious. I always felt sorry for whoever waited on us. I always tried to be extra nice to make up for him being an asshole. I wanted to make sure they only spit on his food, not mine. Worst of all, he was a lousy tipper, and you know how I feel about that. I'd tell him I had to use the ladies' room as we left the restaurant. When he went out to get the car, I would hurry back to the waiter and apologize, and give him another twenty. When the valet opened my door, I would slip him another five. That's why I usually never date any guy more than twice. I want a guy I can respect. If I have no respect for them, they're history. Plus, most men are intimidated by me."

"That's doesn't answer my question. What about Tony?"

She smiled and said, "He's definitely on my To Do List. I like what I see so far. He has a hell of a sense of humor; he makes me laugh. He lets his mother slap him in the head, and he dances with old ladies. He's a lot smarter than he lets on. I especially like that about him. He has a great body and he's hot handsome. If he's as good in the sack as I think he will be, I might just have to keep him around for a while."

"Well, you'd better give me all the details if you get to that point."

She gave me a sad look and said, "Are you sure you want to hear about it? I know you've been having a dry spell."

"I've been living in the Sahara, but it would be good to know somebody isn't. I want details."

"Okay. I'll tell all. By the way, I didn't get a chance last night to tell you, but Tony invited us out tonight to watch the fireworks. A friend of his lives in Narragansett, and he's having a bunch of people over for a barbeque."

I said, "You and Tony go ahead. I'm going to the parade at 6:00. I promised Mac I would come by and watch it with him. I also want to stay close to home and keep an eye on the marina tonight. Everyone will be partying, and I should probably stick around."

"Are sure you don't mind? I feel bad. I came up to see you."

"Don't worry about it, Hel. I want you to have a great vacation. Go have fun with Tony. I have off tomorrow afternoon. How about we grab lunch from Mo and take a ride up the pond on Mac's boat? Maybe if Mac is up to it, he'll join us."

"Okay, sounds good. Tony has to work anyway. He did say he would take off Thursday and Friday so we could do some things together."

I smiled at her and teased, "He did, did he? I think the boy likes you."

She smiled, "They all like me. Speaking of the boy, I told him I'd meet him on his boat, he's taking me for a boat ride. I'll see you before I leave for the party. Tony said we would leave around 5:00."

"Okay, have fun. Thanks for lunch."

She gave me a wave and headed out the door.

At 3:00, I put a Be Right Back sign on the door of the store and went down to the fuel dock to talk to Matt about some charge slips. I was having trouble with the handwriting on a few of them. Brian was in the fish store, and Matt was on the fuel dock finishing up with a boat. While I waited, I noticed a big dog sitting on the dock. He looked like a Chesapeake Bay retriever. Matt finished and came over. I asked him whose dog it was.

He told me, "That's Diesel, Harry Randall's dog. Harry ran in to town to pick up something and asked me to keep an eye on him."

I asked him about the slips and before he had a chance to answer me, another boat pulled up for fuel.

I said, "You go ahead and take care of that boat; I can wait a few minutes."

He went to talk to the customer, grabbed the fuel hose,

and climbed aboard the boat. A small boat went by with two golden retrievers in it. They started barking at Diesel and he barked back. After the boat passed the dock, Diesel took an amazing flying dive off the dock into the water and landed with a big splash. He started swimming after the boat carrying the golden retrievers. I quickly looked back at Matt; his back was to me and he was still busy fueling up the boat. I thought, "Shit, shit." I had visions of Diesel swimming to Block Island or getting hit by another boat or a jet ski.

I kicked off my sneakers, jumped in the water, and started swimming after him. I was on the swim team for six years during grade school and high school. As fast as I swam, I couldn't make any headway on Diesel. I'll never underestimate the doggy paddle again. A boat approached, then slowed down, and I took a quick look. It was Ian on *The Stalwart*. He reached over the side and grabbed Diesel by his collar and hauled him up onto *The Stalwart*. I stopped swimming, and Ian looked at me and extended his hand to pull me aboard.

He had a smirk on his face and asked, "Out for a swim, Meggie?"

I gave him a dirty look, turned, and swam back to the dock. I hauled myself up the ladder to the fuel dock. I was dripping wet and once again humiliated. Matt stood there with his mouth open.

Meekly, he asked, "Meggie, what did you do that for?"

"You said you were watching him for Harry and since you were busy, I went after him. I was afraid he would swim away or get hurt."

Matt told me, a little too late, "Diesel always does that. He jumps off the dock at least five times a day when he's down here. He just swims a little bit and then turns around and swims around to the little beach on the other side of the marina. Five minutes later, he's lying on the dock again. I'm sorry, Meggie."

It wasn't his fault; I didn't want to take my frustrations out on him so I let him off easy. "Don't worry about it, Matt; next time I'll know better. Stop in and see me when you get a chance, and we'll go over the slips."

Luckily, I had handed him the slips and he put them in his pocket before he started fueling up the boat. Even though I was soaking wet, I bent down and put on my sneakers. The last thing I needed at this point was a fishhook in my foot. Ian had tied up and both Sam and Diesel were walking around on the dock in front of *The Stalwart*. Unfortunately, I had to walk that way. I could sense that Ian was looking at me. I tried to ignore him, but I had to stop and wait for the dogs to get out of my way before I could continue up the dock. Diesel stepped in front of me and proceeded to puke up saltwater all over my sneakers. I sneaked a peek at Ian. He looked me up and down and shook his head. His shoulders were shaking and I could tell he was trying not to laugh. Ian was lucky I didn't have a gun because I would have shot him in the head. The dogs finally moved out of my way, and I proceeded up the dock with as much dignity as I could muster. I glanced around the marina to see who might have witnessed my latest mortifying experience. Sure enough, Bob on the *Bite Me* had his camera phone ready. I stopped and struck a nice pose for him. He snapped my picture, gave me a wave, and I stomped over to the cottage to change clothes.

Business was steady all afternoon, and at 5:00 Helen

popped in the store.

She said, "Just wanted to tell you I'm leaving. You have a great night."

"You too."

As she was headed out the door, she turned and said, "Don't wait up."

Some girls have all the luck. I closed up and went over to the cottage. I didn't have a chance to shower after my delightful swim, so I jumped under the welcoming hot water, dried my hair, put a little makeup on, and dressed in a denim skirt and a red and white striped tank top. Since my spare sneakers were history, my only choices of footwear left were sandals or flip-flops, which seemed like the better bet.

I looked around as I walked through the streets of Cozy Harbor on my way to Mac's house. It was so nice to see all the houses decorated in red, white, and blue. Practically every house I passed was in party mode. People were starting to line the curbs with chairs, getting ready for the parade to start. As I approached Mac's house, I could see that his party was underway. I recognized Mac's nephew, Mike. Mac was sitting in a chair next to a woman whom I assumed was probably Mike's wife.

Mac saw me and said, "Meggie, I'm glad you came. Come meet everyone."

I said hello to Mike, and then Mac introduced me to Mike's wife, Nancy. Mike and Nancy introduced me to their son, Kyle, and their daughter, Taylor. Kyle looked to be in his early twenties and Taylor a little younger. A few of Mac's poker buddies sat with their wives at a picnic table in the shade. Mac took me over and introduced me as his favorite clamming partner. Mike handed me a beer, and I helped myself to a hot dog off the grill. I sat in a chair next to Nancy.

I asked her, "How's Mac doing?"

She said cheerfully, "He's bounced back great. Mike and I have been here all weekend. We're going home tonight and I think he'll be fine on his own."

I told her, "I'll check up on him."

"You wouldn't believe all the people who have said that to us. Mac's had a steady stream of visitors."

"I believe it. He's a Cozy Harbor treasure."

I finished off my hot dog and disposed of the paper plate in the trash on the side of the house. When I came back around front, Ian was standing in the yard talking to Mac and Mike. After what happened today, he was the last person I wanted to see. I heard the parade approaching and went and sat in a chair by the curb between Nancy and Taylor.

Leading the parade was an antique fire engine with a big red, white, and blue banner across the front of it that read The Cozy Harbor Fourth of July Parade. Following the fire truck was the bicycle brigade, consisting of about twenty kids of various ages on bikes and tricycles. All had American flags and red, white, and blue streamers dangling from their handlebars.

Next came four antique cars loaded with people dressed up for the occasion. The kazoo band was up next, with about thirty adults playing "Yankee Doodle Dandy" totally out of sync. Behind them was Kathy from *The Dancing Queen* in all her glory. Kathy had a banner across her chest that said The Dancing Queen and behind her was a dance troop from her studio. Kathy and the girls were dressed in sparkling outfits and performed a dance number to Bruce Springsteen's "Born on the Fourth of July." People strolled by in all sorts of wild costumes. Most of them looked homemade and were probably thrown together today. One adorable little boy pulled a wagon with two little girls dressed as mermaids. Four guys, dressed as lobsters, did a little dance. Pulling up the rear of the parade was a group of adults and kids, leading dogs, whom they'd dressed up for the occasion.

The parade continued on down the street. We all got up, picked up our chairs, and went back into Mac's yard. There's nothing like a small town parade. I loved it. I decided to head back to the marina since the party was winding down. I still hadn't talked to Ian, which was fine with me. I said my goodbyes and started down the street. I got halfway down the block when Ian caught up with me.

He said, "Slow down, Meggie. You didn't even say hi to me."

I turned my head to him and said, "Hi, Ian."

"Do you mind if I walk back to the marina with you?"

I shrugged, "Suit yourself."

"Where's your friend?" he asked.

I ground out, "You're too late. Tony already has dibs on her. He took her to a party."

"Boy, you're really pissed at me," he said, probably taken aback by my tone of voice.

I gave him my phony smile and said, "I'm not pissed at you. I'm nice to all the marina customers."

"Meggie, I owe you an apology."

"Not necessary."

He sighed and said, "Look, I'm sorry I laughed at you today. Even you have to admit it was funny."

"I'm glad I'm such a source of amusement for you."

He ignored my remark and continued, "When I saw you in the parking lot hugging that guy at 4:00 in the morning, it took me by surprise. It was the last thing I expected to see on my way to work. I admit I jumped to conclusions, and I should've given you a chance to explain. Yesterday morning, I went over to the Snack Shack to grab some coffee, and I overheard Mo telling Marion the whole story about your old boyfriend showing up."

I barked out, "I told her not to tell anyone about that."

"Well, it's hard to keep anything a secret around here."

"So I've learned."

"Anyway, I'm sorry," he said in a quiet voice.

I stopped and turned to look him in the face. "Ian, you were way too quick to judge me and think the worst. You just assumed I picked up some guy for a one-night stand. That showed me exactly what you think of me."

"Meggie, I don't think of you that way at all."

I said, "Look, it doesn't really matter anyway. Like you said, we shared a few kisses, no big deal."

"I shouldn't have said that. It was a big deal to me. Frankly, I wanted to go over and rip his head off. I was surprised at myself for feeling that way, and I lost my temper. I should have let you explain."

"Don't worry about it."

We had just walked into the marina parking lot.

He gently grabbed my arm and turned me toward him again.

He looked me in the eye and pleaded, "Meggie, can we please start over?

I let it rip. "Ian, you hurt me. You think you can kiss me whenever you want and then ignore me for days. You assumed I'm a slut and didn't give me a chance to explain and then, you laughed at me like I'm some kind of freak show. I recently ended a three-year relationship with a guy who treated me like a piece of furniture. I won't let that happen again. So unless you're willing to treat me the way I deserve to be treated, go away."

I started walking again. I can't believe I just unloaded on him like that. It felt great. I am woman, hear me roar.

He was still walking beside me.

"I would like another chance to start over with you. Do things right this time. Please. Do you have plans for tonight?"

"Not really. I thought I should stick around here and keep an eye on things since everyone will be partying."

"You don't need to do that. People will be heading home soon. Why don't you come over to my house? We can watch the fireworks from my deck."

I knew I would cave. It was fun watching him grovel, though, and I'm glad I stood my ground and let him know exactly how I feel. Out of the corner of my eye, I saw Mo getting out of her car. She waved at us and walked over.

Ian was in front of me and turned to look at Mo. She looked at me and I shook my head no. I was hoping she wouldn't say anything about me going on Big H's boat for the fireworks, since I had just told Ian I was staying around the marina. I could tell she got my nonverbal message.

"Hey, you two," she said, "I'm headed down to Big H's boat. We're gonna watch the fireworks from the water."

Ian smiled at her and said, "Have fun."

She smiled back. "See you tomorrow." She turned and hurried toward the docks.

Ian turned back to me and asked in a low voice, "How about it, Meggie?"

I let him sweat a few seconds, then said, "Okay. I'll follow you in my car. Let me run in and get my keys."

He smiled and said, "Great."

I ran in and brushed my teeth really quick. Thank God I didn't put onions on my hot dog. And I had freshly shaven legs. The gods were smiling on me tonight. I followed him to his house on Sand Hill Cove. I was expecting a little one-story cottage and was surprised by the size of his house. It was a large, two-storied shingled house with an attached garage. I parked behind his truck in the driveway. He opened my car door for me and led me into the house.

I commented, "This is a big house."

He explained, "Originally it was just a small beach cottage, but years ago my grandparents expanded it. They probably would never get the permits to expand now. I wasn't expecting company, or I would have picked up a little bit."

He opened the front door, and we stepped into a hallway with stairs on the left. Sam came down the hall to greet us. I gave him a good scratch, and then we continued down the hallway past a powder room on the right. At the end of the small hall, we stepped into a large room. The downstairs had an open floor plan with a spacious living room, dining area, and kitchen. The floors were hardwood, with a beautiful red oriental rug under the dining table and another one in the living room area. The back of the house was a wall of windows to take advantage of the water view. In the center of the windows was a big French door that led out to a deck. The view was breathtaking.

Impressed, I said, "Your house is beautiful. That's a million-dollar view."

"Thanks. I'm very fortunate that I inherited it. I could never afford to buy this house. I've done a lot of work to it in the past few years. I replaced the roof, all the windows, refinished the floors, and put in a whole new kitchen."

I took a look at the kitchen, and it was a cook's dream. Beautiful natural cherry cabinets, state-of-the-art stainless-steel appliances, and beautiful granite counters. There was a large island in the middle of the kitchen with halogen lights hanging from the ceiling, spotlighting it. Three stools sat at the island counter.

"Are you a cook?" I asked.

He laughed and said, "I can only do the basics. Let me show you the upstairs."

He guided me back through the hallway and up the stairs. At the top was a door that led into a large master bedroom and bathroom, which ran along the back of the house. Here again to take advantage of the views was a wall of windows. A door in the middle opened on to a small balcony where two chairs and a table sat. The bedroom was furnished with a king-sized bed and two dressers. The bed was made, and, other than a couple pair of shoes lying around, it looked pretty neat to me. He showed me the rest of the upstairs, which had two other bedrooms facing the street and another full bath. He had a double bed and a dresser in one, and the other room he used as an office.

It was a beautiful home, although personally I think the

décor needs a woman's touch. Preferably mine.

I turned to him and said, "I'm very impressed."

"I hoped you would be," he said and then suggested, "Let's go downstairs and I'll open a bottle of wine."

We went downstairs and I took a seat on a stool at the island. Ian got a bottle of Pinot Grigio from the fridge and poured us each a glass.

He held up his glass for a toast and looked thoughtfully into my eyes. He said in a gentle voice, "To new beginnings."

We clinked glasses and took a sip.

He glanced at the clock and asked, "Do you want to go out on the deck? The fireworks should start soon."

"Sure."

He grabbed the bottle of wine and I followed him out to the deck outfitted with a table and four chairs, plus two Adirondack chairs and two rockers. All the furniture was white. I sat in one of the Adirondack chairs. Ian pulled the other one close to mine and sat down. Sam plopped down at our feet.

Ian turned to me and said, "So, Mo said that Jimmy asked you to marry him."

He took me by surprise. "Yes, and I couldn't have been more shocked. We went out for three years and never talked about marriage. He never even bought me a piece of jewelry. I do have a nice collection of purses he gave me over the years," I joked.

"Did you want to marry him?"

"I knew I wanted to get married some day, but I never brought up the subject either. I guess I knew deep down that he wasn't the right guy. That wasn't my first proposal, you know."

Amused, he said, "Oh really. How many proposals have you had?"

"Too many to count."

"Really. Tell me about them."

"Are you sure you want to hear about them all? I asked. "It could take a while."

He nodded firmly and said, "We have all night."

"Okay, you asked for it. My first, second, and third proposals were from the same guy. Johnny Deegan asked me to marry him in the sixth, seventh, and eighth grade. He finally gave up when we got into high school and turned his affections towards a friend of mine. They dated all through high school. When they went off to different colleges, their romance fizzled out."

"What's Johnny Deegan doing now? Did he ever get married?"

"He went undergrad to Penn and then to Harvard Law and graduated top in his class. He's working at the best corporate law firm in downtown Philly. He just got married last year. Helen and I went to his wedding."

"What about the other proposals? I'm sitting on the edge of my seat."

I continued, "Well, my brother Charlie's friend Wayne has asked me at least forty-seven times."

"Did you ever go out with him?"

"No. My mom loved us to invite our friends home after school. Our house was the hangout for all the kids. She liked to keep an eye on us, especially my brothers. My dad had finished off our basement and my brothers and their friends always hung out down there. Charlie and his pals were always having contests to see who could make me blush first. They actually took bets on it. Whenever I was home and they happened to come in the house, Wayne would kneel down in front of me and ask me to marry him. He always won the bet, because I would blush like crazy. The worst was when I got my first bra. I was in eighth grade and all my friends were much more developed than I. They all had been wearing bras for a year or two. I was a late bloomer. I kept bugging my mom to take me out shopping. She finally took pity on me and took me shopping. I can't believe I'm telling you this."

"I love it. Go on," he prompted."

"Well, a couple of days after I got my bras, I was sitting in the living room doing my homework and in walked Charlie with all his friends. There were six of them. I'll never forget it, it was traumatic for me. Charlie pointed at me and said, 'Hey look, guys, Meggie is wearing a bra.' I thought I would die right on the spot."

"What happened to Wayne?"

"He still comes around the house whenever Charlie's in town and always proposes. I just ran into him about a month before I came up here. I went out for some drinks with a couple of girlfriends. He was at the bar with some guys and introduced me to them as his future wife."

"Did you blush?"

"Oh, yeah, big time. How about you? Any proposals?" I asked dying to know.

"No proposals. Not a one. After listening to you, I'm starting to feel sorry for myself."

A loud boom signaled the start of the fireworks.

Ian suggested, "I think we can get a better view if we stand up."

I stood and went over to the deck railing. Ian came up behind me, put his arms around me, and rested his chin on the top of my head. It felt so great to have him hold me like that. I leaned back against him and looked up into the sky. We stood like that for a while and watched the beautiful explosions of color. He slowly turned me around and leaned in for a kiss. I tilted my head to give him greater access. He gently brushed his lips against mine and then used his tongue like a paintbrush, sweeping it across my lips. I opened up for him, closing my eyes to enjoy all the sensations flowing through my body. I was backed up against the railing of the deck with his hard body plastered against mine. I ran my hands up his back and reached up to touch the soft hair on the back of his neck. I've never been so turned on by a kiss before. I wanted more. Helen always says that if a guy is a lousy kisser, stop right there.

We broke apart, both of us gasping for breath.

"Fireworks go off when I kiss you, Meggie," he teased.

"Is that your Fourth of July line?" I asked smiling into his eyes.

He shrugged. "I know, pretty corny, but I couldn't resist."

Ian put his arm around me and we watched the finale. When it was over, he gave me a kiss on the cheek and said, "I'm glad you came over."

"Me too."

I wanted him to ask me to stay in the worst way, but I wasn't going to be the aggressor, so I said, "Well, I'm sure you're working tomorrow. I guess I should get going."

He said, "I'll walk you out."

"Okay." I said, disappointed.

Ian and Sam escorted me to my car.

I told him, "Thanks for a nice evening."

He said, "I know your friend's in town, but do you think we could go out some night?"

"I'm sure she'll be spending time with Tony, so it shouldn't be a problem. By the way, what do you have against Tony?"

"I have nothing against Tony. I like Tony. I just didn't want him hitting on you. How about Wednesday night?"

"Sounds good."

"I'll pick you up about 7:30 and, if your friend doesn't have plans, she can come with us."

I said, "Okay," my heart jumping for joy. He leaned in and gave me a quick peck on the lips. I gave Sam a goodbye pet and got in the car. I hope Wednesday comes quick.

What an eventful day. I went from heartbreak and humiliation to romance and fireworks.

CHAPTER NINE

On my way out the door to work the next morning, I decided to peek in Helen's room. It was just as I expected, no Helen. I couldn't wait to hear how her night with Tony went.

When Journey arrived, I went over to the Snack Shack for a cup of coffee. I figured Helen would find me when she got back. Deb was sitting at the counter having breakfast, and Mo was busy filling up the salt and pepper shakers.

I said, "Hey, guys. How were the fireworks?"

Deb said, "Great. Did you see them?"

I said, "Yeah. Ian invited me over to his house, and we watched them from his deck."

Mo looked up and said, "I figured you didn't want him to know you had plans."

"Thanks, Mo."

She leaned on the counter and said, "Okay, spill."

"He apologized to me. He said he overheard your conversation with Marion."

Mo said, "I hope you don't mind, but I did that on purpose. I know you two have a thing for each other, and I just wanted to help things along. As soon as he walked in the door, I started to tell Marion about that devil Jimmy showing up. I probably embellished the story a little too just to get him goin'."

"Well, it did the trick. He's taking me out on an official date tomorrow night. Thanks, Mo."

Mo smiled and said, "I'm glad, honey. Where's your friend?"

"The last time I saw her was 5:00 last night. She was headed to a party with Tony."

Mo started fanning herself and said, "Eeew-eee, I can't wait to hear what they've been up to."

I had to ask, "Any progress with Big H?"

She shook her head. "No. It was nice of him to ask me to go watch the fireworks, though."

Deb said, "His sister Sue is such a nice person. That husband of hers is an idiot. I don't know what he was thinking."

Mo said, "I can tell you what he was thinkin' with, and it wasn't his brain. That bimbo down in Georgia can probably suck the chrome off a truck. Unfortunately, that's all some men care about."

We all laughed.

I asked Mo, "Any dates this week?"

She said, "Yeah, I have a date tonight with a new guy. He's an Elvis impersonator. He asked me out to dinner, and I said Uh-huh."

Deb and I smiled at each other. I said, "I can't wait to hear about this one."

Mo said, "I liked Elvis, but I was never an Elvis fanatic like some people. I've been also chattin' with a new guy on the Net, and we're really hittin' it off. He lives local, and he gets all my jokes. He hasn't asked me out yet, but he's the most interestin' one I've come across so far. He hasn't posted a picture of himself on the website so he's probably ugly as mud but I enjoy cybertalk."

I told her, "Don't give up on Big H."

She winked at me and said, "I'm keepin' my options open."

I said, "Well, thanks for the coffee, and you two have a great day."

I went back to the office to do some paperwork. At about 11:00, Helen popped her head in. She looked like the cat that ate the cream.

"Have a good time?" I asked.

She smirked, "Do I look unhappy?"

I got up, grabbed her arm, pulled her in the office, and shut the door. "You promised me details," I demanded.

She asked, "Are you sure you want to hear this?"

I said, "You bet."

She sat on the edge of the desk and giggled. Then she said, "Meggie, I don't know how to explain it. Just give me a minute." She put her right hand over her mouth and started to giggle harder.

I was on the edge of my seat. This was going to be good.

She pulled herself together finally and said, "Meggie, it was hands down the best sex I've ever had or fantasized about. It wasn't just sex, though. I think the right word would be sensual. It was the most mind-blowing, sensual, sexual experience of my life. There isn't an inch of my body that he didn't do something with. He made me feel like a goddess. He worshipped my body from head to toe and back again. I truly wish every woman in the world could experience what I did last night. Every woman deserves that at least once in their life."

This, coming from Helen, was huge. I didn't know what to say, so I just said, "Wow."

She nodded, "Wow is right. The only bad part about the whole thing is, he's ruined it for me with anyone else. Believe me, I'll never find another guy that good. He's a gift from God."

"What's his house like?"

"I loved it. It's in a private compound with about twenty other homes. Each house is on five acres of land, so it's really secluded. The house is a contemporary design, very open, and it's in a beautiful setting, surrounded by woods. I like the way he's decorated it. We have very similar tastes in furniture and art."

I asked her, "So, when are you seeing him again?"

"He wanted to do something tonight, but I told him I'd made plans with you."

"Oh, Hel, you don't have to worry about me. Enjoy Tony while you can."

She said, "Believe me, I will. But I haven't spent much time with you, and frankly I need to rest up after last night. How was your night?"

I told her about running into Ian and going to his house for the fireworks.

She asked, "Anything happen?"

"No. We kissed a few times, and then I went home. He didn't ask me to stay. He did ask me out for tomorrow night, though. He invited you to come with us if you don't have plans."

She licked her lips, smiled, and said, "I'm going back for a second helping of Mr. Maroni."

I said, "Ian apologized, and I forgave him but not before I told him that he couldn't treat me like that again. I think he got the message because he did finally ask me out, but I'm not going to set myself up again to be hurt. I'm going to try to hold back my feelings. It's going to be hard, though, because I really like him and I'm so attracted to him physically."

"Smart move, keep him on his toes."

"He seems to really like me, but he doesn't seem too anxious to sleep with me. Maybe he's sleeping with someone else, or he just isn't sure he's attracted to me. Remember that guy down at the Jersey shore who told me I was the kind of girl a guy would rather hug than screw?"

Helen shook her head in disgust. "Oh, Meggie, that guy was a drunken asshole. He knew he didn't stand a chance with you, so he tried to make you feel like crap. You're a beautiful, sexy, sweet girl, and don't you forget it. Are we going for a boat ride with Mac?"

"No, Mac has a doctor's appointment. One of his poker buddies is taking him. He wants to meet you sometime before you leave."

"I want to meet him, too. So, what do you want to do today?"

I stood up and said, "How about we go shopping? I need new sneakers, and maybe you could help me pick out a sexy outfit for tomorrow night."

She wiggled her hips and said, "Nobody does sexy better than I do. I'll find you the perfect outfit to knock his socks off. I'm ready if you want to go now."

"Okay."

We walked out to the store and I asked Journey where we should go shopping. She told us we should head for Garden City, and, if we didn't find anything there, to hit the Providence Place Mall. She wrote down directions for me. I kind of had an idea where we were going, but I'm glad she refreshed my memory.

When we got on Route 4, Helen asked if we could stop for coffee.

I said, "I know just the place—Allie's Donuts. Best donuts and coffee in Rhode Island. It's just off the highway on Route 2. Allie's has been around forever. Mom and I always made early-morning trips to Allie's for donuts when we came up here for our family vacations. Mom only eats donuts when she's in Rhode Island. She says if she can't have Allie's, she'll go without."

I found the place without a problem. We both got coffee and an old-fashioned donut with chocolate icing.

Helen was halfway finished eating her donut when she turned to me and said, "I might have to move here. Everything is great up here. The sex, the people, the donuts."

I told her, "Wait until you have a Del's Lemonade."

We got to Garden City and went through several shops until Helen found the perfect dress for me. It was a black strapless with an empire waist and a flirty skirt that ended about three inches above my knees. Of course, then we had to go to Vicky's and get a sexy black strapless bra and panties to match. We both bought a few other items there as well. We had lunch at a cute little restaurant and then went up to the Providence Place Mall, where I continued to do damage to my credit card. To go with the dress, I got a new pair of sexy black sandals and a beautiful Judith Jack necklace with earrings to match. I also picked up a new pair of Nikes, a pair of topsiders, and a cute skirt and top. Helen also made me buy some new perfume. I told her lately, I've been wearing lobster bait. She said a girl has to have a new perfume for a new guy. Helen did some damage herself at a few stores, and then she treated us both to a manicure and pedicure. We both contributed heavily to the economy of Rhode Island. I didn't feel too guilty though because I hadn't really bought any new clothes lately, and I hadn't spent much money since I'd been here.

We got back to the marina in time for me to close up. I was going to make dinner, but Hel said, "You have to be as tired as I am. Let's just order a pizza."

The pizza arrived, I opened a bottle of wine, and we stepped out to the deck to enjoy the beautiful evening. We sat out there for a couple of hours just relaxing and talking. At about 8:30, we went in the house, and I suggested we watch a movie. I had brought a couple of my favorite movies up with me. We decided to watch our ultimate favorite, *Bridget Jones's Diary*.

Halfway through the movie, I started to itch. It suddenly dawned on me that I hadn't put my bug cream on. I lifted up my shorts, and I had about twenty-five big welts on my thighs from mosquito bites.

I jumped up and screamed, "Shit, shit, shit."

Helen looked up in alarm. "What's wrong?"

I lifted up my shorts.

She looked at my thighs and said, "Oh, shit."

"We have to go to the drug store and get some Benadryl and some cortisone cream. I can't believe how stupid I am," I said in a panic.

We went into town to the CVS. When we got back to the cottage, I took some Benadryl and lathered up my legs with the cream. I was sick. What if Ian finally made the moves on me? There was no way I could let him see my thighs. Just when everything was looking up with Ian, this has to happen.

Helen tried to cheer me up. "I'm sure they won't look that bad in the morning, Meggie. Just don't scratch them."

"Believe me, I won't. I don't need them looking any worse than they are now."

Helen commiserated. "You poor thing."

"Well, there's nothing I can do about it. He probably won't want to sleep with me anyway."

Helen trying to reassure me saying, "He will, and tomorrow you'll look a lot better."

"I hope so."

We watched the rest of the movie and went to bed.

When I woke up the next day, the bites looked worse. They had turned darker in color and now looked like really bad bruises. They were still swollen to the size of a half dollar and they hurt like hell. If I could've jumped out of my skin I would have. I put on some more cortisone cream and went to work.

When Journey got in, I went over to the Shack for some coffee. Mo was waiting on a few customers who were getting coffee and bagels to go. I took a seat at the counter, and when everyone left, she looked at me and asked gently, "Honey, who died?"

I stood up and lifted up my shorts.

She looked at my thighs. "What the hell happened?"

I said, "Mosquito bites. I'm allergic, and I forgot to put on my bug repellent cream."

She came around the counter and gave me a big hug. I started to cry. "Mo, why do things like this always happen to me?"

Mo led me over to a stool at the counter. "Sweetheart, you just sit down. I'm gonna get you some coffee and cut you a piece of the ham and cheese quiche I just pulled out of the oven."

She served me the quiche and coffee. Even if I'm not hungry, when I walk into the Shack, all it takes is one whiff of Mo's cooking and my stomach starts to growl.

I moaned, "Mo, can you believe it? Ian finally asked me out on a real date, and I look like this! I just can't get a break."

She said, "Honey, it's not how you look but what's inside."

"Sure," I said sarcastically.

"When I get blue, I go fishin'."

"I didn't know you liked to fish, Mo."

She said, "I'm not talkin' about that kind of fishin'. I go fishin' for a memory, a good one. The one I pull up the most is this one. I once was madly in love with a guy with one leg. It was durin' the Vietnam days, and he lost his left leg in the war. He was a big, strappin' Nebraska farm boy who rode the rodeo in the off-season. I met him when he just got out of the Veterans Hospital on the base I was stationed at in Texas. It didn't matter to me that he only had one leg. He was a great guy and let me tell you, that was some of the best sex I ever had. I don't know if it was ridin' those broncos or what, but he was something else."

"What happened? Why didn't you wind up with him?"

She said, "Well, I was young and I just wasn't ready to marry anyone, and he actually had a sweetheart back home. He was afraid to go home, thinkin' that she wouldn't want him with only one leg and all. By the time I got finished with him, that soldier felt like he could conquer the world. He went home and married her. He wrote to me and thanked me. I didn't sleep with him out of pity; I was attracted to him for the wonderful person he was. I served in the Marine Corps for over twenty years, but nothin' made me feel prouder than when I got that letter from that soldier."

A wave of shame swept over me. Mo's story put things in perspective. Here I was worrying about some stupid mosquito bites when there were people in the world who had real problems.

"Mo, you're one of the best people I've ever met," I told her.

"Back atcha, sweetie."

"How was your date with Elvis?"

She laughed, put her hand on her hips, and writhed seductively.

She said, "Elvis with the thrustin' pelvis? Well, I met him at the restaurant. As soon as I walked in, I knew who my date for the evenin' was. He was standin' at the bar. He had the black Elvis hair. Of course, his was dyed. He wasn't the young-lookin' Elvis, that was for sure. Not that I expected him to be young, but he looked like what Elvis would look like if he was still alive today. He was old, fat, bloated Elvis.

"He had on white tight pants, a black shirt opened almost

to his navel, and around his neck hung so many gold chains it's a wonder he wasn't hunched over. What guy wears white pants these days? His big gut hung over a giant belt buckle I could barely see. It crossed my mind that I should just turn and run, but I then I decided this could be a hoot. He had told me he was an Elvis impersonator online, so I figured he just did it for a job. No, he thought he *was* Elvis. He talked like Elvis and after one glance at him, I could tell he believed he was the sexiest man alive. I had to bite my lip to keep from laughin'."

"Did you stay for dinner?"

"Oh yeah, and then the fun really started. He took me to a karaoke bar so I could hear him sing."

"How was he?"

"I'll give him credit, he was great. He sang 'Are You Lonesome Tonight' and when I closed my eyes, I almost believed it was the real Elvis himself up there singin'. Well, when the song was over and I opened my eyes, I knew I wasn't that lonesome. I thanked him for dinner and high-tailed it out of that bar."

"Oh, Mo. I knew if anyone could make me laugh today, it would be you. You're amazing."

She looked at me seriously and said, "Honey, Ian is a good guy, and I think he really cares about you. You get yourself all gussied up and have fun tonight. What will be, will be."

"Thanks for the pep talk and the quiche Mo; it was great."

As I was walking out the door, she said, "Hey, how was your friend's date with the Stallion?"

I laughed. "I made her promise me she would come over and tell you all about it. She should get up in a little while."

She rubbed her hands together in excitement. "That gives me somethin' to look forward to. Have a great time tonight."

I nodded. "I promise."

I went over to the cottage on my lunch break and found Helen and Tony sunning on the deck.

Helen was concerned. "How are the bites?"

I groaned. "They don't itch as much, but they still look bad."

Tony lifted his head up off the deck chair and said, "Let me see, they can't be that bad."

I figured, what the hell, and lifted up my shorts.

He took a good long look and asked, "You want me to kiss them and make them better?"

Helen gave him a light smack on his arm.

I told him, "Tony, if I thought it would work, I'd let you have a go at it."

Helen said to Tony, "Meggie doesn't think she's sexy."

Tony winked at me. "Hey, I didn't call you Red Hot for nothing. Believe me, you're smoking hot. All men have an internal hotometer, and the first time I saw you, mine went off like a shot."

Helen arched her brow. "How about me?"

He shook his head. "Princess, you broke it. It'll never be the same again."

I was convinced. "Well, nothing will probably happen tonight anyway, so I'm not going to worry about it. Ian doesn't seem too interested."

Tony disagreed. "He's interested. He's just taking his time with you because of the code."

I asked, "What's the code?"

Tony whispered, "It's a secret code guys have."

Helen narrowed her eyes at him. "Okay, Maroni, spill."

He put up his hands. "Okay, but in order for me to tell you, you have to promise not to divulge this information to anyone. I need you both to cross your hearts, promise, and then lift up your shirts and show me your breasts."

Helen rolled her eyes. "God, I haven't heard that one since the sixth grade."

Tony said, "Okay, just cross your hearts."

We humored him.

He continued. "Well, the code is, you never date a friend's sister unless you really mean business. Meggie, you said Ian hung around with your brothers in the summer and went to school with one of them."

"Yes," I answered.

He said, "Well, Ian isn't going to make any moves on you unless he is absolutely sure he's in for the long haul."

Helen agreed. "That makes sense."

I thought about what he said for a minute. "I can buy that. None of Jack's or Charlie's friends ever asked me out, and I've been around a bunch of them over the years. I would've even said yes to a few of them."

Tony said, "As far as the bites are concerned, don't give it another thought. A guy could have a hell of a lot of fun connecting the dots."

We all laughed.

I asked them, "What have you two got planned for the afternoon?"

Tony said, "Well, I worked this morning, and this afternoon I'm gonna repair the bilge pump on my boat. I want to take my Princess to Block Island tomorrow."

"I'll help you," Helen offered.

Tony looked surprised. "Really?"

Helen said, "Sure, I'm an engineer. I can fix anything. Bring it on."

He took her hand and said, "Baby, you're turning me on again."

"Well have fun," I told them.

Helen said, "I'll help you get ready later for your date."

They walked down to the boat, and I went back to work.

CHAPTER TEN

Helen kept her word and helped me primp for my big date. She's great with hair and makeup. I never felt comfortable wearing a lot of cosmetics. Helen doesn't wear too much either, but she always knows just the right way to apply enough so that it looks good, but not overdone. Thank God the mosquitoes only went for my thighs. The bites were well hidden underneath my dress. I looked at myself in the mirror and was pleasantly surprised. The dress looked great, and I must say, I felt pretty.

Helen looked me over and exclaimed, "Meggie, you're beautiful. You've always had the most beautiful skin. You have the classic peaches-and-cream complexion."

Being Irish, I always burned. Basking on the beach was never an option for me unless I applied three tubes of sunscreen. I guess I'll be thankful for that when I get older. I'm always jealous when I see a beautiful woman with a great tan, though.

"Thanks Hel," I said and gave her a big hug. "I'm so glad you're here."

"Meggie, in all the years we've been friends, I've never

seen you this worked up about a guy. You were never this excited about a date with Jimmy."

I laughed and said, "Well, it's not like I dated a lot. But no, I've never felt this way about anyone. For the first time in my life, I'm looking forward to a first date. Maybe it's because I've known him for years. It's strange. I feel comfortable with him, but he also makes me a nervous wreck. I'm so attracted to him. He literally makes me weak in the knees. I can't wait for you to meet him."

Ian showed up at 7:30 on the dot. He knocked on the screen door, and I went to let him in. He looked so handsome. He had on a pair of creased khaki pants and a sage-colored, short-sleeved silk shirt, which made his gorgeous green eyes smolder. In his right hand, he held a beautiful bouquet of summer flowers. Helen was behind me, and I kept my eyes fixed on Ian's smiling face. If he briefly looked at me, then stared at Helen, I knew that would be a sign that he wasn't really into me.

He didn't let me down. Ian only had eyes for me. He looked me up and down and back again. This outfit was worth every plastic penny it cost. He said, "Meggie, you look beautiful."

He handed me the flowers, and I could feel the blood rush to my face.

I finally found my voice and said, "These are beautiful. Thank you."

I then turned to Helen and introduced them.

Ian smiled. "Helen, it's great to meet you. Meggie was looking forward to your visit."

"It's nice to meet you, Ian, and I have to say, I love Rhode

Island."

He said, "It's a great place. I hope you've been enjoying yourself."

"I've been having a great time. The people here are fantastic," exclaimed Helen.

"You're absolutely right," said Ian. "We're a lucky bunch around this marina."

Helen offered to put the flowers in a vase for me and started waving us out of the cottage. As Ian and I walked away, I looked back at Helen who gave me a two-thumbs-up.

I had only seen Ian in his truck, so I was surprised when he escorted me over to a beautiful, classic, silver Mercedes coupe.

Excited, I asked, "Ian, is this yours? It's beautiful!"

"It's a toy. You know guys; we have to have our toys. I don't take it out often, but I wanted tonight to be special."

I gave him a warm smile and said, "I feel honored."

He opened the door for me, and I got in the car. I was careful to make sure I held my dress down so he wouldn't see my bites and run for the hills.

I asked him, "Where are we going?"

"I made reservations for us in Newport."

"Oh, that's great. I haven't been to Newport since I got here."

He said, "It's always packed over there in the summer, but during the week it usually isn't too bad. I never go over there on the weekends; it's a zoo."

"I told Helen she needs to visit there before she leaves. I want her to tour the mansions and see the wharf area."

Ian suggested, "Maybe we could all go over some night

before she leaves."

"She'd love that."

Ian put some soft rock on the radio, and I settled back to enjoy the ride over. You have to go over the Jamestown and Newport bridges to get to Newport. The views of Narragansett Bay from those vantage points are breath-taking. We lucked out and found a parking space across the street from Bowen's Wharf. We walked hand in hand across the street and down a cobblestone street to a nice restaurant situated at the end of the wharf.

The restaurant had great ambience with handsome, dark wood paneling and large windows to maximize the views. The host showed us to an intimate table for two by a window overlooking the docks and water. The table was set with beautiful, crisp white linens, china, silver, and crystal. In the center of the table sat a candle and a small vase of roses with petals of pure white, penciled with pink at the edges. Newport is the sailing capital of the world, and there were several large, sleek sailboats docked at the wharf. I was definitely impressed. So far this is the best date I've ever had and the night is young.

The waiter came, and I ordered a cup of lobster bisque and the roasted striped bass with braised fennel. I love the licorice flavor of fennel. Ian ordered a cup of chowder, and mahi mahi with avocado melon salsa. He also ordered us a nice bottle of Chardonnay to go with the meal.

When the waiter left, Ian asked me how things were going for me at the marina.

"Good. There is something I wanted to talk to you about, though. About five marina customers have come up to me in the past several weeks, and they're all missing things from their boats."

He frowned, "You're kidding. That's unusual. People have always been able to leave their boats unlocked and nothing ever gets stolen. What's been taken?"

"Well, just small stuff like sunglasses, a flashlight, a bucket. Things like that. What do you think I should do?"

"Well, I would keep an eye on it. If more stuff goes missing, then you should probably call the police and get it on record. There's probably nothing they can do about it, though. You should also call a meeting of the marina customers on a Saturday when most of them are down on their boats. Let them know what's been going on so they can start locking up and tell them to keep an eye out for people wandering around the marina who don't belong there."

"That's a good idea. I hope it won't come to that."

He said, "I'm glad you told me. I have a lot of expensive equipment on my boats. I'm going to tell my guys to start buttoning the boats up at night. Do you leave the cottage open when you're in the store?"

"Yes, I do."

"Well, you should start locking it. When you're home at night, if you have the door open, make sure that screen door is locked. If there isn't a lock on it, let me know, and I'll install one for you. It's probably just some kids stealing small stuff, but better to be on the safe side." He winked at me and said, "I don't want anything happening to my girl."

His concern for me warmed my heart and his last comment made my face turn red.

I told him, "I'll let you know if anything else goes missing."

He said, "By the way, you're quite the hero at the marina."

"What do you mean?" I said cautiously. I had no idea what he was talking about.

He laughed and said, "All the guys are talking about how you jumped in the water to save Diesel. Don't be surprised if you're on the dock and a couple of guys jump in the water and start thrashing around."

"I could get my picture posted on the pilings again."

He smiled and said, "When I saw you with that lobster bait all over you, I knew you were going to be trouble."

"What do you mean—trouble?"

"The good kind."

Our food was served, and we enjoyed a great meal. Ian's a foodie, too, and we had fun sampling each other's dishes. Between courses, Ian reached across the table and held my hand. An elderly couple walked by us, and the woman said to her husband, "Isn't that romantic, George; they're holding hands." I blushed, and Ian smiled at them. I've got to get a grip on my blushing.

We skipped dessert since we were both full. Afterward, Ian suggested taking a walk around the dock since it was such a nice night. It had gotten dark and the wharf was all lit up with twinkle lights. It was beautiful. With a full belly and enough wine to be a little fuzzy, I felt I was in a romantic wonderland. This was the perfect night. One of the restaurants had an outdoor seating area, and they had a three-piece band playing. People sat enjoying their meals and some couples on the wharf were dancing to the music. They started to play an old slow song, "You Belong to Me." Ian took me in his arms and started to dance with me. It was the most romantic moment of my life. He held me close, and we swayed to the music. When the song was over and we drew apart, I felt a little dizzy. He pulled me back to him and gave me a little peck on the lips, then took my hand, and we continued our stroll around the wharf.

After a while, we passed by an ice cream store.

He asked, "Are you ready for dessert?"

"I've never been known to pass up ice cream."

He ordered himself a cup of coffee ice cream, and for me, my favorite, strawberry ice cream in a sugar cone.

I told him, "When I die, I want to be buried in a vat of strawberry ice cream."

"My mom used to say something like that. Whenever we went out for breakfast, and they had Eggs Benedict on the menu, she had to have it. Then she'd say she wanted to be buried in a vat of hollandaise sauce."

"Hollandaise would work for me, too."

We finished off our ice cream on the way to the car. I was proud of myself. Not one drop landed on my new dress.

When we got back to the cottage, Ian came around to open the car door for me. As we walked up to the cottage, Ian said, "Let me know what night Helen and Tony want to go to Newport. Or, if you would all like to come to my house for dinner, we could do that instead. Has she had a lobster yet?"

"I don't think so. That would be fun."

He laughed. "Well, I know where we can get some."

He put his hands on my upper arms, and pulled me in for a kiss. He gave me a long, delicious ice-cream-flavored kiss.

We took a breath and I softly whispered, "Would you like to come in?"

He bent down and touched his forehead to mine.

"Meggie, if I come in, I won't want to leave. I want to make love to you in the worst way, but I want to do this right. I want us to get to know each other a little better. I knew you years ago as a child, but I want to get to know the grownup Meggie. I feel it's important that we don't rush into anything. I would like to wait a little bit before we go to the next step."

I took a deep breath and said, "I'm so relieved."

"Why? You didn't really want me to stay?"

"No, I definitely want you to. It's not that. I'm allergic to mosquitoes."

He looked confused. "What's does that have to do with sleeping with me?"

"The other night Helen and I sat out on the deck talking for a couple of hours, and I forgot to put my bug repellent on. I have huge bites on my thighs."

He started laughing. "You know, I think I changed my mind. I want to see those bites," he teased.

"No, I like your idea better."

He shook his head. "Meggie, you're a mess."

"Yeah. I guess it's a good thing you're finding that out now."

He wrapped his arms around me and gave me a warm, sensual kiss. Then, softly whispered in my ear, "I like messes."

I murmured, "I'm glad."

He said, "I'd better get going or I'll never leave. I'll stop by and see you after work tomorrow."

I looked up at him. "Ian, I had a great time tonight. Thank you."

He winked at me and said, "Me, too, Meggie the mess. Goodnight."

I watched him walk away, and then I went into the cottage. I undressed, put some cortisone cream on the bites, and went to bed smiling.

When I got up in the morning, I checked Helen's room. She was MIA again, so I left a note on her bed to stop by and see me when she got back. Since I had a few minutes, I decided to check my e-mails. There was one from my parents, and one from Laura. I checked the one from my mom first.

Hi, Meggie:

Have you heard from your grandmother again? She's been on my mind a lot. Your father and I are having fun, but I'm getting a little homesick. Our flight home is all set for August 5th and I can't wait to see you. Maybe Dad and I will come up for a little visit while you're still there. I hope things are going well at the marina. We're very proud of our special girl.

Love, Mom

Ah! I answered her back.

Hi, Mom:

Everything here is going okay. Helen is here for a week and we've been having fun. The last time I talked to Gram she sounded really happy, so I think this vacation has been a good thing for her; I'm sure she's fine. I miss you all and can't wait to see you.

Love, Meggie

Laura wrote:

Hi, Meggie:

What have you and Helen been up to? Have you been out with that guy yet? Has Helen met anyone? A cop showed up at the door the other day and wanted to know who called 911. Aidan was standing beside me and said Eddie did it and ran down the hallway. The cop asked me who Eddie was and I shook my head and told him it was the dog. So, while my four-year-old is calling 911, I've been very busy potty training Danny. Thank God it's summer and I can let him run around naked half the time. Throwing Cheerios in the toilet seems to help, too. It gives him something to aim at. Such is my exciting life. Hope all is well.

Love, Laura

I replied.

Dear Laura:

I have so much to tell you. First of all, Jimmy showed up late one night and begged me to take him back. He even went so far as to ask me to marry him. Can you believe that one? I told him no, of course. I actually was nice to him, even though he didn't deserve it after the way he treated me. Whatever feelings I had for him are long gone, I'm happy to say.

After a rocky start with Ian, that's the guy I told you about, he and I had our first real date last night. It couldn't have gone better. He's the whole package. He's handsome, fun, romantic, and he's a great kisser. That's as far as we got, but I'm hoping things will progress. I'm developing feelings for him, but I'm trying to hold back. My track record with men, as you know, hasn't been the greatest. My head tells me what the smart thing to do is, and then my heart and body tell me something entirely different.

Things at the marina are going well enough. There have been some thefts I'm worried about, but so far they've been minor. I heard from Gram. She said she's having a great time, but I'm still worried about her. I probably won't stop worrying until she is standing in front of me and I can see her with my own two eyes.

Helen is having a ball. I'll be surprised if she goes home. I'll have her call you and fill you in.

Good luck with the potty training and maybe you should hide the phone. Give the boys a hug.

Love, Meggie

I hit the Send button and went to open up the store.

At around 9:00, Helen stopped by. The first thing out of her mouth was, "How was your date?"

"It was great. No, it was perfect. We had a romantic dinner and then went for a walk around the wharf. When he brought me home, I invited him in, but he said he wanted us to get to know each other better before we took the next step."

"Boy, Tony was right on the money with the code thing. I think that is really sweet. This could be serious, Meggie."

I sighed, "I know it is for me, I'm halfway in love with him already. I refuse to get my heart stomped on again, though. How do you do it? I don't think I've ever heard you say that you were in love. Lust yes, love no."

"I don't think I've been in love. You know what a cynic I am. I told you before, if you believe the worst, you usually won't be disappointed," she joked.

"Maybe Tony will be the guy to break that barrier down and turn you into a believer in true love."

She pointed her finger at me. "You need to stop reading romances."

I laughed, "Never."

Helen said, "Ian's really handsome. He reminds me of

that hot doctor who was on the TV show 'Lost.' He has the same tall, lean, muscular body, and the strong facial features."

"You mean Matthew Fox? Now that you mention it, he does look like him. How was your night?"

"Tony picked me up right after you left and took me back to his house. He made me a fantastic dinner. The guy's a gourmet cook. He learned from his mother and grandmother. He made veal Marsala and roasted asparagus. It was delicious. When he was in college, he shared a house with three girls. He did all the cooking, while they cleaned and did his laundry. He is just too good to be true. I keep looking for the flaw, but so far I haven't found one."

"Are you going to Block Island?"

"Yeah, I'm just on my way down to the boat. We were going to spend the night out there, but Tony's mom called and a friend of the family died. He has to go to a viewing tonight. Do you have plans with Ian?"

"No. Great, we'll do something fun together. By the way, Ian wanted to know if you and Tony would like to come over his house for lobster some night."

Helen said, "Definitely. How about tomorrow night? Saturday night is my last night here, and Tony said he has big plans for us."

"Okay. I'll tell Ian Friday sounds good. Have fun on the island."

She started towards the door, looked back, and smiled, "Oh I will."

Later that morning, a few more customers came in to see me. Dino from *Atsa Ma Boat* was missing some fishing pliers, and Donna and Dave on the *Tireless* were missing a fender. I informed them about the other missing items, and suggested that they start locking things up. I added their things to the lost-and-found list posted on the bulletin board. I made up a flyer informing everyone of the missing items and asked everyone to be on the lookout for strange people walking the docks.

Since I didn't eat breakfast, by lunchtime I was starving, so I went over to the Snack Shack. Sitting at Mo's counter were Big H, Sexy Cathy, and Dancing Kathy. I took a seat next to Dancing Kathy who turned to me and asked, "How's it going?"

I said, "Pretty good, but more people have reported things missing from their boats. I'm going to put a flyer on all the boats this afternoon to warn people to lock things up."

Big H said, "That's a good idea. What a shame. We've never had a problem like that down here."

Mo suggested, "You should talk to Deb about it. Bein' a retired cop, she might have some good ideas for you."

I said, "That's a great idea. If any of you see her, tell her I'd like to talk to her."

Mo said, "Sure. What can I get you?"

I ordered a roasted veggie wrap and an iced tea.

I asked everyone, "So, what else is new around here?"

Sexy Cathy said brightly, "Well, Just Howard has a new girlfriend."

Big H immediately stood up and said, "Well, I'm out of here. I'll leave you ladies to your gossip." He was out the door in a flash.

I turned back to Sexy Cathy to get the scoop. "Really?"

Sexy Cathy laughed and said, "Yep. He's been strutting

around the marina like a rooster."

I laughed and said, "Good for him. What does she look like?"

Dancing Kathy thought a moment. "Well, I would say she looks to be a couple of years younger than he is, probably mid-forties. She's short, which is good, since he's vertically challenged. Her name is Barbara. She has short blond hair and she's cute. She's a high school music teacher, and she directs all the high school plays. Just Howard also bragged that she's a songwriter."

Mo added, "She's multitalented."

Sexy Cathy chimed in. "I thought I was hearing things the other day when I heard Barbra Streisand and show tunes coming from B dock. Barbara was playing the soundtrack from the *Sound of Music*. When I saw Mikey Murphy do a twirl on the dock like Julie Andrews did in the movie, I almost fell in the water laughing."

Mo chuckled, "Those Murphy brothers crack me up. I'm happy for Just Howard. He's had a hard time with the ladies, bein' so shy and all. I guess he must be gettin' lucky if he's lettin' her play show tunes."

Dancing Kathy started swaying back and forth on her stool. "Oh yeah. His boat's been a rockin'."

We all laughed.

Sexy Cathy asked Mo, "Any new dates this week?"

Mo said, "I'm goin' out with that tall widower again. There were no sparks flyin' last time we went out, but I thought I'd give him another try just to make sure. I'm still talkin' on the Net with that one guy I really like. We have great chats, but he hasn't asked me out yet. Also, I've been chattin' with a new one, but he's a taxidermist and I just can't get past him stuffin' dead things. I wouldn't want those hands touchin' me."

Sexy Cathy said, "I don't blame you.

Mo asked me, "So, how was your date with Ian?"

Sexy Cathy said, "Oh, he's a cutie."

I agreed, "He sure is. We had a great time. He took me to Newport for dinner."

Dancing Kathy sighed. "I remember those days when you're first dating and the guys are all charming and they take you to nice places. Now Mike thinks he's Mr. Wonderful if he picks up a pizza. I guess after twenty-five years of marriage and four kids, I should be thrilled with the pizza."

I said, "Wow, you have four kids?"

Dancing Kathy laughed and said, "Yep, two boys and two girls. I'm a very busy woman."

Sexy Cathy said, "Meggie, I saw your friend and Tony take off on his boat."

I said, "Yeah, they went to Block Island for the day."

Dancing Kathy said, "She's caused quite a stir on the docks. The guys are all drooling over her. I thought I was going to have to put a bib on Mike."

Sexy Cathy nodded, "When any of the guys see her, they yell to each other 'Goddess alert.' When is she leaving? She's making the rest of us look bad. Kenny loves tall, thin women with big boobs."

Mo shrugged. "What guy doesn't?"

I smiled and said, "She's always had that effect on men. She's leaving on Sunday."

Mo said, "Tony's gonna be heartbroken. I thought I'd never see the day, but that boy's a goner."

Sexy Cathy asked me, "How does she feel about him?"

"She likes him a lot."

Mo said, "Well, maybe they'll keep it goin' long distance. If anyone should breed, it's those two. Their kids would be beautiful."

I smiled and said, "Tony's mother would love that."

Matt came into the shack grinning ear to ear. "You ladies need to come down and see the fish hanging on the dock. *The Bonnie Blue* just got back from being out overnight. They got a 655-pound giant tuna."

Mo said, "Holy cow! Who caught it?"

Matt said in awe, "Bonnie hooked it and reeled the fish in all by herself."

Mo said, "Now that's girl power. Let's go check it out."

We all went down to see the fish, the largest I've ever seen. Everyone was congratulating Bonnie, and Jim was taking pictures of her with the fish, telling everyone Bonnie was his lucky charm, his Queen of the Ocean.

Matt turned to me and said, "Once word gets out about this fish, everybody in Cozy Harbor will be coming to take a look. You might be pretty busy this afternoon in the store. You should also order more frozen mackerel and butterfish. Everyone's gonna be going fishing now that they know there are giants around, and they'll want bait."

I went back to the office and did indeed have a busy afternoon. All anyone could talk about was the giant tuna. Journey and I sold a lot of fishing lures and T-shirts that afternoon. Ian came by the office later in the day.

My heart took a little leap in my chest when I saw him standing at the office door.

He gave me that melt-my-heart smile. "How was your day?" he asked.

"Good. Really busy. Did you see the tuna?"

"Pretty impressive. Bonnie makes a hell of a first mate."

I nodded. "I talked to Helen and she said Friday would be a good night to get together."

"Good. I'll bring home the lobsters and pick up some corn and potatoes at the farm stand."

"I'll make a salad and a dessert."

"Sounds like a plan. What are you doing tonight?"

"Tony has to go to a viewing, so Helen and I are going to do something together."

"Great. I have a meeting of the Lobstermen's Association. You girls have fun."

He looked out into the store, then pulled me out of my chair and kissed me. As soon as his lips touched mine, my knees went a little weak. After he left, I had a hard time concentrating.

After I closed up the store at six, I went down to the docks to deliver the flyers about the thefts. I saw Tony's boat at the dock, but it didn't look like anyone was on it, so I assumed Helen must be at the cottage. As I went down B dock, I saw a crowd in front of the *Tuna Kahuna*. Standing on the boat were the Murphy brothers and Helen. They all had a beer in hand. I walked up to the guys on the dock and asked Randy from the *Blood, Sweat and Beers* what was going on.

He said, "The boys got a new radar installed, but they were having trouble getting it to work. We've been trying to figure out the problem all afternoon. Your friend came over and it took her all of about five minutes to solve the problem."

I laughed and said, "She's a smart girl."

Randy said, "Beauty and brains." He shook his head. "That Tony is one lucky son of a bitch."

Helen looked up, saw me, and waved.

Don Murphy said, "Meggie, Helen's not allowed to go home. We need her around here."

I said, "Fine with me."

Helen smiled and handed Don her empty beer bottle. "I'm glad I could help, guys. See you later." As she climbed off the boat, all the guys scrambled to give her a hand.

As we walked up the dock, Don yelled, "Hey, Meggie, I've got dibs on the next friend of yours who comes to visit."

Helen and I laughed.

Helen said to me as we walked up the dock, "Between Bonnie bringing in that fish and me fixing the radar, it was a bad day for the guys down here. I hope they all don't have pecker problems tonight."

I laughed. "Don't you love it?"

She said, "Damn right I do."

CHAPTER ELEVEN

Since Helen had spent most of her time on Tony's boat, I decided to take her for a drive around the area and give her a little tour. First I took her over to the Pier Area in Narragansett and drove down Ocean Road so she could see the Towers and the sea wall. Then I drove over to Galilee and took a little spin through the village. Both of us were hungry by this time, so I pointed the car toward Kelly's. A burger sounded good. When we got there, all the tables were taken, so we sat down at the bar and ordered our burgers and a couple of beers. I asked the bartender if they had a band tonight, and he said they had an Irish band.

Helen and I devoured our burgers and ordered another beer. We decided to stay and listen to the band for a set. More people started to come into the bar, and a little skinny, nerdy-looking guy with a buzz cut came in and sat next to Helen. I had an older couple next to me. The nerdy guy looked at us and said, "Okay, now I know who's responsible for global warming."

Helen looked at me and rolled her eyes.

The guy said, "Hi, my name is Pete."

Helen said, "I'm Helen, and this is Meggie. Is that your best line?"

He said, "I have a million of them. Maybe you girls could help me out and tell me which ones you like best."

We both said, "Okay."

He said, "Do you have a quarter? I need to call my mother and tell her I met the woman of my dreams."

We both made a face and he said, "Can I buy you a drink or should I just give you the money?"

We shook our heads no.

He said, "I may not be Fred Flintstone, but I bet I can make your bed rock."

Helen laughed and said, "Keep going."

He said, "Do you believe in love at first sight, or should I walk by again?"

I said, "I like that one."

He said, "My name is Pete. Remember it because you'll be screaming it later."

Helen said, "You'll get smacked with that one."

Then he said, "Okay, this is my last one." He looked Helen up and down and said, "Wow, all those curves, and me with no brakes."

She said, "That's my favorite. Where do you get all these lines from?"

He said, "The Internet, where else. Can I buy you ladies a drink for putting up with me?"

We looked at each other and said, "Sure."

I felt someone behind me, and then that someone kissed me on the neck. I turned around and Ian was standing there. Whenever I see him, it's as if a light goes on inside me.

He said, "I was on my way home and saw your car, so I thought I'd stop by. I hope you don't mind?"

"No. I'm glad you did."

"I hope I'm not infringing on a girls' night out."

"Not at all. We came for a burger and decided to hear one set of the band, then head home."

I asked him, "How was your meeting?"

"Lively as usual."

Ian ordered himself a beer, and then Helen introduced him to Pete. The band was setting up and the bar was getting crowded. A tall, pretty brunette came up to Ian and draped her arms around him.

She said, "Hey stranger, I haven't heard from you in a while."

Ian looked at me and then back at her. He said, "Cindy, I want you to meet my girlfriend, Meggie."

Cindy looked at me in surprise and said, "Well, that explains a lot. Hello, Meggie."

I blushed and said hi. I looked over at Helen, and she smiled and raised her eyebrows.

Cindy unwrapped herself from Ian and said to him, "Well, this is a sad day for a lot of ladies. You're a lucky girl, Meggie. It was nice to meet you. Bye, Ian."

He said, "See you around, Cindy."

Pete said to Ian, "I guess the red one's taken."

Ian put his arm around me and said, "Afraid so."

Pete said to Helen, "How about you, blond one?

She said, "Sorry, I'm taken, too."

Pete said, "Well, I guess I'll mingle and try my lines out on some other girls."

Helen rubbed his crew cut and said, "Don't give up, Romeo. Keep working on those lines."

He gave us a bow and wandered off down the bar. Helen moved over, and Ian sat between us.

Ian said, "I'm looking forward to tomorrow night. Why don't you come over about 7:30?"

I said, "7:30 is good."

The band started to play. They were great. They started a real lively tune and Helen turned to me and said, "Hey, Meggie, you up for a dance? We can show off our old stuff."

"Sure."

When I was in the fifth grade, my mom decided I should take Irish step dancing. I didn't want to because I didn't know anyone else taking it. She called Helen's mom and asked her if Helen could take them with me. So Helen became the only Polish Irish step dancer in the class. We took lessons for three years and had a lot of fun. We got to dance in all the local parades, with the highlight being Philadelphia's annual St. Patrick's Day Parade. To this day, whenever we're at an Irish bar, we always get up and do our favorite routine. We kicked off our flip-flops and got out there and did our number. The dance floor cleared as people watched us and clapped to the music. When we finished, everyone gave us a big round of applause.

We went back to the bar and Ian said, "That was great. You're both terrific dancers."

I said to him, "I have a lot of other talents, too."

He looked me up and down and said, "Believe me, I intend to discover each and every one of them."

It suddenly got very warm in the bar.

We finished our beers and, when the set ended, we got up and left. Ian walked us to my car, gave me a quick kiss, and said goodnight.

As we drove home, Helen said, "Meggie, did you love the look on Cindy's face when Ian called you his girlfriend?"

"I can't believe he did that. I was floored."

"No one deserves a nice guy more than you do, Meggie. I'm happy for you but sad at the same time. I have a feeling you won't be coming back to Philly. What will I do without my best friend?"

I said, "I don't know what will happen. Maybe you'll wind up in Rhode Island with Tony."

Helen said, "You never know."

I said, "I guess it would be hard for you to give up your job. Maybe Tony would move to Philly."

"No way. After college, he worked on Wall Street for five years. He gave himself five years in New York with the goal of making a lot of money and then moving back to Rhode Island. After his five years were up, he did just that and bought his business and his house. He hates big cities. If we ever got to the point of marriage, no way could I ask that of him. Besides, it would kill his mother. I'm very marketable, and I wouldn't have trouble getting a job here. If I left Philly, my mother would still have my brother and sister to torture."

"God, Hel, wouldn't it be crazy if we both wound up here."

"Time will tell. I'm still looking for Tony's flaw."

"What are you doing tomorrow?"

"Tony is taking me to Newport to tour the mansions."

"You'll love Newport. I'm gonna owe Tony for entertaining

you."

She gave me a wicked smile and said, "Don't worry about it. He's been paid in full, over and over again."

When we got home, I decided to just go to bed. I wanted to get a good night's sleep so I would feel great tomorrow. Helen decided to do the same thing. I was enjoying working my way through Gram's Elizabeth Adler collection, and I was halfway through *Peach*. I read for a while and fell asleep.

Friday mornings are always really busy, and this one was no exception. Around 10:00, Deb and Terry stopped in.

Deb said, "Hey, Meggie. I heard you wanted to talk to me."

I said, "I need some advice."

She said, "Shoot."

I took them over to the bulletin board and explained about all the thefts. I asked them, "Do you think I should call the cops?"

Deb said, "Since it's just small stuff, I can almost guarantee it's kids. An adult would go for the more expensive stuff. Terry and I are going to be down here all weekend. We'll do a little stake-out. I'll catch the bugger. There really is nothing the police can do at this point. They're not going to station a cop down here for a missing pair of sunglasses and a bucket."

I said, "I told everyone in the flyer I left on the boats to watch out for people walking around the docks who don't belong here."

Deb said, "That's good. But the average person doesn't usually know what to look for. Don't you worry, Meggie; I'll be on the job."

I said, "Thanks so much. I've been really worried about

this. Things have been going missing for a couple of weeks now."

I asked Terry, "How's Sue's divorce coming along?"

She grinned. "By the time I finish with that son of a bitch, I'll have his balls hanging from the piling next to Bonnie's giant tuna tail."

I laughed and told them to have a great weekend.

At about two o'clock, since things had calmed down, I left Journey in charge and slipped out to run a few errands. I stopped by Mac's house to check on him and see if he needed anything at the grocery store. He looked great and said the doctor told him he could start clamming again next week. I filled him in on my big date with Ian and our dinner tonight with Tony and Helen. Mac took me out back and gave me some beautiful tomatoes from his garden. He said he was all stocked up with food and didn't need a thing. I gave him a kiss and continued with my errands. Since Mac gave me the beautiful tomatoes, I decided to make a Caprese salad. I picked up some fresh mozzarella and basil for the salad, and then I took a look at all the berries on display and decided to make a fresh fruit tart, which I baked back at the cottage. I would make the salad at Ian's house.

I went back to the store and closed up. Helen was at the cottage when I got back. She had a great day and loved Newport.

I asked her, "What mansions did you tour?"

She said, "The Breakers and the Astor's Beechwood. It's hard to believe people lived that lavishly."

I shook my head and said, "I can't imagine what that would be like."

I jumped in the shower first, then dried my hair and put on a little makeup. I chose a tailored, white knee-length skirt and my favorite pink shirt. Helen was right behind me. She looked her gorgeous self by the time Tony arrived to pick us up.

I handed Tony the tart and his eyes lit up. He said, "Wow, did you make this?"

"Yes. I love to cook."

He said, "Can we have dessert first?"

I gave him a stern look and said, "No. You'll have to wait."

Tony drove us over to Ian's where they got a tour of his house, and then Ian made vodka tonics for everyone. Ian took Helen and Tony out on the deck, and Sam did a few tricks for them. I went into the kitchen to make the salad while Ian cooked the rest of the meal. The guys had fun teaching Helen how to take apart a lobster, a skill I had learned years ago from my mother and grandmother. Dinner was delicious. I served my tart and everyone went crazy over it. When we finished, we were all so full that Ian suggested we go for a little walk down the beach. Ian held my hand as we strolled along the sand.

When we got back to the house, Tony said, "Helen and I are going to take off. Thanks for a great dinner."

Helen said, "That was delicious."

Tony asked me, "Meggie, do you want a ride home?"

Ian quickly answered, "I'll take her."

Sam, Ian, and I walked them out. Ian shut the door and I said, "Let me help you clean up."

"Okay."

We made quick work of it. When we finished, I looked at

the clock and saw that it was 11:00.

I said, "Ian, it's getting late. Do you want to drive me home now?"

He came over to me, put his arms around me, and kissed me. He said, "Meggie, I don't want you to go."

I said, "I thought you wanted to wait and get to know me better."

He took my hand and put it over his heart. "I know you in here."

I touched his cheek and said, "I know you, too."

He gave me a long, scorching kiss, then worked his way down my neck, nibbling on my ear lobe on the way. I was melting. He kissed me again. His hands moved down my back and he pressed me closer to him. We couldn't get enough of each other. He finally stepped back and scooped me up in his arms and carried me upstairs. He gently laid me down on the bed and lit some candles. The moonlight shone in the windows.

He took off my sandals and kicked off his shoes and lay down next to me. He kissed me again and started to unbutton my blouse.

He said, "You're so beautiful. I want you so much. I've wanted you from the first moment I saw you standing on the dock."

I put my arms around his neck and said, "I've wanted you, too."

He undressed me like I was a beautifully wrapped present, savoring every moment. I lay there naked in his bed and watched him remove his clothes. I finally got to see his lean, hard, muscular body. It was even better than I imagined.

He was perfect. I wish I could just freeze-frame this moment.

After we made love for the second time, he turned to me, brushed my hair back and said, "Oh, Meggie. What am I going to do with you?"

I said, "I hope you'll do more of what you just did."

He laughed and kissed me. "You can count on it."

I had to ask him, "Ian, did you tell Cindy I was your girlfriend because you wanted to shake her loose, or did you really mean it?"

He said, "Meggie, I promise you, I'd never say anything like that unless I meant it."

"Good. I want you to know that I only date one guy at a time."

"Meggie, I think you're wondering if we're going to be exclusive."

"I know I was going to be because that's the way I am. But you said you have a lot of girlfriends."

He smiled and said, "I was kidding. You're the only girl I want to be with. Now, let me have another look at those mosquito bites."

I don't know when we fell asleep, but when I woke up, Ian was lying on his side looking at me.

I asked him, "Did you sleep?"

He nodded and said, "I woke up about five minutes ago. I wish we could stay in bed all day, but I've got to go to work."

"What time is it?"

"Four o'clock."

"I've got to open up the marina."

He said, "I'll jump in the shower and get some coffee going."

Then he kissed me and said, "Meggie, last night meant a lot to me."

"Me, too."

When Ian got out of the shower, I jumped in. When I got down to the kitchen, he handed me a cup of coffee.

I said, "I'll just take this with me."

When we got to the marina, it was just starting to get light. He said, "Have a great day. Can I see you tonight?"

I said, "I'd love that. Helen and Tony are going out."

He said, "I'll pick you up at 7:30."

He kissed me and went down to the docks.

When I got into the cottage, I had to do a happy dance. Today my life is perfect.

CHAPTER TWELVE

I couldn't stop smiling all morning. I'm so in love I can't stand myself. Helen stopped in mid-morning and found me in the office.

She took one look at my face and said, "So, I can see he didn't let you leave last night. It's written all over your face."

I sighed and said, "Being with him was everything I knew it would be and more. Hel, I love him. I know what you're thinking. I've fallen hard fast but I've never been more sure of anything in my life. He's it."

She smiled and said, "I like him, Meggie. He seems like a great guy. Just be careful. Just so you know, if he hurts you, I'll have to beat the crap out of him."

"Deal."

I asked her how her night was.

She said, "It was super-fantastic as usual. He's taking me to the beach today, then I'll be back to get ready for our last night. Tony has special plans, and I'm supposed to dress up. Are you seeing Ian tonight?"

"Yeah, I don't know what we're going to do, but he said he would pick me up at 7:30."

"Oh good, we can get ready together. I don't want to go home tomorrow," she whined.

"Hel, you're welcome to stay as long as you want."

"Thanks, but I can't. I've got a big meeting on Tuesday, and I've got to do a presentation. I need to get back and get ready for it. Tony is going to come down to Philly next weekend."

"That's great."

"Yeah. I'll show him our stomping grounds."

"Well, enjoy your last day."

"I'll see you around 6:00."

At the end of the day as I closed up the store, I realized that no one had been in to report any more thefts.

Helen and I helped each other get ready that evening for our big dates. She looked stunning in a gorgeous, strapless blue dress that matched her eyes. I wore my blue sundress with the tiny spaghetti straps. Tony showed up first, looking like he stepped off the cover of GQ. They made the most gorgeous couple. I saw them off and waited for Ian. He showed up in a pair of jeans and a light blue chambray shirt. He looked at me and said, "Sweetheart, you look beautiful, but I think you're going to have to change."

"Where are we going?"

"The Rhode Island Philharmonic is doing a concert tonight at Narragansett Town Beach. I've picked up a couple of different salads, some bread and wine. We're going to meet up with some friends of mine. They went early to save a spot."

"Okay. That's sounds fun. Just give me a minute."

He said, "Make sure you put on your bug cream, and bring a sweatshirt, too."

I put on another dose of bug cream and threw on some

capris and a long-sleeved shirt. I grabbed a sweatshirt and walked out into the living room.

Ian looked me over and said, "You look great no matter what you wear."

We were walking to the door when he stopped, put his arms around me, and gave me a long, deep kiss.

When we finally pulled apart, he smiled and said, "I've been looking forward to that all day."

I was a little nervous about meeting Ian's friends. We found them without a problem and Ian introduced me to Kristen and Jake and Tammy and Steve. Steve and Jake were childhood friends of Ian's. It was a great night to be on the beach. The music was beautiful. We all shared the food and wine and I got to know Ian's friends. After the concert was over, Ian took me back to his house where we spent another amazing night making love. I haven't been getting much sleep, but I've never felt better.

The next morning, I was in the store when I saw Tony's car pull up. I went out to say hi. Tony went down to his boat and said he'd be back to say goodbye after Helen got packed up. I went with her into the cottage.

I asked her, "So, where did Tony take you last night?"

She said, "We went to his favorite restaurant on Federal Hill. He knew the owner and half of the wait staff. The food was amazing and we were treated like royalty. Then he took me to Waterfire in downtown Providence. They have all these wood-burning cauldrons in the middle of the Providence River, which flows through the city. There was opera playing and tons of people strolling along the river. Tony arranged for us to take a gondola ride. I felt like I was in Venice. It was really romantic."

"Any flaws yet?"

"Not a one."

"Well, at least you'll see him next weekend."

She said, "It's going to be a long week."

I helped her pack, then we loaded up her truck.

She said, "Meggie, this was the best week ever. I love you."

I gave her a hug and said, "Love you too, Hel. Drive carefully."

Tony walked up, and I left them to say goodbye. As I walked away from them, I felt my eyes welling up. In a little over a month from now, I'll have to say goodbye to Ian.

Late in the afternoon, Deb and Terry came into the store.

Deb said, "Meggie, we caught the thief. It's a little boy about nine years old. We saw him sneaking on the *Breaking Wind.* He was on the boat for a couple of minutes and then left. We followed him out of the marina, and he pulled something out from under his shirt. We kept following him. He lives about two blocks away."

I asked her, "How do you think we should handle this? I don't want to call the police on a nine-year-old."

She said, "How about if Terry and I go talk to his mother?"

"I'd go with you, but Journey's not here today."

"No problem, Meggie. We'll handle it."

They came back an hour later.

Deb said, "The boy's name is Sean and his dad died in May. His mother said he's been having a really hard time dealing with his dad's death and he's been acting out."

I asked, "How did the dad die?"

Terry said, "Roadside bomb in Afghanistan. He was in

the National Guard."

My eyes welled up for the second time today.

I said, "Poor kid."

Deb said, "The mother's name is Marybeth. She called Sean in the room and asked him about the stolen items. He started crying and confessed. He had all the stuff he'd taken hidden under the cottage in the crawl space. Marybeth is making him load all the items in his wagon, and she's going to come down to the marina with him so he can return everything and apologize to everybody."

I said, "Do you think that's necessary? He's had a rough time."

Deb said, "He has, but he's acting out in a bad way. If he gets away with it, or gets off too easy, then he'll do something worse the next time."

I said, "I guess you're right. God, that's so sad."

Terry looked at Deb and said, "Maybe we could talk some of the guys into taking the kid fishing. They could teach him how to fish and maybe take his mind off his dad's death."

Deb said, "That's a great idea."

I hugged them both and said, "You two are the best. Thank you so much for taking care of this for me. I don't know what I would have done without you."

Deb said, "It felt good to have my old cop skills kick in."

Terry said to Deb, "Let's go twist a few arms."

I took all the notices off the bulletin board and breathed a sigh of relief. My heart was breaking for Marybeth and Sean, though.

Ian popped in the store on his way home. I invited him over for dinner. He went home to clean up, so I closed up and ran to the grocery store. I made a nice salad for us. I layered Bibb lettuce with broiled tomatoes, sprinkled some blue cheese on top, and then I drizzled some aged balsamic over it. For the entrée, I made shrimp scampi with roasted red peppers and spinach. He loved it. After dinner, we sat on the deck for a little while.

Ian turned to me and asked, "Do you run?"

"I do, but I haven't done much since I've been here. Why?" I wonder if he thinks I'm getting fat.

"The Blessing of the Fleet is a couple of weeks from now, and I usually run in the road race. I was wondering if you would like to run with me. They have a walkers' division, too, if you'd rather walk."

"I'd love to run with you, but I'll have to start training for it."

"Sam and I usually go for a run when I get home from work. If you came over right then, we could go together or I could meet you here when you close up."

I said, "That would be great. How many people run in the race and how long is it?"

"The road race is put on by the Lions Club. All the proceeds go to their various charities. Last year about 2600 runners ran in it. It's a ten-mile race through Narragansett on the Friday night before the Blessing, which is on Saturday at noon."

"I'll give it a try. I just hope I don't slow you down."

"He said, "I'm sure you'll be fine. I'll send in entry forms for both of us."

"Okay."

"Meggie, can we go to my house? I want to spend the

night with you, but I don't feel comfortable staying at your grandmother's cottage."

I laughed and said, "You're kidding."

He said, "Hey, I've known your grandmother my whole life. I don't feel comfortable ravishing her precious granddaughter in her house. Call me old-fashioned."

"You win. Let me grab some clothes for the morning and a toothbrush."

Monday after work, I met Ian at his house for our first run. We decided to try for five miles and work our way up a mile every day before the race. It felt good to run. I know Ian can run faster and farther than I, but he held back and kept pace with me.

On Tuesday morning, I wandered over to the Snack Shack for a cup of coffee. Mo was by herself.

She said, "What's up, honey?"

I said, "Well, things couldn't be better with Ian. We've been seeing a lot of each other. He asked me to run in the Blessing of the Fleet road race with him, so we're training for it."

"Good for you."

While she was pouring my coffee, Big H walked in and sat at the counter. Mo poured him a cup of coffee, too.

Mo asked him, "Hey, do you know a good handyman?"

He asked, "What's the problem?"

She said, "One of my bedroom windows is broken. I can't get the thing shut. I'm hopin' I can just get someone to fix it rather than havin' a whole new one put in. I'd fix it myself, but I'm about as handy as a back pocket on a shirt."

He said, "I'll fix it for you. Give me your house keys, and

I'll go over there right now."

She said, "Do you know where I live?"

He said, "On Cypress Street at the end on the left."

Surprised, she said, "That's right. Thanks."

She handed him the keys and he left with his cup of coffee in hand.

Mo turned to me and said, "That man is gonna drive me friggin'crazy."

The door opened and Tony walked in.

He said, "Hey, Meggie, I wanted to do something nice for you as a thank-you for introducing me to Helen."

"Tony, I should be thanking you for entertaining my company."

He put his hand out and said, "How about giving me your car keys and I'll fix that dent on the left side of your car. I think the guys can just bang it out, but I may have to keep the car for a couple of days."

I reached in the pocket of my shorts and pulled out my car keys. I handed them over and said, "That's okay. Gram wants me to drive her car once in a while anyway."

He looked at Mo and said, "Mo, you're looking good today. Did you do something different to your hair?"

She put her hand on her hips and gave him a big smile and said, "I got it colored a shade lighter than usual. You're the only one who's noticed. You notice everything about women, don't you?"

He gave her a wink and said, "I only notice the really beautiful ones."

We laughed.

Tony continued and said, "Now that I've met my Polish

Princess, though, I'll only be admiring beautiful women from a distance. You beauties have a nice day."

After he swaggered out of the Shack, Mo said, "Your friend is one lucky gal."

"That's for sure. They're pretty hot and heavy. He's going to Philly to see her this weekend."

"Well, if that don't put pepper in the gumbo."

"Anything knew with you, Mo?"

"I had a busy weekend. I went out Saturday night with an accountant. I met him for dinner. Before we ordered, he wanted to make sure I knew that we were goin' Dutch. I don't mind payin' my own way, but we met at a diner. How expensive could the bill be? I bet he squeezes a quarter so tight the eagle screams."

"I take it you won't be seeing him again."

"No way. Last night I went out with a truck driver. A nice guy, but he's on the road three weeks out of the month. I want a guy full-time, not part-time. So, I'm back to square one. I'm tryin' not to get discouraged."

"Are you still talking to that local guy?"

"Oh yeah. He says he lives right here in town, and he has a boat somewhere down here. We have the best time chattin' on the Net, but he still hasn't asked me out. I'm startin' to think maybe he's married. Otherwise, why wouldn't he want to meet?"

"I can see your point. Have you had a lot of married men hit on you on the Net?"

"Oh yeah. I set them straight right away. I've never dated married men and I never will. That's just lookin' for trouble."

"Good for you. Well, I'd better get back. You hang in

there."

"I will. See you later, Sweetie."

I went clamming with Mac in the afternoon. I didn't let him do any of the work, though. I let him drive the boat and sit and relax while I did the digging. I dug up a half of bucket full and we had a fun time. He looked good and was really glad to be out on the water again. I enjoy my time with Mac so much. He's such a wise man and has the sweetest nature about him.

The rest of the week flew by. Things were calm at the marina, and I was able to catch up with a stack of paperwork. Every minute I wasn't at work was spent with Ian. We would meet after work and run, have a little dinner, and than I would spend the night with him at his house. The more time I spend with him, the more in love with him I am. Saturday night he suggested we take a night off and go out. He made an exception to his rule about not going to Newport on the weekends and took me over there for dinner. Afterward, we went to a blues bar to hear some music. The band was great, and we danced a lot. I was surprised because when I ran into him at Kelly's that night, he said he wasn't much of a dancer. Truth is, he's a great dancer, and we look great together. Most guys I've dated wouldn't dance, and whenever we went to hear music, I'd be left tapping my feet the whole night wishing I were on the dance floor.

The following Wednesday, I was sitting in the Snack Shack having lunch with Deb and Sexy Cathy when Tony walked in. I hadn't seen him since he'd taken my car keys last week.

He smiled at us and said, "Hello, ladies."

We all said, "Hi."

I asked him, "How was your weekend in Philly?"

His face lit up and he said, "Great. Helen showed me all around and took me on a tour of the sports complex she just finished. She's an amazing woman. She's coming up for the Blessing of the Fleet."

I said, "Oh, good."

He said, "I've got your car outside. You want to take a look?"

I said, "Sure."

Sexy Cathy, Mo, and Deb followed us out to the parking lot to look at the car. I almost didn't recognize it. He not only fixed the dent, but he painted my station wagon. I was floored.

I screamed, "Oh my God! Tony, it looks brand new. I can't believe it's the same car! Oh my God!"

He said, "I owe you big time."

I went over to him and gave him a big hug.

Cathy, Mo, and Deb were all checking out the paint job.

Mo said, "Lordy, Lordy, it looks beautiful. I should have you work on my car."

I kept shaking my head in disbelief. I couldn't believe he did that for me.

I asked him, "Does Hel know about this?"

He said, "Yeah, I told her not to tell you because I wanted it to be a surprise."

"Well, Tony, I couldn't be more surprised." I had to hug him again.

He said, "Well, ladies, I've gotta get back to work. One of my guys is sitting over there waiting to give me a ride back to the shop. Have a great day."

I pointed at him and said, "Tony, you're the man."

He laughed and gave me a wave.

Mo said, "Do you think we could get him coned?"

I asked, "You mean cloned?"

She said, "Yeah. We need to get him cloned. Then I could order me up one of him. Hell, I'd order two."

Deb winked at me and said, "Hell, I'm a lesbian and even I want one of him."

We all cracked up laughing.

CHAPTER THIRTEEN

The weather has been unbelievable this summer. I knew we were bound to get a rainy weekend sooner or later, and it finally arrived. It started on Thursday and the forecast was for rain all weekend. Since I knew it would be slow at the marina because of the rain, I gave Journey Friday and Saturday off. She's been doing such a great job, I thought she deserved it. When I told her, she was thrilled. Her boyfriend, Dash, was up in Boston working on a small documentary film. She was going to go up to visit him for the weekend.

Ian and I still ran every evening. The Road Race is held rain or shine. At least we'll be prepared if it rains the night of the race. I haven't spent one night at the cottage since the first night we slept together. We're practically living together. I've never lived with a guy before, and I always thought it would be a big adjustment, but with Ian it's so easy. I still have all my clothes and things at Gram's, but I did leave some toiletries at Ian's. The fact that we're joined at the hip will make it especially hard when I have to go back to Philly. I've been trying not to think about going home, but it's definitely in the back of my mind. I have to be back a week before school starts for some meetings and to get my classroom together. That means I only have a little over three weeks left here.

On Saturday, Gram called me at the marina. She said she'd called me a few times at night at the cottage, but I wasn't home and she didn't bother to leave a message because they'd been traveling. I explained that I'd been seeing a lot of Ian, and she was thrilled for me. Of course, I didn't tell her I stayed at his house every night. Gram said Cal had taken her to San Francisco for a few days, then to Yosemite National Park to see the redwood trees and beautiful waterfalls. I asked her when she thought she would be back, and she said they had reservations to fly home on the seventh. Gram explained that she would be staying at Cal's house in Newport and would give me a call when they got home. They want to take me to dinner, so I can meet Cal.

I started to panic because I thought she would say I didn't need to stay and that she would be taking over the marina when she got back. I was relieved when she asked when I had to be back home and then asked if I would stay until then. I told her, no problem. Gram said she was going to take Cal down to meet my parents. I filled her in about the happenings at the marina, and she said she was very proud of me and the great job I was doing.

Cal and Gram must be serious if she is taking him to meet my parents. This whole senior romance thing is blowing my mind, but I couldn't be happier for her. I guess if they were serious, she would have to decide whether to keep the marina or sell it and move to San Diego. I couldn't imagine my grandmother selling the marina, but then again, I couldn't imagine her going off for the summer and shacking up with an old boyfriend. I guess I'll find out more when I see her. I can't wait to get a good look at Cal.

Sunday morning was extremely slow at the marina. It was still raining and the wind had kicked up. I closed up the store at noon and went over to Ian's. He didn't go out to work because the seas were too rough, so he had a rare day off. I picked up some chowder and clam cakes for lunch, and we spent the whole afternoon in bed watching the storm. I could look out the windows at Ian's house forever and never get tired of the views. In stormy weather, the sea was a beautiful, powerful thing to watch. Of course, that wasn't the only thing we did all day, but I won't go into details. I will say, however, that there was an old line I'd heard once: "There are only two things to do on rainy days, and I hate cards."

Monday morning the sun was shining and by Tuesday, the seas had calmed down and a nice high-pressure system hovered above New England. People started to return to the marina and things got busy. I called Mac to let him know I couldn't go clamming because we were too busy in the store. He said he would get a friend to go with him. At lunchtime, I wandered over to the Snack Shack to grab a bite to eat.

Mo was by herself in the Shack. She had her chalkboard down and was in the process of changing the menu.

I said, "Hi, Mo. What's up?"

She said, "Well, I'm revampin' the menu a bit. All the guys are on diets and they want more low-cal things so I thought I'd add a few nice salads."

I said, "What inspired them all to go on diets?"

She said, "Your friend Helen. I guess she told one of them she heard there was this doctor on Oprah once who said that if a guy lost so many pounds, he'd gain an inch on his penis."

I laughed. "I wonder how that came up in conversation?"

"Yeah," she snickered. "I would have loved to have been a fly on the wall."

"That's too funny. I'll have to ask Hel about that one."

Mo said, "Hey, I figure if they lose weight and their penises get larger, maybe their wives and girlfriends will start comin' down here, and I'll get more business."

"It's worth a shot. Do you think if I lost weight, my boobs would get bigger?"

Mo laughed and said, "Your boobs are fine, honey. You don't want them any bigger." She grabbed her own breasts and said, " I've been carryin' these girls around a long time. It's fun when you're young and they're pointin' at the moon, but when you get older, your back starts hurtin' and gravity takes over. Pretty soon these puppies will be down to my knees."

We both laughed and I asked her, "Can I get a club sandwich? I'll have some chips with that, too. I don't feel as guilty eating chips since I've been running every night with Ian."

"Do you think you'll be ready for the race on Friday?"

"Yeah. I think I'm going to be fine. Helen is flying up on Friday morning, and she and Tony are going to cheer us on and make us dinner after the race."

She handed me my sandwich and said, "So, I guess things are goin' well with Ian."

"Couldn't be better. Oh, I heard from Gram. She's coming home on the seventh. She wants me to meet Cal, and then she's taking him to meet my parents."

Mo said, "Holy guacamole! Things must be serious."

I said, "I think so. She asked me to stay and run things until I have to go back for school. She's going to stay at Cal's house in Newport. I guess he's got a house in San Diego and one in Newport."

Mo said, "Wow. It sounds like he's loaded. Maybe he knows somebody who would like a real woman like me."

"I'll ask him for you."

"Do that. Hey, you never know. When do you have to be back?"

"The last week in August. I have some meetings to go to before school starts."

"I'll hate to see you go. What about you and Ian?"

"I don't know. We haven't talked about it. I haven't brought it up because I'm having too much fun, and I'll just get depressed thinking about it. Besides, we haven't been seeing each other all that long and I don't want to scare him off."

Mo said, "If I was a bettin' woman, I'd bet you aren't goin' to be teachin' in Philly anytime soon."

"We'll see. How's the dating scene?"

She said, "Well, I'm still chattin' it up on the Net with the local guy. He calls himself Fisher Man. He still hasn't asked me out yet, but I keep talking to him anyway. He's a fun guy. I still think he might be married, though."

"I hope not. Maybe he's just shy. Maybe he'll be worth the wait."

"Yeah, I hope he doesn't wait too long. Little Mo's gettin' cobwebs."

I laughed and said, "Any new cyber men?"

"Yeah. A pretty hot one, too. He sent his picture and he's

definitely eye candy. His name is Dave, and he's about my age, divorced with no kids. He owns his own company. I think he makes cardboard boxes or somethin' like that. Anyway, I'm seein' him on Saturday night. We're meetin' at a restaurant in Westerly."

"Sounds like a hot one."

"I hope so."

"Hey, I saw Sean and his mother Marybeth get on the Murphys' boat."

Mo said, "Yeah, all the guys are fightin' over who's gonna take Sean fishin' next. The kid seems to be enjoyin' himself."

"Oh, that's good to hear."

Mo looked up from her board and said, "How does a Greek salad sound? I'm also gonna put on here a salad Niçoise. Since there's fresh tuna around, I thought that would be good."

"Sounds great."

By the time I was halfway through my sandwich, the Shack had a crowd of people. I finished up my lunch and went back to work.

After closing, I went right over to Ian's, and we did a ten-mile run. It was the first time we actually ran that distance. I was dragging the last mile, but I made it. We went back to his house, took showers, and grilled some chicken and veggies. We celebrated our run with a vodka tonic. Another great night together followed, and I woke up Wednesday feeling great. Actually, I've never felt better in my life. It's amazing what exercise and a lot of sex will do for a girl.

When I opened up the store at 4:30, people were already waiting. I let in five guys and a girl. The girl looked a little out of place. First of all, she really wasn't dressed for fishing. She was a chesty blond with a tight, sparkly V-neck T-shirt on that said "Too Hot" and cut-off jeans short shorts. She had a ton of makeup on, but the weirdest thing was, she wore high heels. I never saw anyone get on a fishing boat with high heels. One of the guys told me they were here for a charter on the *Blood, Sweat and Beers.* They bought a few T-shirts, and then I pointed them toward the boat. About an hour later, I got a call from Randy on the *Blood, Sweat and Beers.*

He said, "Meggie, you have to do me a huge favor."

I wondered why his voice sounded so panicky. I asked, "What's up?"

He said, "That charter I've got on my boat is a bachelor party. The guys thought it would be fun to bring a hooker along."

I couldn't believe what I was hearing. "You're kidding. I saw her this morning, and I didn't think she looked the fishing type."

He said, "Well, she isn't. She's been sick as a dog ever since we left. I'm halfway to Block Island, and I'm turning around to drop her off at the marina, then I'm heading out again with these bozos. I was wondering if you could do me a favor and give her a ride to the bus stop so she can catch a bus back to Providence?"

"Sure. What's her name?"

I heard Randy yell to the guys, "Hey, what's her name?" The guys yelled back in chorus, "I don't know."

I said, "Don't worry about it, Randy. Call me back when you get close to the marina and I'll meet her at the dock."

Randy said, "Try and keep this under your hat. If my wife, Sarah, finds out about this, she'll sell my boat. She's a scary broad."

I said, "Well, I'll try to keep it on the QT, but you know how things are around here."

He said, "Thanks, Meggie. I owe ya."

I hung up and laughed. Just when you think everything is normal around here, something comes up out of the blue.

Randy called me back about a half-hour later, and I went down to the dock to meet the hooker. The guys helped her off the boat and the poor thing looked like death warmed over. Her skin had turned green and her hot pink lips were pressed together in a tight grim line. As soon as her feet hit the dock, she laid down. The guys got back in the boat and took off to go fishing.

I said to the hooker, "Hi, my name is Meggie. How are you feeling?"

She looked up at me and said, "I've never been so sick in my life. I feel like I'm gonna die. I didn't know I'd get seasick. I've never been on a boat before."

I asked her, "What's your name?"

She said, "Lolly. Lolly Lovelick."

I bit my lip so I wouldn't laugh and asked her, "Do you think you can stand? I'll give you a ride to the bus stop."

She said, "I can't go anywhere right now. I just want to sleep for a while. Can I just lie on the dock and take a nap?"

I knew I couldn't let a hooker sleep on the dock. The marina would be buzzing with people in about an hour. I wasn't about to offer Gram's cottage, so I decided I would put Lolly on Tony's boat and let her sleep for a bit. When she got up, I would take her to the bus stop.

I said, "I'm sorry, but I can't let you do that. How about

I help you on one of the boats, and you can sleep there until you're feeling better."

"There's no way I'm getting on another boat."

I said, "The boat won't be moving. You'll be fine."

She looked skeptical but agreed to give it a try. I helped her up off the dock and we headed over to Tony's boat. I helped her on board, thanking God that Tony hadn't locked it up. When I got her below, she stretched out on the berth, and I threw a blanket on her. With luck, she won't sleep too long, and I can get her off the boat before Tony shows up.

I told her, "Come find me in the store when you wake up, and I'll give you a ride to the bus."

I went back to work and I had to tell Journey. It was just too funny. The rest of the morning went by and no Lolly. At lunchtime, I went down on Tony's boat to see if she was still there. There she was, still sleeping away. I decided to go have lunch at the Shack. If she wasn't up and about by the time I finished, I would wake her.

I walked in the Shack and sitting at the counter were Dancing Kathy, Big H, Bob from the *Bite Me*, and Joe Turner, without Number One or Number Two. I sat down and ordered a salad. The guys were all talking about fishing. I was almost finished when Tony walked in and said, "Does anybody know anything about that Goldilocks sleeping on my boat?"

I thought, shit. I didn't know what to say, so I blurted out the truth. "I do. She's a hooker."

Everyone's jaw dropped.

Dancing Kathy laughed and said, "Oh my God."

Tony smiled at me and said, "That's really nice of you, Meggie, but it's not my birthday."

I said, "She's not for you. I just put her on your boat to sleep because she got seasick. Randy took out a charter that was a bachelor party, and they brought her along. They got halfway to Block Island, and she got violently ill. They dropped her off. I was going to give her a ride to the bus stop, but she was too sick. So I let her sleep on your boat. I hope you don't mind."

Tony said, "Just make sure you tell Hel I had nothing to do with this."

I said, "Don't worry, I will."

Everyone was laughing.

Mo said, "This is a first. A seasick hooker."

Joe Turner said, "Next time that happens, Meggie, put the hooker on my boat."

Bob said, "Mine's available also. Hookers are always welcome."

I pleaded with them. "Randy doesn't want his wife to find out, so keep it under your hat."

Bob shivered and said, "Scary Sarah. I don't blame him."

Just as I stood up to go wake up Goldilocks, she walked in the door. All the guys looked her up and down.

I asked her, "Are you feeling better?"

Much to the guys' pleasure, she stretched like a cat and her boobs almost fell out of her low-cut T-shirt. She said, "I feel like a new person. I thought I was gonna die out there."

Bob said, "Meggie, aren't you going to introduce us?"

I said to Lolly, "This is Tony. It was his boat you were napping on, and that's Bob, Big H, Joe, and Kathy. Oh, and behind the counter is Mo."

Lolly said, "Hi, I'm Lolly Lovelick."

Everyone smiled and said hi. Mo had to turn around and face the grill. I could see her shoulders shaking.

Lolly asked, "Could I get a cheeseburger and a coke?"

Joe Turner said, "You should try the Italian sausage."

I looked at Tony and rolled my eyes. He was laughing.

Lolly licked her lips and smiled at Joe. She said, "I had two of those yesterday. I think I'm in the mood for a cheeseburger."

Mo said, "One cheeseburger comin' up. Have a seat."

I could tell none of the guys were going to leave while Miss Lolly was in the Shack.

Lolly looked at me and said, "Thanks for helping me out this morning. I really appreciate it."

I said, "No problem. I guess you lost a day's work."

She said, "They were nice. They gave me two hundred dollars and all I did was get seasick. I guess I won't be going out on the water anytime soon. Actually, I only do this occasionally for some extra money. I'm a full-time dancer."

Dancing Kathy perked up and asked her, "Where do you dance?"

Lolly said, "I'm a dancer at a gentlemen's club in Providence."

Kathy said, "What kind of dancing do you do?"

The boys started to snicker.

Lolly said, "I'm a featured pole dancer."

Kathy said, "Really. That is the new craze. It's supposed be really good exercise. I own a dance studio, and I've had a lot of calls from people wanting to know if we offer pole-dancing classes."

Lolly said, "It's becoming really popular since it was featured on Oprah."

Kathy said, "Hey, would you be interested in teaching a class at my studio?"

Lolly said, "I'd love it. I could use the money and maybe I could give up my side job."

Kathy said, "Give me your number and I'll call you. What nights are you free?"

Lolly wrote her number on a napkin and gave it to her and said, "Wednesdays are good for me."

Dancing Kathy said, "Let me make some calls and see if I can get some people to sign up. How many do you think should be in the class?"

Lolly said, "As many as you can fit in your studio."

Kathy said, "I can fit about twenty."

Lolly said, "Sounds good."

Mo said, "I'll sign up and I'll get my friends Sandy, MaryAnn, and Val to sign up too. They'll love it and so will their husbands. How about you, Meggie?"

I said, "Sure. I can always use more exercise."

Dancing Kathy got up to leave and said, "I'll call you in a few days, Lolly, when I get things set up. This could be lucrative for us both."

Joe said, "Hey, I'd pay just to watch the class."

Dancing Kathy gave him a dirty look and said, "Forget it, Joe. I'm surprised you don't have a pole on your boat."

Everyone laughed.

Dancing Kathy said, "Speaking of poles, I wonder where I can get some quick."

Tony said, "I know just the guy to call." He wrote a number on a piece of paper and gave it to Dancing Kathy.

Dancing Kathy said, "Thanks, Tony. Lolly, I'll be in

touch."

Lolly said, "Thanks."

Dancing Kathy said, "No. Thank you," and walked out the door.

Lolly looked around at all of us. "Boy, this is my lucky day." She raised her eyebrows and said to Tony, "Thanks for letting me take a nap on your boat. Can I do anything for you as a thank-you?"

I thought the guys were gonna fall off their stools. Tony laughed and said, "No, I'm good."

Since she had finished her burger, I asked her, "Are you ready to go catch the bus?"

She smiled and said, "Yeah. It was nice meeting all you people. Thanks again, Tony."

The guys gave her a sad smile and waved goodbye. They were like children, and I was taking their favorite toy away from them.

I dropped her off at the bus stop and told her I would see her soon. I can't wait to tell Ian about my day.

Before I went over to Ian's for our nightly run, I checked my e-mail. There was one from Helen.

Hi, Meggie:

I'm looking forward to seeing you on Friday. I miss it up there. How's Tony? I hope he's missing me because I can't wait to see him. I hope you're keeping an eye on him for me. I'm so glad I can get off Friday. Tony will be picking me up at the airport. I get in around 10:00 in the morning. Just so you know, I'll be staying with him.

Lonely in Philly,

Hel

I wrote back.

Hi, Hel:

Looking forward to seeing you, too. I've been keeping not just one eye, but two, on Tony and you have nothing to worry about. He looks like a lost puppy without you. Also, I haven't seen any flaws. Have a good flight. Pop in the store if you guys make it down to the marina before the race.

Love, Meggie

P.S. Ian and I are still going strong.

CHAPTER FOURTEEN

Race day is finally here. I'm excited. I feel great and I'm ready to go. I went over to the Snack Shack and had a late lunch. Mo made me a big pasta salad to fortify me. Helen and Tony popped in the office in the mid-afternoon to wish me luck and to tell me they'd be at the finish line. At 4:30, I left Journey to close up, and I went over to Ian's. We got to the Pier School where the race would start and did some stretches. Then we were off.

About two miles into the race, I could tell it was frustrating for Ian to hold back and run with me.

I told him, "Ian, go ahead. I don't mind a bit."

"Are you sure?"

"I'm positive. Go."

He smiled and gave me a wave. "Okay. I'll be at the finish line waiting for you."

I waved him off and said, "Have fun."

I continued on, and was about halfway through the race running up Point Judith Road when I heard someone calling my name. There was a crowd of people cheering everyone on. I looked into the crowd and spotted Sexy Cathy and Kenny.

They were smiling and waving at me. I waved back. About a half a mile up the road from where I saw them, I noticed my right sneaker was untied. A vision quickly popped in my head of me tripping and getting stampeded by all the people behind me. I went off the road to tie my sneaker. The last thing I wanted to do was trip up anyone behind me.

Mission accomplished, I ran back to the road to continue the race when I realized I had just stepped in something. I looked behind me and saw a dead skunk. I can't believe I didn't smell it first, but I could sure smell it now, coming from my sneakers. I had been on the lookout for a good place to jump back in the pack instead of watching where my feet were going. For the rest of the race, the other runners gave me a wide berth and picked up speed as they passed me. I thought about quitting, but I got used to the smell, and I'm not a quitter.

When I approached the finish line, I could see people pointing at me and a few aimed their cameras my way. I found Ian, Helen, and Tony in the crowd waving at me and laughing. I crossed the finish line and bent over to catch my breath. When I looked up, Ian was standing in front of me while the others kept their distance. He must love me; either that or his sense of smell must be off.

He gave me a hug, handed me a bottle of water, and asked, "Meggie, are you okay?"

I smiled at him and said, "A little stinky, a little embarrassed, but I finished. I guess the people who passed me came in and told everyone about the skunk woman."

"I was hoping it wasn't you, but I had a feeling it was. I'm so proud of you for finishing."

I looked over at Helen and Tony, who had their hands over their noses.

Helen yelled, "Congratulations. We'll see you at Tony's in a little while."

I yelled, "Okay."

Ian said, "Let's get you home and showered."

We had dropped Ian's truck off earlier at the finish line and took my wagon to the Pier School. When we got to the truck, Ian said, "Take off your sneakers and socks, and throw them in that bucket in the back of the truck."

I said, "I guess these sneakers are history."

He said, "Yep."

"That's the third pair this summer."

He said, "I think I should start buying stock in Nike."

Ian dropped me off at the cottage and went home to shower and change. I soaped myself up good, paying special attention to my legs and feet. I then put on a khaki skirt, a black top, and a pair of black sandals. Hooray! I don't smell like skunk anymore. Thank God my sneakers got the worst of it.

Ian picked me up, then stopped at the liquor store to pick up a bottle of wine to take to Tony's. I was excited to see Tony's house. We drove on a private road about a half-mile into the woods, and then turned into Tony's driveway. The house had a big sweeping front lawn with woods on either side of it. The house itself was a large contemporary design, with gray shingles, white trim, and a black front door. Helen and Tony met us in the driveway and ushered us around back to check out the pool. It was a good-size, rectangular in shape and surrounded by a beautiful flagstone patio. On the patio sat two chaise lounges and a glass-topped table with six chairs. Beautiful flowering scrubs and perennials enhanced the entire backyard.

I said to Tony, "Wow, this is beautiful. I love the pool. We should have brought our suits."

Tony said, "You guys are welcome anytime, even if I'm not home. I had it heated so I can get more use out of it. Make the season last longer."

Helen said to Ian and me, "You both must be exhausted after that run."

Ian said, "I'm a little tired. How about you, Meggie?"

"I'm more than a little tired. I'm also embarrassed about the skunk. I hope they don't put my picture in the paper."

Ian smiled and said, "They probably will. The local papers are always looking for a good story like that."

Tony asked, "How about a drink? Helen made some killer margaritas."

I said, "I'd love one."

Needless to say, the margaritas went down too easy, and by the time we ate, I was feeling no pain. Tony barbequed some big beef ribs with a bourbon sauce that was to die for. With the ribs, we had potato salad, and corn on the cob, and, for dessert, Tony made my favorite, strawberry shortcake. After dinner, he took us on a tour of the house, which was impressive. I could tell from looking around that Tony's a neatnik, which is a good thing because so is Helen. I think it's the engineer in her. We had one more margarita after dinner and my eyes started to droop. Ian took one look at me and decided it was time to get me home. When we got to his house, we went straight to bed. It was the first night we didn't have sex before we went to bed. We made up for it in the morning however. Sex sure takes the edge off having to get up at 4:00!

Today is the Blessing of the Fleet. Most of the boats that weren't out fishing were going to be heading over to Galilee for the blessing at noon. The blessing usually attracts a couple hundred boats when the weather is good, and today is a stellar day to be out on the water. The boats parade by a grandstand where a priest—occasionally a bishop— blesses each and every boat. On the grandstand is a panel of celebrity judges, who award prizes for the most originally decorated boats.

At 10:00, I decided to take a break and walk around the marina to check out the decorations on the boats. Most of the fishing boats were out, but A dock, where the cabin cruisers are, was a buzz of activity. Boat owners had friends and family down to help decorate and participate in the parade. The *Grain Man* went with a Hawaiian theme and had a couple of blow-up plastic palm trees strapped to the deck. The guys wore shorts and Hawaiian shirts, and all the women and little girls were dressed as hula dancers.

The *Lady Marion* was doing "Gilligan's Island" with all the characters. Pierce was the Captain, and Marion was Marianne. They enlisted Don and Geri from *She's the Boss* to be Mr. and Mrs. Howell. They invited some other friends to make up the rest of the cast of characters. The *Dancing Queen* went disco, with seventies' music and a disco ball hanging above the deck, where the dancers were practicing their routine for the judges. The *Bite Me* had several large plastic blow-up sharks, and the *Summa Home* decided on a pirate theme. All the other boats were festooned with colorful flags, streamers, and balloons.

As I was walking up the dock, Tony and Helen were

boarding his boat.

I looked *The Stallion* over and asked, "Where are your decorations?"

Tony said, "I wanted Helen to wear her new blue bikini, and then I was going to make up a sign that said, "Who needs decorations?"

Helen shook her head and said, "Can you believe him?"

Tony said, "It's just as well. There'll be too many boats out there, and one look at her and they'd be crashing into each other."

I asked, "Are you going over to the blessing?"

Tony said, "Yeah. I want Helen to see it. Can you come?"

"I wish I could, but I need to get back to work. Have a great time, though."

Helen said, "We will. I'll see you later before we leave."

The rest of the day was really busy. Tony and Helen popped in the store around 4:00 to say goodbye.

I said to Helen, "So, when will I see you again?"

"I'll be back up in two weeks." She put her arm around Tony. "Tony's coming down next weekend and I'm taking him to the Jersey shore."

I said, "Tony, you'll love it."

He gave Helen a kiss on her cheek and said, "I'll go anywhere my Polish Princess wants to take me."

I asked Helen, "When is your flight tomorrow?"

"It's at noon. It's the only flight I could get."

I asked them, "What are you doing tonight?"

Tony said, "We're going out to dinner with some friends of mine. Would you and Ian like to come?"

I said, "I'd better say no. Ian said that when he got back

in today he was going to have to repair a water pump on the *Miss Kay.*"

Helen gave me a hug and said, "I'll see you in a couple of weeks."

On Monday morning, Ian gave me a kiss in the parking lot and headed down the dock. I went and opened up the store. Today is my twenty-ninth birthday, but I haven't told that to anyone here. I'm kind of shy about things like that. I wouldn't want my friends to think I expected them to do anything for me. I especially didn't tell Ian because I didn't want him to think he had to buy me a present or go to any trouble. Not that he wouldn't want to, but I just felt funny telling him.

Around 7:00, the phone rang. I picked it up and said, "Good morning, Harbor Marina."

A voice said, "Good morning, sweetheart, happy birthday."

I smiled.

I said, "Hi, Dad. How's New Zealand?"

He said, "Very picturesque. We've really enjoyed ourselves. Your mother and I are exhausted, though. We're ready to get home and back into our usual routine."

"Are you still coming home on the fifth?"

He said, "Yes. How are things at the marina?"

"Good."

"I hear you're dating that Brady boy."

"Yeah, Dad. He's really nice."

"Well, he'd better treat my little girl right or he'll have to deal with me."

"I'll tell him that, Dad."

He asked me, "When are you coming home?"

"Well, I have to be back the last week in August for

meetings before the start of school."

"Have you heard from your grandmother lately?"

"Yes. She's coming back to Rhode Island on the seventh. She mentioned that she was going to come down and see you while I was still here."

"Well, that will make your mother happy."

"How's Charlie doing?"

"Your brother is fine. He's taken us on the pub tour of New Zealand."

I laughed and said, "It figures."

Dad said, "I'm just kidding. We've seen a lot here, but we've also seen quite a few pubs."

"Mom must have loved it."

"You know your mother. She makes friends wherever she goes. She's invited half the population of New Zealand to come and visit us. She's tried to fix up Charlie with at least a dozen women, and she's shown your picture to a few guys. She won't be happy until she's a grandmother."

"Don't I know it. Is Mom with you now?"

"She's right here. Happy birthday, sweetheart."

"Thanks, Dad."

He put Mom on the phone.

"Meggie, happy birthday, honey."

"Thanks, Mom."

"I can't talk long. Charlie has us signed up for a bus tour. Do you have plans with Ian for your birthday?"

"Yes. We're going to do something tonight."

"Oh, good. Well, I heard your father's half of the conversation, so I'll get all the info from him. I miss you. Have a great birthday. I bought you a nice present here. I'll give it to you when you get home. Oh, and Charlie said happy birthday, too."

"Thanks, Mom. Have a great time."

"Love you, honey. Bye."

At about 11:30, I was in my office working and Matt popped in.

He said, "Meggie, Mo wants you to come over to the Snack Shack."

I asked, "What's up?"

He said, "She wants you to taste one of her new recipes."

I said, "Journey's off today."

He said, "I'll cover for you. Brian's down on the fuel dock."

I smiled at him and said, "Okay. Thanks."

I walked into the Shack. It was crowded with people, and I wondered if everyone had come to taste Mo's latest recipe. Big H was there, along with Tony, Sexy Cathy, Kenny, Dancing Kathy, Deb, Marion, Bob, Mac, and Don and Geri from *She's the Boss*. Everyone turned to look at me when I walked in the door, yelling, "SURPRISE! HAPPY BIRTHDAY, MEGGIE!"

I could feel the blood start rushing to my face. I asked them, "How did you know it was my birthday?" Then I said, "I know, Helen?"

Mo said, "Yeah, and I'm glad she told me. Come look at the cake I made for you."

I went over to the counter and feasted my eyes on a beautiful sheet cake with chocolate frosting and pink roses around the edges. In the middle was written "Happy Birthday, Meggie" and around the writing were some candles. Mo lit the candles and everyone sang to me. I made a wish and blew them all out in one breath. I went behind the counter and gave Mo a big hug. Mo handed me a cake knife and I started slicing. Underneath all that delicious-looking chocolate frosting was a moist chocolate cake with raspberry filling. My mouth and eyes started to water. I was just going to let today pass like any other day.

I cut pieces of cake for everyone, and we all dug in.

I said, "Mo, this is sinfully good. I'm enjoying every bite."

"No way would we let your birthday go by without celebratin'."

I turned to everyone and said, "This is so nice. Thanks, everyone."

Tony said, "It isn't over yet. Time for presents. Sit down on a stool, Meggie."

I sat down and he handed me a big box. He said, "This is from me and Hel. It's something you need."

I opened the box and in it were three pairs of Nikes. I started to laugh.

Tony said, "We thought maybe three pairs would be enough to get you through the rest of the summer."

I said, "God, I hope so." I gave him a hug and said, "Thanks."

He gave me a wink. "You're welcome."

Dancing Kathy gave me a gift certificate for my first pole-dancing class. I asked her when the first session would be and she said next Wednesday. Bob gave me two framed 5 x 7 pictures of myself that he took—one with the lobster bait all over me, and the other one the picture he took of me after I went for my swim with the Diesel dog. Sexy Cathy gave me two new romance novels that had just hit the bookstore;

Marion's present was a gift certificate for a manicure in town. Deb gave me a beautiful pair of blue sea-glass earrings from her and Terry. Don and Geri gave me a baseball cap with their boat name, *She's the Boss*, on it.

I reached inside Mac's gift bag and pulled out an "I don't give a clam" hat. He gave me a big smile and said, "Now we'll have matching hats when we go out clamming." I gave him a big hug.

To my surprise, Big H handed me a beautiful bouquet of daisies. He said, "A pretty girl has to have flowers on her birthday."

I was overwhelmed. I said, "Thank you all so much. This was so sweet."

Mo said to me, "Come over here and cut the rest of this cake up."

I said, "I'll slice a piece for Brian and Matt."

Everyone else said goodbye and filed out of the Shack. I turned to Mo and said, "I can't believe all of you."

Mo said, "Honey, you deserve it. Everyone down here has taken quite a shine to you."

I said, "Well, the feeling's mutual. They're all great people. Hey, how was your date Saturday night?"

She smiled and said, "Pretty darn good if I must say so myself. He was really handsome. The best-lookin' one yet. Not only that, but he was a charmer. We had a nice dinner, and he was a perfect gentlemen. After dinner, he walked me to my car and kissed me goodnight. It was a whoppin', make-your-toes-curl kinda' kiss."

I said, "Oh boy. When are you seeing him again?"

She smiled and said, "Thursday night. I'm meetin' him for

drinks and dancin'. I'm gonna break out my lucky underwear and my dancin' shoes. I think this might be the one."

I said, "Wow. Now I can't wait for Friday morning so I can hear all about it."

She asked me, "Does Ian know it's your birthday?"

I said, "No, and please don't tell him. I would hate for him to think he had to buy me a present."

She said, "Are you sure? I could let it slip out in front of him."

"No, thanks. But, this was great, Mo. Thanks so much for the beautiful cake. I'm going to take Brian his piece and then relieve Matt. I'll be back later to pick up my presents. I still can't believe everyone went to so much trouble."

"Well, have a great birthday, sweetie."

"It's already been."

I went down to the fuel dock and gave Brian his cake and then to the store with Matt's piece.

His eyes lit up when I handed him the cake. He said, "Happy birthday, Meggie. Doesn't my Aunt Mo make the best cake you ever tasted?"

"She sure does. Thanks for holding down the fort."

He blushed and said, "Anytime. I'd better get back."

It was so nice to know that someone else around here blushes, too.

Ian came by the store around 4:00.

He said, "I'm done for the day and I'm starving. Let's go out to eat tonight. I feel like Italian food."

"I love Italian food."

"I'm going to go home and take Sam for a run and do a few things. I'll pick you up at 7:00."

"Okay. How should I dress?"

He smiled and said, "You always look beautiful, but I'd love to see that black dress again."

"The black dress it is."

He kissed me quickly and went out the door.

I had a funny feeling someone told him it was my birthday.

I closed up a little early at 5:30 and went over to the cottage. I took a long shower and was drying off when the phone rang. It was Gram.

"Happy birthday, Meggie."

"Oh, Gram. Thanks."

"Any big plans for the evening?"

"As a matter of fact, Ian is taking me out to dinner, and I'm supposed to dress up."

She said, "I always liked that boy."

I asked, "How are you?"

"I'm looking forward to getting home next weekend. We get in on Saturday. I want you to save Sunday night to go to dinner with Cal and me. We'll celebrate your birthday then. I'd tell you to bring Ian, but there are some things I want to talk to you about."

"Okay. I'll plan on Sunday night."

"I'll call you on Sunday and set up a time."

"I'll look forward to it, Gram, and have a great trip home."

She said, "Happy birthday. Bye."

I hung up the phone and it rang again. To my surprise, it was my brother Jack.

He said, "Hey, Meg. Happy birthday."

I said, "This is a surprise. I can't believe you remembered my birthday. Where are you?"

"I'm a sentimental kind of guy. Of course, I'd remember my baby sister's birthday. I'm in Singapore. Hey, I hear you're dating Ian Brady. Tell him he'd better be nice to you and remind him that I'm bigger than he is and my punches pack a wallop."

I laughed and said, "He's taking me out to a fancy restaurant for dinner."

"Well, good. Tell him I said hi. I haven't talked to anyone for a few weeks. What's been going on with everyone?"

I filled him in on all the family news.

He said, "Wow. Gram has a boyfriend. I don't think I'll ever be able to get my brain around that one."

I asked, "When are you coming home?"

"I'll be home at the beginning of October for three and a half months, which means I'll be home for the holidays."

"Great. It seems like I haven't seen you in a long time."

"You'll be sick of me after three and a half months."

I laughed and asked, "Broken any hearts lately?"

"You know me. I've left a trail of broken-hearted women all over the world."

My brother Jack is gorgeous. All my friends drool over him.

Joking, I said, "Are you bringing me home a nice present from Singapore?"

"Only the best for you. I've gotta go, but have a great time tonight. Happy birthday."

"Thanks, Jack. Bye."

I decided to wear my hair up tonight since it was really humid. I put on a little makeup and slipped on my black dress and a pair of black sandals. I sprayed some of my new perfume on, and I was ready for my evening. I had a few minutes before Ian showed up so I checked my e-mail. There were e-mails from both Laura and Helen wishing me a happy birthday.

Ian showed up promptly at seven and he looked devastatingly handsome in a pair of black pants and a beige, silk, short-sleeved Tommy Bahama shirt. As soon as I saw the Mercedes, I knew someone must have told him it was my birthday. On the way to dinner, I filled him in on my day, leaving out the birthday parts in case by chance he didn't know. It was about a twenty-minute drive to the restaurant. Ian pulled up in front, handed the keys to the valet and escorted me in. The interior was beautifully decorated and air-conditioned. The walls were painted a warm gold Tuscan color, and the tables were adorned with vases of big gorgeous dahlias in a variety of bright colors. The host, Nick, was also the owner and, as it turns out, an old friend of Ian's. Ian introduced me, and Nick sat us at a beautiful, quiet table for two.

I said to Ian, "This is really nice."

He smiled and said, "Wait until you taste the food."

Nick came over with two glasses of champagne. He said, "I hear this is a special occasion."

Ian said, "Yes, it is."

Nick gave me a smile and said he'd send a waiter over in a few minutes.

Ian picked up his glass and said, "Happy birthday, Meggie."

I blushed and said, "Thank you. I guess Helen told you."

"I never reveal my sources."

The waiter came over and delivered a small bowl that contained a variety of olives. He also brought a plate of dates that he explained were soaked in brandy, stuffed with gorgonzola cheese, wrapped in prosciutto, and then broiled. He said they were compliments of Nick.

I ate a date and said to Ian, "That is the best thing I've ever tasted."

He smiled and said, "The night is young. We haven't even ordered yet."

We looked over the menu and decided our next course would be a terrine of roasted vegetables, which was served with slices of Italian bread. For my entrée I decided on the chicken with a porcini mushroom sauce, and Ian ordered the osso buco. We had finished the champagne, and Ian ordered a bottle of wine to go with the meal. Everything was excellent and, coming from a foodie like me, you know it was good. Ian asked me if I would like dessert.

I said, "I'm so full."

"It's your birthday. Why don't we split some of their tiramisu, and I'll order us a couple of cappuccinos?"

I said, "Since you're twisting my arm, how can I say no?"

He ordered our dessert, and when the waiter walked away, Ian placed a small, beautifully wrapped box on the table.

He said, "Happy birthday. Open your present."

I gushed, "Dinner was enough. You didn't have to get me anything."

He said, "I wanted to and guess what?"

"What?"

"It's not a purse."

I laughed and said, "That's a relief."

I took my time unwrapping the box. I took off the paper and recognized the blue Tiffany's box. My heart started beating really fast. I removed the lid and opened the velvet box. Inside were beautiful diamond stud earrings. Each diamond looked to be about a carat in size, and they were set in platinum. I was floored. I've never received jewelry from a guy before, let alone beautiful diamond earrings. I was a little choked up, and I could feel my eyes starting to tear up.

Ian asked, "Do you like them?"

I swallowed hard and said, "Ian, they're the most beautiful gift I've ever received."

He smiled and said, "Put them on. I want to see how they look with that dress."

I took out the silver earrings I had on and slipped them in my purse. Then I put on the diamonds and took a mirror from my purse for a close look. They were gorgeous.

Ian said, "I didn't think you could look more beautiful, but those earrings are perfect for you."

I was overwhelmed. I smiled at him and said, "Thank you. This has been the best birthday I've ever had. Ian, you have made me feel so special."

A tear escaped and I could feel it sliding down my right cheek.

Ian reached across the table and gently brushed the tear away with his thumb.

He said, "That's because you are special. Now, no more crying."

We enjoyed our dessert and cappuccinos and then went back to Ian's house. He gave me a few more birthday presents of a more private nature, but I don't think I want to share them with anyone. A girl has to keep a few things to herself.

CHAPTER FIFTEEN

Today is Friday and I've been on a birthday high all week. Yesterday, I stopped in the Snack Shack and told Sexy Cathy, Marion, and Mo about my birthday dinner with Ian. They made me run back to the cottage and get the earrings he gave me. I showed them off and they oohed and aahed over them. I haven't worn them during the day because I'm afraid I might wind up in the drink again.

I was starving and since it was already 11:30, I went over to the Shack for an early lunch. The only one sitting at the counter was Big H. I said hello to him and Mo and took a seat next to him.

Mo said, "What are you in the mood for today, honey?"

"I think I'll try the salad Niçoise."

Mo said, "Comin' right up."

I turned to Big H and asked, "How's the fishing been this week?"

He said, "Good. I went to the Dump yesterday."

I said, "The Dump?"

He said, "Yeah, it's an area south of Martha's Vineyard."

"Why do they call it the Dump?"

He said, "Because it's an old World War II dumping ground. They dumped a bunch of old surplus stuff there. They haven't dumped anything there in years, and it's a prime tuna fishing area."

I asked, "Did you have any luck?"

He nodded and said, "We had a good day. We got a couple yellowfin and some mahi. We also had a white marlin in the area, but we couldn't hook him."

"Did you see the marlin jump?"

"No, but he was coming up and eating bait."

I shook my head and said, "I really have to take a day off and go tuna fishing before I have to leave."

Big H smile and said, "Well, Meggie, you're welcome anytime on my boat."

"Thanks, Big H." Mo served me my salad and it looked delicious. I asked Big H, "Did you catch this tuna?"

He sat up tall on his stool and said, "As a matter of fact, I did."

I decided it was time to needle Big H a little more about Mo, so I asked her, "Hey, how was your date last night?"

As soon as the words were out of my mouth, Big H was putting his hat back on and standing up. He said, "I've got work to do, ladies. Meggie, enjoy your salad."

I said, "Have a great day."

Mo looked at me and rolled her eyes.

I said, "So, how was your date?"

She leaned on the counter and said, "Meggie, it was a nightmare from hell. I got all dressed up, and I was feelin' really positive about this one. I got to the bar and we ordered some drinks. Then he proceeds to tell me he invited a friend of his along, and she should be showin' up any minute. Well, I thought that was odd. He then proceeded to ask me how I felt about threesomes."

Shocked, I said, "No way."

Mo raised her hand and said, "I kid you not. I told him that wasn't my thing and he said that was too bad because he told his friend all about me, and they thought we would all have a good time."

I asked her, "What did you do?"

She said, "Well, I told him I hope they have a good night, but count me out."

"Are you still going to date on the Internet?"

Mo shook her head and said, "No. I'm still going to e-mail with the Fisher Man, but I'm taking myself off the website for now. I did meet a few really nice guys like that widower, but, of course, I wasn't into them."

"That's too bad, Mo."

She shrugged her shoulders and said, "Oh well. Sometimes you meet the best people when you're not lookin'. Maybe if I stop lookin', Mr. Wonderful will find me."

I said, "I wish we could light a fire under Big H's ass."

Mo said, "He must be seein' someone. Maybe that Fisher Man will come through."

"I hope so. Hey, I guess the first pole-dancing class is next Wednesday night. Do you know if Dancing Kathy got enough people to sign up?"

Mo nodded and laughed, "She got just about every woman at the marina."

"That's great."

Mo wiggled her hips and said, "The women of Cozy

Harbor are gonna get their sexy back."

"I think it'll be a riot."

Mo laughed and said kiddingly, "Maybe that's just what I need. I know it's impossible to imagine me being any sexier than I already am, but even an old dog like me can learn a few new tricks."

On a more serious note, I said, "My Gram comes home tomorrow and I'm having dinner with her and the mysterious Cal Sunday night."

Mo perked up and said, "I can't wait to lay my eyes on him myself. He must be one hell of a guy to snag your grandmother."

"I know. I can't wait to see how it all plays out."

Concerned, Mo said, "Do you think she'll sell the marina and move to San Diego with him?"

"I don't have a clue, Mo. My Gram is seventy-two years old. I know my parents don't want to move up here and run the marina."

"Meggie, you've done a good job of it. You should run it permanently."

"It's up to Gram. Whatever she wants to do is fine with me. I just want her to be happy. Right now I'm still planning on going home in a few weeks."

"Ian hasn't said anything about you goin' back?"

"Not a thing and I haven't brought it up. I *want* him to bring it up but I can't throw away my teaching job when I don't have a clue what Ian's thinking or what Gram's plans are."

Mo said, "Well, I'm sure Betty will let you in on her plans on Sunday."

"I hope so, Mo. I'd love to stay and run the marina, but if she wants to sell it, I would understand."

Mo said, "I sure don't feel like gettin' used to a new owner. What if they don't want to keep the Shack open? They could run my sorry ass out of here."

"Mo, people come from miles around for your good cooking. I wouldn't worry about it. I'll let you know as soon as I find out anything. Keep this all under the counter."

"Sure thing."

I got up to go. "See you later."

I went back to work and had trouble concentrating. My mind kept wandering to the issues I had just discussed with Mo.

Around 4:00, I was in my office paying some bills when I heard voices in the store. I recognized Ian's voice, but not the other guy's. I tilted my head toward the door so I could hear better.

The guy said, "Ian, I haven't seen much of you this summer. I hear you're almost a married man."

Ian laughed and said, "Far from it. I'm just having some fun."

My birthday high just flew out the window.

The guy chuckled and said to Ian, "Hey, are you still trying to buy the marina from the old lady?"

Ian just said, "I've gotta run. I'll drop by your boat sometime for a beer."

The guy said, "You do that."

I heard the door shut and I stood up and looked out into the store. Ian had walked out with the guy. Journey turned around and looked at me. She raised her eyebrows but didn't say anything.

I said, "Well, I guess I know where I stand."

Journey said, "It was just two guys bullshitting, Meggie."

"I wonder."

I felt sick. I was starting to believe Ian had feelings for me. Not only did I find out he's far from marriage, but that he wants to buy the marina from Gram. I started to remember some of the things he said about Gram. He told me on several occasions how much he cared about her. Maybe he was just being nice to me to get on her good side. Feelings of doubt washed over me like a tidal wave. I was deep in thought when Matt came in the office. He was all red in the face and looked upset.

I asked him, "What's up?"

He said, "I've got some drunks at the dock. They came in for fuel, and I filled the boat up, then the guy handed me a credit card, I ran the credit card and it was declined. I went and told him and he got all pissed off. He handed me another card and the same thing happened. He started ranting and raving and demanded to talk to the owner."

"Do you know these guys?"

He shook his head no. "I've never seen that boat before."

"How many guys are on the boat?"

He answered, "Three."

"I'll go talk to them. Is Ian on his boat?"

"No."

"Go see if Big H is around and tell him what's going on."

"Okay, Meggie."

I went down to the fuel dock where I saw the boat tied up. It was a thirty-four-foot cabin cruiser. There were two guys on it and another guy stood on the dock. The one on the dock was thin and just a little taller than I am with dark brown hair and a face like a weasel.

I went up to him and said, "I'm the owner. I understand there's a problem."

He and the other guys laughed. One of the guys said, "She can't be the owner. She's probably just 'doing' the owner." They started laughing harder.

I repeated, "I am the owner."

He said, "Well, if you're the owner, you need to teach your flunkies how to run the credit card machine."

Calmly, I said, "Give me your credit card, and I'll try it again."

He handed it over, and I went into the fuel shack and ran the card. It was declined again.

I went out and gave him back the card.

I said, "I'm sorry but your credit card was declined. You'll have to pay in cash."

He got really red in the face and started waving his arms around, cursing and swearing. I stepped back away from him. He turned toward me with his back to the fuel shack. He came at me and started to point his finger at my chest while he screamed at me. I could smell the alcohol on his breath.

He said, "Look, lady, you need to get your fucking credit card machine fixed."

Out of the corner of my eye, I could see Big H walking down the dock with a furious look on his face. I expected to see steam come out of his ears at any moment. The next thing I knew, Big H grabbed the guy's finger-pointing arm and twisted it behind his back. He hauled the guy up and away from me.

In a low, threatening voice, Big H said in the guy's ear, "You touch her one more time with that finger of yours, and I'll break your fucking arm."

The drunk's buddies started to climb off the boat until they heard the thunder of running feet coming down the dock. I looked up and ten guys from the marina were coming at us full speed. Leading the pack were the Murphy brothers. The other two drunks changed their minds and quickly jumped back on the boat.

Big H spoke to the one he had in a hold. "You and your friends need to hand over as much cash as you can to pay for the fuel, and then you can take your piece-of-shit boat out of here. I'd better never see you around here again. If I do, trust me, it won't be pretty."

He let go of the guy who scurried over to his boat. The men with him handed him some cash, and he reached in his pocket and pulled out some more. His fuel bill was $420. He handed me the money and said, "I only have $310 in cash."

I knew I'd never see a dime of the rest of the money but I said, "You can mail me the rest."

He jumped on his boat, and they took off.

I was shaking. Big H put his arm around me and gave me a squeeze. He asked, "Meggie, are you okay?"

"Yeah. Thanks a lot. I'm sorry you had to do that."

He laughed and said, "Are you kidding? I haven't had that much fun in a long time."

I asked him, "That doesn't happen very often, does it?"

"At least once a summer we get a boatload of knee-walking drunks in here."

I said, "I thought about pushing him in the water."

"That would've worked."

"What does Gram do?"

"She gets one of us to go take care of it. She knows we love kicking ass for her. If this ever happens again, don't even come down here. Just come and get me or one of the other guys. If we're not around, get Greg."

I gave him a hug and then thanked all the other guys.

Matt came over to me and said, "Meggie, I called the marine patrol. Those guys shouldn't be out on the water."

"That was a good idea, Matt."

He looked over at Big H and said, "Big H is one bad-assed dude, isn't he, Meggie?"

I laughed and said, "He sure is. Lucky for us."

He nodded and said, "Yeah."

I went back to the store. I can't get the conversation I overheard in the store out of my mind. Ian never mentioned he was interested in buying the marina. Why wouldn't he tell me he was? That's probably why he hasn't asked me when I'm going back to Philly. He probably doesn't care. He entertained Betty's granddaughter all summer. He should gain points for that. His mission's been accomplished.

At 6:00, I said goodnight to Journey and was just getting ready to close up the store when Ian walked in. He still had on his work clothes, and he wore a very concerned look on his tanned, handsome face.

He came right up to me and put his hands on my shoulders. He said, "I just heard what happened. Are you okay?"

I swallowed hard and said, "I'm fine. It shook me up a little bit, but Big H and the guys came to my rescue."

"Big H told me what happened. I told him I owe him one. I went to pick up some parts for the *Intrepid*. I wish I had been here." Then he gave me a big hug.

I lied and said, "That's the only bad thing that's happened around here all summer. I guess I've been lucky."

Ian ran his hands through my hair. He said, "I never want anything bad to happen to you."

Then he kissed me with such tenderness, my eyes started to water. It was hard for me to believe this is the same guy who a few hours ago said he was far from marriage and just having fun.

He said, "I have some repairs to do on the *Intrepid*. Do you want to just get a pizza when I'm done?"

"Sure. I'll be over at the cottage. I want to do some cleaning before Gram comes home."

He gave me a quick kiss and said, "I'll come by for you when I'm ready."

I finished locking up and went over to the cottage. I did a little cleaning and straightening up. The cottage wasn't that dirty because I haven't spent much time there. I've either been at work or at Ian's house. The more I thought about Ian, the more upset I got. The more upset I got, the more cleaning I did.

I had just finished scrubbing the bathroom when the phone rang.

It was my mom.

She said, "Hi, honey, just wanted you to know that we're home."

"Oh, Mom, I'm glad you called. How were your flights?"

"Good, but it was a long trip. Your dad and I are so glad

to be home. What's new?"

"Well, Gram is coming home tomorrow and she's coming to see you next week."

"That's what your father said. I can't wait to see her and hear all about her trip out west. I can't wait to see you, too. When will you be home?"

"In a couple of weeks."

"Are you going to keep seeing Ian?"

"I don't know, Mom."

"I'm sure you'll work it out. Well, I'd better let you go. I've got a lot to do around here after being away for so long."

"Talk to you soon, Mom."

"See you later, sweetie."

I didn't mention Gram's friend Cal to my mom. I figured I'd let Gram have that honor. I wonder what my mom will have to say about it all. I think it will really throw her for a loop. She'll be happy for her, no doubt, but she'll be surprised. I remember hearing my mom say many times over the years that she wished Gram would meet someone. When my mom was a young girl, she used to try and fix Gram up with any single guy she came across. When she married my dad and moved away, she felt terrible leaving Gram behind in Rhode Island.

I can't wait for Sunday. I'll get to meet Cal and hopefully, I'll find out what Gram is going to do with her life and the marina. I'm going to ask her if Ian had approached her about the marina. After I find out all that, maybe I'll be able to make some decisions about my own life. I know what I want to do. I want to stay and run the marina, and I want to be with Ian. At least, I thought I did.

When Ian came to pick me up, I put on a happy face even though my heart wasn't in it. I wanted to ask him about the marina, but I think deep down I wasn't ready to hear what he had to say. We ate our pizza and talked about our day and went to bed early. When we hit the sheets, I jumped his bones. He jumped on the bandwagon and it was passion with a capital P. I figured it might be my last night with him. I needed to find out what he was up to and how he felt about me but I wanted one more amazing night.

CHAPTER SIXTEEN

Another busy Saturday morning at the marina was underway. This morning was especially hectic, and I had to be out in the store with Journey. The tuna were around, and everyone was coming in for tackle. The forecast for today wasn't all that great for offshore fishing. A cold front was coming through this afternoon with scattered thunder showers forecasted. Tomorrow, though, was supposed to be a great day, and all the fishermen planned to take advantage of it. The only boats that went offshore today were the lobster boats. I think this morning will be a record money-making morning for the marina. Things slowed down after lunch, and I was finally able to go into the office and do a little paperwork.

I was poring over some customer accounts when Mac appeared at my office door. As much as I needed to get some work done, nothing could keep me from spending a few minutes talking to one of my favorite people.

I said, "Hey, Mac. Did you go clamming today?"

He smiled and said, "I sure did and I brought you some." He pulled a bag from around his back and handed it to me.

Preparing to give him a lecture, I asked, "Did you go out

by yourself?"

He shook his head no and said, "I didn't lift so much as a pinky."

"Who went with you?"

He said, "Mike's son, Kyle, came down with his friend, Ryan. They're going to a clambake tonight, and they have to bring the clams. Kyle called me last night because he knows I know the best spots."

I laughed. "They needed the Clam Man."

"Well, Kyle's been clamming with me for years. I think he was killing two birds with one stone. He checked up on me and got his clams."

"He seemed like a really nice kid when I met him on the Fourth."

"He's a great kid. Mike and Nancy have done a wonderful job with those kids. Kyle is going to Northeastern next fall to get his MBA in business. He always comes down to see me when he gets a chance. He's also a hell of a guitar player."

"Oh, really. Does he play in a band?"

Mac said, "As a matter of fact, he does. They're cutting their first CD in a couple of weeks."

"Well, when they do, I want one."

He beamed with pride and said, "You got it."

"You must've had fun going out with two young guys for a change."

"Oh, yeah. But you're still my favorite clamming partner. All I had to do was take them to my favorite spots and watch them do all the work. Kyle's friend Ryan is six-four and can rake like a champ. He's the Murphy brothers' nephew. He was an NCAA champion rower. He went to Harvard and is preparing for the next Olympics. I'm hoping I'll live long enough to see that gold medal around his neck. It does this old heart good to see young men today who are so driven and have such pride in their country."

"I love watching the Olympics."

Mac said, "I guarantee you that kid will be representing the good old USA."

On a more serious note, I asked, "How are you feeling, Mac?

"Meggie, I feel great. I've had a life revelation. I think that scare I had was good for me; I'm learning to take it easy. I'm going to let the younger people do things for me without putting up a fuss. I've finally realized that I'm an old man. There is no shame in admitting you're old and you can't do what you used to do."

"Mac, you're not only still handsome, but you're smarter."

He laughed and asked me, "Now it's my turn. How are things going with Ian?"

"Okay. We've been seeing a lot of each other. Hey, Mac, do you know if anyone has approached Gram lately about buying the marina?"

"I know a few people have over the years, but I doubt she ever gave it any thought. The marina is her life."

I decided to press him a little further. "Has anyone I might know approached her?"

He shook his head no and said, "I don't think so. Why are you asking?"

"Just wondering, that's all."

"Well, I've got to go, honey. Enjoy the clams."

I stood up and gave him a hug and a kiss. I said, "Mac,

you're the best."

He said, "No, you're the prize, Meggie. Don't ever forget that." He gave me a wink and walked out the door.

I didn't want to tell Mac that I heard Ian wanted to buy the marina, because I'm still not sure how I feel about it. When I'm with him, I believe that he has genuine feelings for me. When I'm away from him, the doubts start rolling around in my brain. I know I'm in love with him. At least, the person I think he is. I can't accept that he would use me to get to my grandmother. My gut is telling me he isn't that kind of guy. Then again, look what happened with Jimmy. I was shocked when he dumped me. I didn't see it coming at all. Okay, he wasn't Mr. Wonderful but the rejection hurt. It was a big blow to my self-esteem, which was never high to begin with. Maybe I need to step back? Ian has never said how he feels about me. He's never asked when I'm going home or talked about doing anything together beyond next week. I need to look at this as just a casual thing until I find out the truth. How am I supposed to do that, though? How do I shut off my feelings?

Tonight Ian and I were going out to dinner with his friends. Ian said he'd come and pick me up about 7:00. Mid-afternoon, we got a pretty good thunderstorm. I have always loved thunderstorms, but now that I'm dating someone that makes his living out on the water, I've changed my mind about them. After I finished closing up the store, I went out on the dock to see if Ian was back. The *Intrepid* and *Miss Kay* were tied up at the dock, but the *Stalwart* wasn't back yet. Ian usually gets back around 4:00. Occasionally he puts in a longer day but since we had plans tonight, I was surprised he wasn't back yet. I was getting a little worried. I decided to go over to the cottage and get ready, and then when he came in I would just go home with him, and we could leave from his house.

I took a shower and put on a beige skirt and a brown blouse and brown sandals. I decided to wear my hair down because Ian likes it that way, and I put on a little makeup. I went down to D dock. The *Stalwart* still wasn't back. Okay, now I'm really worried. I walked over to A dock. Sexy Cathy and Kenny were sitting on their boat, but I didn't see anyone else around. Since it was dinnertime, I assumed a lot of people probably went out to eat. I went down the dock to talk to them.

Sexy Cathy looked at me and said, "Meggie, you look really pretty."

I said, "Thanks. Ian and I are supposed to go to dinner with some friends of his, but he's not back yet and I'm worried."

Kenny said, "I'm sure he's fine. He knows what he's doing out there. I heard on the marine radio that there was a squall out on the water today when that front came through. Ian has all the latest electronics and he would have seen it on his radar and avoided it. Maybe he had engine problems."

I asked, "What exactly is a squall?"

Kenny said, "It's a sudden violent increase in wind speed, which is usually associated with active weather such as the thunder showers we had this afternoon. Most times, they only last a few minutes, but they can cause damage."

Worried, I said, "I hope he's okay."

Kenny said, "Let me see if I can scare him up on the radio." Kenny got on his marine radio and called Ian several times, but Ian wasn't picking up.

Sexy Cathy said, "He'll be coming in soon, Meggie. How about a beer or a margarita?"

I said, "No, thanks, but I think I'll hang out here with you, if you don't mind."

Kenny said, "Come on board and have a seat."

I stepped onto their boat and sat in one of the deck chairs.

I asked, "Have you eaten dinner yet? I wouldn't want to hold you up."

Cathy said, "We had an early dinner on the boat. I decided I was tired of eating out, so I made a bunch of food yesterday to bring down for the weekend. Hey, I'm looking forward to our pole-dancing class."

I laughed and said, "It should be fun. I guess Dancing Kathy got a lot of the women down here to sign up."

Sexy Cathy said, "Even Just Howard's new girlfriend, Barbara, signed up."

Kenny smiled and said, "I've been looking into getting one installed at our house. I can't wait for my first private recital."

We all laughed. Kenny tried again to reach Ian on the radio but got no response. They continued to talk about this and that. I could tell they were trying to keep my mind off Ian. I checked my watch—7:30. I looked over to B dock where the sportfishing boats were and saw some of the guys standing around. They must have come back from dinner.

I said to Kenny and Cathy, "I think I'll go over and see if any of the guys have heard anything."

Kenny said, "I'll go with you."

I said, "Cathy, thanks for the company."

She smiled and tried to reassure me. "I'm sure he'll be

back any minute."

Kenny and I went over to talk to the guys. Standing on the dock were Medium Howard, the Murphy brothers, and Randy. We informed them that Ian wasn't back yet and asked them if they heard anything. They hadn't, but they had heard about the squall. Randy said it would have been out where Ian usually goes, but he also said Ian would have seen it on the radar and avoided it. They all concluded that he must have had engine problems. Randy went on his boat to call Ian's other two boat captains, John and Tim, to see if they knew anything. He came back and said he could only reach John, who said he had talked to Ian this morning on the radio but hadn't talked to him since. The guys talked about squalls and told a few sea stories. By now it was almost dark and I checked my watch again. It was 8:15.

I asked them, "Do you think we should call the Coast Guard?"

Medium H said, "Give him a little more time. Ian would be upset if we sent the Coast Guard out looking for him for no reason."

Don Murphy said, "Oh look. Here he comes."

I breathed a sigh of relief. We all headed over to D Dock. Ian docked the *Stalwart* and Randy said, "You're late. Did you have problems out there?"

Ian said, "Did you hear about the squall?"

We all said, "Yes."

He said, "I saw it coming on the radar and avoided it. When I went back after it passed through, I came across a sailboat that was in trouble. Their mast snapped in the squall. I gave them a hand and a tow back to Bristol." He said, "Meggie,

I'm sorry I'm late. I've tried to call you at the cottage for the last hour, but I guess you were out here."

Kenny said, "You got your girl here a little worried. I tried calling you on the radio, but you weren't answering."

Ian said, "I turned it off. Too many people rambling on it. I needed some peace and quiet. I've had a long day."

The mosquitoes were out in full force tonight, and I waved one off my arm.

Ian said, "Meggie, you'd better go up to the cottage and wait for me before the mosquitoes make a meal out of you. I called Jake and told him we weren't going to make dinner. I'll be up in a few minutes."

I said, "Okay. Thanks, guys."

I got almost to the end of the dock when I heard Ian call my name and say something. I didn't quite hear him, so I turned around and yelled, "What?"

All the guys yelled back, "He said you look really pretty."

I smiled, blushed, and hurried back to the cottage. I can't believe he said that in front of the guys.

Since our dinner plans were canceled, I decided to make us something at Ian's. I didn't have a lot in the fridge, but I did have the clams Mac gave me this morning. Suddenly I realized I was starving and quickly hunted through the cupboard. In the vegetable bin I found garlic, fresh parsley, and some beautiful plum tomatoes that Don and Geri from *She's the Boss* gave me from their garden. I also found a bottle of clam juice in the cupboard and a box of linguine. I knew Ian had plenty of white wine at his house. Linguine with fresh clam sauce sounded pretty good to me. I was loading up a bag with the ingredients when Ian walked in.

He came over to me and put his arms around me and gave me a big hug.

I said, "I was worried about you."

He said, "I'm sorry. I'm not used to someone worrying about me. I think I kind of like it. You know, Meggie, the sea and weather can be unpredictable, but I take every precaution to keep myself safe out there."

"I know. That was nice of you to help those people. You're a hero."

He said, "Not really. I just gave them a tow. It was a couple and their eight-year-old daughter."

I said, "Well, I bet they were glad you came along."

"They were. They kept thanking me. I'm sorry about dinner."

"No problem. I'm going to make you a quick dinner at your house. How does linguine with clam sauce sound?"

He gave me a grateful look. "Like heaven. I'm tired, hungry, and I need a hot shower."

I said, "Let's go."

He said, "Do you mind driving yourself? I can sleep in tomorrow a little bit. I've got repairs to do on the *Miss Kay* in the morning. John's going to take the *Stalwart* out.

I said, "No problem."

I prepared dinner while Ian took a shower. The pasta turned out great. Ian finished first and put down his fork. He sighed and said, "That was delicious. You're an angel."

"You're welcome."

"You said you're going to have dinner with your grandmother tomorrow night, right?"

"Yes."

"I think I might take a ride up to Boston and have dinner with my cousin Christine. I'll call her in the morning."

"You're pretty close, aren't you?"

He said, "Yeah. She's my only cousin. We're a small family. Her father is my mom's brother. Chris is an only child, too. Her parents live in Florida near mine. Chris and I try to get together at least once a month."

"That's nice."

"You must be excited about seeing your grandmother and meeting her boyfriend."

I had told Ian about Cal.

"I am."

"Do you think she'll come back to work soon?"

"Gram said she wanted me to keep running the marina until it was time for me to go back."

"When do you have to be back?"

Finally! I thought he'd never ask.

I told him, "In two weeks."

"Wow. The summer has sure flown by."

I gave him a smile and said, "I've had a great time."

He smiled back and said, "Me, too. What do you say we clean up and go to bed? I'm exhausted."

I couldn't believe that's all he had to say about me going back. I was so disappointed, but I tried my best not to show it. We did the dishes and went upstairs. In the short time it took me to wash my face and brush my teeth, Ian had fallen asleep. I set the alarm for 4:00 for myself and climbed into bed. I looked over at him and watched him sleeping peacefully. If I slept at all tonight, I would be surprised. There was too much on my mind. I fell asleep for a little while, woke up at 2:00, and couldn't go back to sleep. I decided to do what I usually do under these circumstances and started saying Hail Mary's. When I next looked up at the clock, it was 3:45. I quietly got out of bed and turned the alarm off so it wouldn't wake Ian. I got dressed and went downstairs to the kitchen. I left him a note and told him to have a good time with Christine.

I opened up the store and my day began. I kept busy all morning, which was good as it took my mind off Ian. Gram called around 11:00 and said they would pick me up at 6:00 for dinner. At 2:00, Ian came into the store.

He said, "I got in touch with Christine this morning. I'm going to go home and shower and then head up to Boston. I just wanted to tell you to have fun with your Gram and tell her I said hello."

"I will."

"I'll call you when I get back."

"Okay."

Since no one was in the store, he kissed me goodbye and left.

I closed up early and went home to shower and change. I'd just finished getting ready when I heard Gram's voice calling me. I walked out into the living room, and there she was, looking better than ever. Standing beside her was a distinguished-looking gentleman. He was about five-eleven, slender, with a full head of white hair and warm brown eyes.

I ran to Gram and gave her a hug.

I said, "It's so good to see you. You look beautiful."

She said, "So do you. Rhode Island always agreed with you. Meggie, I want you to meet Cal."

I went over to Cal, who had a big smile on his face. He

took my hand and said, "Meggie, I've heard all about you and you're even more beautiful than your Gram said."

I blushed and said, "Would you like to have a glass of wine before we go to dinner?"

Gram clapped her hands and said, "That would be great. We have a lot to tell you."

I went quickly into the kitchen, opened a bottle of wine, and brought them each a glass. I went back to get one for myself and took a chair. They were sitting on the couch together holding hands. This was so weird for me. A good kind of weird. Gram looked so unbelievably happy.

Gram cleared her throat and said, "Meggie, we have some big news to tell you."

I asked hesitantly, "What?"

Gram said, "Cal and I got married two weeks ago in San Diego."

I was stunned. "Wow! Congratulations!" I stood up and went over to them and hugged them both. I asked, "Does Mom know?"

She said, "No. You're the only one who knows besides my friend Dossie. At our age, we didn't want to make a fuss with a wedding, and we didn't want to wait. When you get to be our age, long engagements aren't a good idea. I don't even buy green bananas at this point in my life."

I said, "You said you were old friends. When did you first meet?"

Cal said, "We met the summer your grandmother got out of high school. I was home from college and met her when I went into the restaurant she was working in for the summer. We dated that whole summer, and then I went back to college in California. I went to Stanford. We wrote letters to each other that following fall, but we were young and decided the distance was too great and we should see other people. I still had two years of school left. Back then, it wasn't like it is now with people jumping on planes right and left."

Gram said, "Last winter, Dossie and I went over to Newport for lunch, and Cal was there having lunch with some old friends. He recognized me after all these years and came over to our table. We had a grand reunion, and then he asked me out to dinner. He still has a home in Newport and one in San Diego. He goes back and forth. When he was in town, we would go out, and rekindled our romance after all these years."

Cal said, "My wife died about ten years ago. I have a son, Michael, and a daughter, Marissa. They both live in San Diego with their families."

I shook my head and said, "I'm floored. I'm so happy for you both. Where will you live?"

Gram said, "We talked a lot about that and decided to live the winters in San Diego and the summers in Newport."

"Are you going to sell the marina?"

She said, "That's up to you and your brothers. You see, I always intended to leave it to the three of you. I told your mother this years ago. I would hate to sell it because it's been in the family for so long. Cal and I have an appointment in two weeks with a lawyer, and I'm going to leave it in a trust for you and your brothers to inherit it when I die. If I gave it to you now, it would cost a fortune in taxes. Since your brothers are both traveling the world with their careers, I was hoping you would stay and run the marina. I've gotten the impression that you enjoy doing it."

"I've had the best summer, and I do love running the marina."

Gram said, "Why don't you think about it? You can give me an answer when we get back from Philly."

I said, "Okay, I'll think about it. I have a question for you, though."

"Shoot."

"Has Ian ever offered to buy the marina from you? I overheard some guy in the store ask him if he was still trying to buy it from you."

She said, "Yes. He has made me offers, but I told him I wasn't interested. Why do you ask?"

"Well, I was just wondering if he was trying to get on your good side by dating me."

Gram looked surprised. She said, "I doubt that. Ian isn't that kind of guy, Meggie. You're a beautiful girl; that's why he's dating you."

"Gram, are you sure? You've known him a lot longer then I have. I want to trust him, but I'm afraid I'm setting myself up for a broken heart."

"I'm sure, honey. He's a good guy. You can trust him." She looked at Cal with love in her eyes and said, "If you don't take a chance, you could miss out on something wonderful."

I smiled at them and said, "Mom's going to be blown away by your big announcement."

Cal reassured me. "Meggie, I'll take good care of your Gram. Don't you worry."

I said, "I'm glad she has someone like you to take care of her. She deserves the best."

Gram said, "Well, I don't know about you two, but I'm

starved. Let's go get some dinner."

I went and grabbed a sweater. It was a little chilly tonight. We had a nice meal, and I got to know Cal a little bit. He was a really warm person with a quick wit and keen intelligence. I could see why my Gram fell for him again. They were so cute together, and she was beaming with happiness. I told them about Lolly and the pole dancing class and filled them in on some of the other funny things that have happened at the marina over the summer. They told me about all their travels and what a good time they had. They planned to go to Philly on Tuesday and return the following Sunday. Gram said she would call me when she got back and we'd talk again.

They dropped me off at the cottage around 9:00 and I checked my messages. Ian hadn't called. Since I had a lot to think about, I decided I wanted to be by myself tonight. I left him a message on his machine that I got home early, I was going to bed, and would see him tomorrow.

CHAPTER SEVENTEEN

I spent another restless night thinking about Ian and Gram and trying to figure out what I should do about the marina. By noon, I was starving and since Journey was off today, I put a sign on the door that I'd be back at 1:00 and went over to the Shack for lunch. Mo was there by herself, chopping up some veggies, when I walked in.

She took one look at me and said, "Honey, you look tired."

"I'm exhausted, Mo. I've barely slept the past two nights."

"What's on your mind?"

"Well, Ian finally asked me when I had to go back and I told him in two weeks. All he had to say was that the summer is flying by."

She leaned on the counter and said, "I'm might have to smack that boy upside his head."

I said, "He's got me so confused. I get mixed messages from him. On the one hand, he is so sweet to me and says really nice things, but he never talks about the future. I also heard that he has offered to buy the marina from Gram. Since I heard that little bit of news, I've been worried. What if he's just dating me to get on Gram's good side so she'd sell him the marina?"

"Well, I've heard he's made offers to her, but a lot of other people have, too. Big H told me he talked to her once about it, but she said she isn't interested in sellin'. Push those doubts about Ian out of your head."

"I'm trying to, Mo, but it's so hard. If I lived here, it would be different; we would have more time to date. I'm only here for the summer, which puts a different spin on the situation. I don't need more time to figure out if he's the one; I know it. I guess he needs more time, or maybe he looks at our relationship as just a summer fling."

Mo said, "Well, don't push him. All a guy needs is a girl to corner him, and he'll be runnin' down the road like the devil himself is chasin' him."

"Believe me, I haven't said a word, and I'm not going to. I wouldn't want a guy who didn't want me."

"He might surprise you, Meggie. Guys are funny. They avoid commitment for years, and one day it's like they wake up in the mornin', they shit, shower, and shave and decide it's time to get married, and that's it. I've seen the way he looks at you. That boy's in love."

"There is something else on my mind, but you have to promise to keep this way under the counter. It's big news."

"Mum's the word. What's up?"

"I had dinner with Gram and Cal last night. You should see her, Mo. She looks radiant. I've never seen her happier. They got married two weeks ago in San Diego."

"NO WAY!"

"I said, "Yep."

"Oh boy. What's he like?"

"He's a very distinguished, handsome, older gentleman. I liked him. He was warm and funny, and it's obvious he adores her."

"Well, holy cow. I'm so happy for her."

"She doesn't want anyone to know until she gets back from Philly and tells my mom. I can't wait to talk to my mom. She's going to be shocked, but I think she'll be over the moon that Gram has a great guy in her life after all these years alone."

Mo smiled and said, "Hey, maybe there's hope for me. Where will they live?"

"They said they would spend the winters in San Diego and the summers at Cal's house in Newport."

Mo got a worried look on her face and tentatively asked, "What about the marina?"

"Well, that's the other thing that's been keeping me up at night. She said she was leaving it to me and my brothers and asked me if I wanted to stay and run it."

Mo smiled and said, "That's great. You're gonna do it, aren't you? You love it, and you're good at it. It would give you and Ian more time to figure things out."

"Yes, it would. Running the marina part is easy. I *do* love it. The problem lies with Ian. I just don't know what to do."

Mo shook her head and said, "You need to tell him your Gram asked you to stay, then see what he has to say about it."

"I know. I'm going to tell him tonight. Gram said to think about it this week while they're in Philly and give her my decision when she gets back. If I'm going to stay, I also have to let the school know next week that I'm not coming back. I feel kind of bad about that, too. I'll be leaving them in a pinch, but I'm sure they can get substitutes until they find someone permanently."

Mo said, "Well, I can see why you haven't been sleeping, honey. You need a good lunch. What are you in the mood for today?"

"I would love a chicken salad sandwich with roasted red peppers on wheat bread, some chips, and a coke. You make the best chicken salad I've ever had."

Mo winked and said, "I put a little lemon juice in it. It gives it a little zing."

She turned around to make my sandwich. The door opened and in swaggered Tony, with a big smile on his face.

I said, "Look who's here. Mo. It's Mr. Happy."

Tony wiggled his eyebrows and said, "I'm Mr. Very Happy."

I asked him, "How was your weekend?"

He took a seat next to me and said, "Great. Helen and I went down the shore on Saturday and spent the night. She took me to some of your favorite hot spots. We ran into some friends of yours, Frannie and Sue. I got to hang out with three beautiful women all evening. Oh, Sue told me to tell you that she has a new boyfriend. He's an assistant coach for the Flyers."

I said, "Good for her. I'm sure the girls loved you."

He smiled and said, "Well, I did turn on the Maroni charm."

Mo said, "I just bet you did."

I asked him, "What else did you do?"

Mo handed me my sandwich, and Tony asked, "What is that?"

I told him and he said, "Mo, I'll have what she's having."

Mo nodded and said, "Comin' right up, handsome."

Tony continued, "Helen took me to her parents for brunch on Sunday."

My jaw dropped, and I almost fell off my stool. The only guys Helen has ever brought home were prom dates and that was because Mrs. Jakowski threatened her. Mrs. J wanted to take pictures before the prom.

"Wow. That's huge, Tony. Helen never brings anyone home. Did you meet everyone?"

"Yeah. I met the whole fam-dam-ly. Her mom put on a great brunch. The food was great, and I loved the whole family. I fit right in."

"I love her family, too. When we were growing up, we were either at my house or hers. They're my second family. Will Hel be coming up soon?"

"This weekend. She has to work a full day on Friday, so she's flying up Friday night. I'm going to have a pool party Saturday night. I hope you and Ian can come."

"We don't have any plans that I know of. I'll check with Ian."

Tony said, "Mo, you're welcome, too, and feel free to bring anyone you want."

Mo said, "I just might do that, but I'm not gettin' in a bathin' suit."

He looked her up and down and said, "Mo, I'd bet you'd be pretty hot in a thong. You could warm up the water in my pool."

We all laughed.

Tony finished his sandwich way before me and went back to work. I'm a slow eater.

I said, "Mo, all we've done is talk about me. What's new

with you?"

She said, "Well, the Fisher Man finally asked me out."

"That's great. Why aren't you excited?"

"After my Internet disaster dates, I've kinda' lost my lust for lust."

"Are you going out with him?"

Rather unenthusiastically, she answered, "Yeah, I said I'd go. He's gonna pick me up on his boat at the fuel dock Friday night about 6:30 and take me to a restaurant up in East Greenwich."

"Good."

"Meggie, I was hopin' you'd do me a big favor?"

"Sure, you name it, Mo."

"Well, I've always met these Internet guys in public places, so I'm leery of goin' on a boat alone with one of them. I was thinkin' maybe you could go down to the dock and check him out before I get on the boat. With my luck, he'll pull up in an old rust bucket, and he'll only have two teeth in his mouth."

"I'll meet you at the Shack after I close up at six. I'll keep an eye out and then go down and check him out. If he looks like a creep, I'll tell him you got sick and couldn't make it. If I think he looks okay, I'll come back and get you."

Mo said, "Deal. I really appreciate you doin' that for me. You never know about people these days."

I got up to leave, and I felt a lot better than when I came into the Shack.

I said, "Mo, thanks for lunch and for listening to me."

She smiled and said, "I can't wait to meet your new grandpa."

I said, "Hey, that's right. I have a grandfather. I never

knew my real grandfathers. They both died before I was born."

"Everythin' will work out, sweetie. Just you wait and see."

"I hope so."

Ian came and found me in the store after he finished work.

He said, "How about I cook dinner tonight? I'll pick up some steaks on the way home."

"That sounds good. I'm going to close up early and take a nap at the cottage. I'll be over around 7:00."

He said, "I'll see you then, and you can fill me in on your dinner with your grandmother. He pulled me in for a kiss and said, "By the way, I really missed you last night."

"I missed you, too." He kissed me again and walked out the door.

I sighed and watched him cross the parking lot to his truck and then quickly closed up the store. I was pooped.

When I got to the cottage, I plopped down on the couch and slept for two hours. I felt like a new person when I woke up. It's amazing what a nap will do for you. After I showered, I put on a short, candy-apple green shift that I picked up at a shop in town, and headed over to Ian's. Sam greeted me at the door, and I gave him a good scratch on his rump. I followed Sam into the kitchen where Ian was making a salad.

Ian looked at me and said, "You look revived. I love the dress. That's a great color for you."

"Thanks. Can I help?"

"No. Why don't you pour us both a glass of wine? I have some white opened in the fridge."

I got up and poured us each a glass.

He said, "Come out on the deck with me while I cook

the steaks, and you can tell me about your dinner last night."

I picked up both glasses and followed him out to the deck.

I said, "Well, it was full of surprises. You have to promise not to tell anyone, though."

"Sure. I promise."

"Gram and Cal got married two weeks ago in San Diego."

"Really. Wow. That's a surprise. Do you like him?"

"Yeah, I do. He's a really nice man and seems to adore her. I couldn't be happier for both of them. They're going to Philly tomorrow to tell my parents. She doesn't want people up here to know before she tells my mom."

"What's she going to do about the marina? Do you think she'll sell it?"

Those words couldn't come out of his mouth fast enough. Well, I guess it's the moment of truth.

I said, "I heard that you offered to buy it from her a few times."

He looked surprised when I said that. He said, "I have. She told me if she ever decided to sell, she would give me first crack at it."

Well, at least he was honest about it.

I said, "I'm surprised you never mentioned that to me."

He shrugged his shoulders and said, "I guess it just never came up in conversation."

"Well, Ian, I'm sorry to disappoint you but she still hasn't changed her mind. She asked me if I would like to stay and run it. She told me to think about it this week and let her know my answer when she gets back. They'll be back on Sunday."

"What do you think you'll do?"

I said, "I'm not sure." I couldn't wait to hear what he said next.

He said, "I'm happy for your grandmother. I've always liked her. She's been great to me."

I tried not to show the disappointment on my face. I was hoping he'd tell me he loved me. That he wanted me to stay.

He swatted at a mosquito and said, "The bugs are starting to bite. Did you put bug cream on?"

"Yes. I'm okay." Since he didn't seem too anxious to talk about whether I should stay or not, I decided to change the subject. I asked, "How was your dinner with Christine?"

"Good. We had an early dinner. Then I went back to her condo and hung some pictures for her. She just moved in last month."

He pulled the steaks off the grill, and we went into the kitchen.

Ian was really quiet during dinner. I told him, "Helen is coming up Friday night and Tony is having a pool party Saturday night. Do you want to go?"

"Sure. That'll be fun."

I couldn't finish my steak. I lost my appetite. I cut up the rest of it and put it in Sam's dish. He gave me a doggy smile, wagged his tail, and ate it up in two seconds.

Ian laughed and said, "That's it. He's officially in love with you."

I smiled. I guess there is always a bright side. At least the dog's in love with me.

We did the dishes together and talked about Boston. I've only been there once when I was little. He told me he would take me up there sometime and give me a tour. When we finished the dishes, I picked up my purse.

Ian looked at me wide-eyed. He said, "You're not leaving, are you?"

"Yeah. I think I should go home. I have a mountain of laundry to do."

"Is there something wrong, Meggie? You don't seem yourself tonight."

"I'm fine."

He came and stood in front of me and pulled me toward him. He kissed me and then gave me a big hug.

He said, "I'll miss you tonight. Can I change your mind?"

I said, "No, I'd better go."

He walked me to the door and said, "I'll stop by after work tomorrow. Are you sure you're okay?"

I smiled at him and said, "I'm sure. See you tomorrow."

As soon as I pulled away from his house, the floodgates opened and I cried all the way home. If he was going to say anything about his feelings for me, it would have been tonight. Obviously, I was right. He just wanted a summer fling.

When Journey got into work the next morning, I went to the Shack for breakfast. When I walked in, Mo was just pulling a coffee cake out of the oven. It smelled so good my stomach started to growl after just one whiff.

Mo said, "Hey there, sweetie. What can I getcha?"

"Can I have a piece of that? I'm starving."

"Sure. Would you like a cup coffee to go with it?"

"Sure."

Mo served me my cake and coffee.

She said, "How goes the battle. Any big decisions yet?"

"Oh, Mo, I don't know what to do. I saw Ian last night

and told him about Gram. He immediately asked me if she was going to sell the marina. I told him no and then told him she wanted me to stay and run it. I didn't tell him she was leaving it to me and my brothers."

"What did he say?"

"That's the problem, Mo. He didn't say a thing. I was so disappointed. I told him I heard he wanted to buy the marina and asked him why he never told me that. He said it never came up. He asked me if I knew what I would do and I said that I didn't. I wanted him to give me some sign, some reason to stay. I'm not sure I believe he was seeing me to get on Gram's good side, but I'm convinced now he just wanted a summer fling. If he wanted more, he would have tried to convince me to stay."

"I think you're wrong, Meggie. I've seen the way he looks at you. I can usually read people pretty well. Except, of course, some of the guys I date. It's hard to see clearly when you're in the situation."

"I wish I could just enjoy the next two weeks with him and not worry about it. I know myself well enough, though, to know I can't do that. I'm in deep, Mo, and it'll be even harder to say goodbye to him if I spend the next two weeks with him. I want to stay more than anything, but if I do and then he dumped me, I would be crushed."

"Are you gonna break it off with him?"

"I think I'm just going to avoid him for a few days. I need time to think about things and I can't do that when I'm with him."

"I sure hope you decide to stay. I'd miss you."

I smiled at her and said, "I'd miss you too, Mo. Hey, are

you doing anything tonight?"

"Nope."

"Want to go to the movies?"

"Sure. I haven't been to the movies in a long time. I'll check the paper and let you know what time? Maybe there'll be a movie with that Russell Crowe guy in it. Now that is a sexy man."

Just then, Matt came running through the door.

"Aunt Mo, Meggie, the girls are getting ready to take the *You Go Girl* out. You don't want to miss the show," he said.

"I've got nothin' on the grill, come on, Meggie. You don't want to miss this. It's a riot," Mo said.

She grabbed my hand, and we both followed Matt over to C dock to join the crowd. I was wondering if anyone was going to pass around popcorn.

Mo pointed to a boat pulling out of B dock in a hurry. She said, "There goes Jim gettin' out of the way fast. Everyone gets out of the girls' way when they're maneuverin'."

Deb was on the boat manning the tiller and Terry was standing on the dock.

"I think I should push off, Terry," Deb said.

Terry said, "The last time you pushed off, you fell in the water."

"That's because I tripped on the line you left lying all over the dock. I keep telling you that you should always coil it up."

"You fell in the water because you're not fast enough. Now I'm going to push off and jump on the boat, so get ready."

Terry pushed the boat away from the dock, jumped on, tripped and fell on Deb. That's when the screaming started.

"Jesus H. Christ, Terry, you trying to friggin' kill me here."

Terry got herself upright and shouted back, "Just hold on to the goddamn tiller. I'll put the jib up. Don't hit anything."

Deb yelled, "You are such a bitch."

Terry tried to get the jib up. The boom swung around and hit Deb in the head, knocking her backwards. She put her hands on her head and screamed, "My God, I'm gonna wind up in the friggin' hospital. I'm seeing stars."

"Quit your whining and watch out for the freakin' jet skiers."

Deb rubbed her head some more and said, "I've got a big lump on my head. Terry, I swear I'm never going sailing with you again. It's too much stress on my nerves and my body."

"Just shut up, will ya. You're giving me a headache."

"Yeah, well, you almost took my friggin' head off with the goddamn boom."

They rounded the corner, and everyone on the dock started laughing.

I turned around and saw Mac standing beside me.

He was laughing and said, "Those girls should start charging people for the show."

A little concerned, I said, "Hey, Mac. I hope they make it back okay."

"They don't stay out very long, and so far they've always made it back. Everyone keeps tabs on them. We'll all be watching to make sure they get in."

"How are you feeling today, Mac?"

"Like a new man. You look a little tired, though. You feeling okay?"

"Just a little tired. My Gram is back. She went to see my parents, but I'm sure she'll stop in when she gets back to say hello."

"Did she have a good trip?"

"She sure did. I'm sure she'll tell you all about it when she sees you."

"I'll look forward to it. You get some rest. I'm going home to take a nap myself."

"See you later, Mac."

It was around 4:00 when Ian appeared in my office doorway.

He looked his usual gorgeous sexy self. It took all the will I could muster up to keep from throwing myself at him. It doesn't matter if he smells like lobster bait or diesel fuel, I want him and I want him now.

He said, "Hi. How's your day going?"

"Good. The girls took their sailboat out this morning. That was funny."

He laughed and said, "Oh, yeah. That's always amusing."

"How was your day?"

"Good. I've got some repairs to make on the *Stalwart*, but I should be done in a couple of hours. What would you like to do tonight?"

"Oh. I'm sorry, but Mo asked me to go to the movies."

Okay, I lied, I asked Mo but I'm not telling him that.

He looked a little hurt but said, "Well, you have a great time. Maybe we can do something tomorrow night?"

"Gee. The pole-dancing class is tomorrow night."

He said, "Maybe you can stop by afterward?"

I said, "Yeah. I'll call you if we get done early."

He looked puzzled and asked, "Meggie, are we okay?"

I said, "Yeah. We're fine."

He pulled me out of my chair and kissed me. The kiss started out as a tender little kiss and then I thought he was going to swallow me whole.

He let me go and stepped back into the doorway. He said, "Have fun." He turned and walked out the back door of the store.

I sat down and fought the tears back.

CHAPTER EIGHTEEN

Tonight is the first pole-dancing class. I closed up at 6:00 and ran to the cottage to change into some black workout shorts, a blue tank top, and a pair of my new Nikes before heading over to the Dancing Queen Dance Studio. When I walked in, the only people who were there were Mo and her friends. Mo introduced me to Val, who was a petite lady with short, dark-brown hair and the biggest blue eyes I've ever seen. Next was Sandy, a tall, blonde, attractive woman who wore her hair in a short bob like Mo. Then there was MaryAnn who sported short, spiky red hair. With her body language and personality, she was like a white Tina Turner. We chatted for a few minutes, and then everyone else started filing in. From the marina there was Sexy Cathy, Marion, Joyce, Geri, Scary Sarah, Bonnie, and Just Howard's new girlfriend, Barbara. I didn't know the rest of the people. Kathy and Lolly must be pleased, though, because the room was filling up.

Dancing Kathy escorted us into a room with four poles where Lolly was setting up her boom box. Dancing Kathy said, "Ladies, I would like to introduce you to your instructor, Lolly."

Everyone said, "Hi, Lolly."

Lolly gave us a big smile and asked, "Ladies, are you ready to get sexy?"

We all laughed and yelled, "Yes."

She said, "Since there are twenty of you, I want you to get in groups of five. Five to a pole."

I joined up with Mo and her friends.

Lolly said, "Okay, ladies. The first thing we need to do is loosen up those muscles. I want you to do some stretches with me."

She took us through several stretches. We extended our arms and legs and rolled our shoulders and shook it out. We did a five-minute warmup.

She asked, "Ladies, are you ready to start?"

In unison, we said, "Yes."

She said, "I'm gonna turn on some music, but before we start working with the poles, I want you to do a few moves with me."

She turned on some music. The first song we heard coming out of the boom box was Marvin Gaye's "Sexual Healing."

"Okay, ladies. I want you to move your hips. Follow my lead."

We all started to swivel our hips.

She said, "Okay, let's try a bump-and-grind." She demonstrated and we all tried to imitate her. We practiced the bump-and-grind for at least ten minutes. Lolly went around the room and gave us each some personal instruction.

She said, "Now I want you to bump and grind and lift your left leg out. Always point your toe. I see you all have tennis shoes on. Next class I want to see you in heels, the highest heels you can stand. Nothing is sexier to a man than high heels. I know they're a bitch, but if you want to do a little pole dance for your man, they're essential."

MaryAnn said under her breath, "Easy for her to say; she hasn't seen my bunions."

Val sympathized. "I haven't worn high heels since I retired."

Sandy laughed and said, "I'm gonna need a hip replacement after this class."

Lolly tried to encourage everybody, "You're doing good, ladies. Let's see you point your left foot, and then slowly flick it up behind you. Good job. Now move like a cat. Move your hips left, right, left, right. Now I want you to put your arms up like you're holding onto a pole. Got the grip? Okay, now pretend you're slowly sliding down the pole. Just go about halfway. Point that left leg out. Good, ladies. You're getting it." We practiced that move for about five minutes. Lolly said, "Okay, ladies, it's time to move onto the poles."

We all gathered around our assigned poles.

Lolly asked, "Okay, who's going first?"

Mo turned to me and said, "You're the youngest, Meggie. You're up."

I went to our pole.

Lolly said, "Okay, I want you to wrap your right leg around the pole. Put your right arm high up on the pole and swing yourself around pointing your left leg out." I pointed my left leg out and took a good swing around the pole.

Lolly said, "Meggie, you're a natural."

Who knew I had a hidden talent?

Everyone took their turns in my group as Lolly went

around the room giving tips to everyone. MaryAnn was the last one to work with the pole. She got in position and twirled around the pole. In mid-twirl, she farted like a machine gun. Our group immediately burst out laughing, and MaryAnn slid down the pole onto the floor. The rest of us were doubled over laughing.

Lolly announced, "Ladies. This was a great class. You all did great. Next week we'll work on some more moves."

Our group was still laughing hysterically and the rest of the women were looking at us a little funny. I laughed so hard I was afraid I was going to pee my workout shorts and quickly headed over to Dancing Kathy to ask where the bathroom was. When I came out, Mo and her friends were waiting for me.

Sandy said, "We thought martinis were in order. Want to come?"

I said, "I'm right behind you."

We left the class and went to the nearest bar down the street.

We all took seats at the bar and Sandy asked me, "What kind of martini would you like, Meggie?"

I said, "I'm a lightweight, Sandy. I'll have a Coors Light."

She ordered my beer and martinis for everyone else.

Mo said, "Hey, Meggie, did you see Barbara on the pole? She looked like a professional. She can bump and grind with the best of them. No wonder Just Howard is struttin' like a peacock."

I said, "I thought the same thing. She had all the moves down."

MaryAnn said, "I can't believe I farted. Are you sure no

one else heard me?"

I laughed and said, "Yeah. We were the only ones. That was so funny."

MaryAnn said, "I guess I'll be known as the farter now."

I said, "Well, I almost pissed my shorts laughing."

Sandy said, "MaryAnn, you're the farter, and Meggie, you're the pisser.

We all laughed.

I stayed for another beer and then went home. I checked the answer machine when I got home and there were two messages. The first one was from my mom telling me to call her back. The second one was from Ian.

"Meggie, it's Ian. I guess you're at your class still. I just wanted to let you know I had to go up to Maine to pick up some parts for the boat. I'm spending the night and I'll get the parts in the morning. I'll be back in the afternoon. I want you to save tomorrow night for me. I'll see you tomorrow."

God, I miss him. My body aches for him. This is torture. I need to make up my mind soon before I go nuts. I should just confront him and tell him I love him and see what happens? He'll either say he loves me back or he doesn't. If he does, I'll stay and see what happens. If he doesn't, I'll go home. The other scenario is to not say anything and enjoy the next week with him and live out the summer fling. I'll have a broken heart, but wonderful memories.

I listened to his message two more times and then looked at the clock. My parents are usually up till 11:00. It was only 10:00 so I dialed their number. I can't wait to hear what my mom thinks about Gram and Cal. Mom picked up after two rings.

She said, "Hello."

I said, "Hey, Mom, it's Meggie."

"Oh my God, Meggie. Can you believe your Gram got married? I'm in shock."

"I hope you're happy for her, Mom. I met Cal and I think he's great."

"Oh, honey, I'm so happy I can't stop smiling. My face hurts. I never thought I'd see the day. She's like another person. There is a light in her eyes I've never seen before and I think she looks ten years younger."

"Me too, Mom. I think she looks great. What do you think of Cal?"

"I couldn't have hand-picked anyone better for her. He and your father have really hit it off. We are going to have to plan a big party when both your brothers get home. Maybe we'll do it up in Rhode Island. Speaking of Rhode Island, are you going to stay up there? Your Gram said she asked you to run the marina."

"I'm still thinking about it, Mom. I'll let her know next week."

"I almost forgot. The school called and they want you to give them a call. They said it was about some meetings you need to attend."

"Okay. I'll call them next week, too."

"What's wrong, Meggie? Why are you having such a hard time making a decision about the marina? I know you really don't like teaching; you've told me that many times. Your Gram said you told her you've loved running the marina, so what's stopping you?"

"Mom, I've loved running the marina. It's Ian. I'm not

sure how he feels about me and if I stay and it doesn't work out, then I'll have to see him all the time and it'll hurt too much."

"Oh, I see. You're in love, aren't you?"

"Hook, line, and sinker."

"You need to tell him how you feel, Meggie. Give him a chance. Guys don't ever say how they feel. You have to pull it out of them. Your father was like that and still is sometimes. Tell that boy how you feel. How could he not love you, Meggie? You're my precious little girl."

My eyes were starting to water.

"Thanks, Mom. I'll let you know what happens."

"It will all work out, honey. I promise."

"Talk to you in a few days, Mom, and say hi to everyone."

"I will. Bye."

"Bye, Mom."

Mom and Mo are right. I need to talk to Ian and tell him how I feel. I don't know when or where I'll get the courage to do that, but I have no choice.

The next morning, I was walking out of my office when the phone rang. I went back and picked up the phone.

"Harbor Marina."

"Meggie, it's Ian. I'm still up in Maine. They had the wrong part, so I'll have to stay up here until tomorrow morning. There's a truck due in early with another shipment and they swear to me the part I need is on that truck. I'm sorry, but I'll have to cancel for tonight but can we do something tomorrow night?"

I was disappointed but relieved. I'll have one more day to get my courage up for our big talk.

"That's fine. I'll keep tomorrow night open."

"Good."

"Good luck with the part."

"Thanks. Talk to you tomorrow."

"Bye."

I love his voice. It's deep and it goes right to my soul.

I hung up the phone and headed out to the fuel dock. I had to talk to Matt about the bait order I needed to fax.

I got halfway down the dock and saw Bonnie waving at me from the *Bonnie Blue.* I retraced by steps and headed over to C dock.

Bonnie said, "Hey, Meggie. I wanted to let you know that we're going offshore tomorrow. The Murphy brothers are coming with us and I wanted to see if you would like to go."

"I would love to, Bonnie. I'm sure Journey can handle things, but I would have to be back by 5:30."

"That's no problem. I'll make sure we're back in time."

"What should I bring?"

"Just yourself. We've got all the gear and bait and the Murphys are bringing food. If there's anything special you want to eat or drink, bring it, but we'll have plenty. Looking at your pale skin, you might want to bring some sunscreen. I have some onboard, but it might not be strong enough for you."

"Don't worry. I never leave home without it."

"Oh, and a hat. You'll need it."

"What time are you leaving?"

"About 4:30."

I smiled at her and said, "Okay, Bonnie. I'm excited. I'll see you tomorrow."

She smiled back at me. "Sure thing, Meggie."

I went down to the fuel dock, talked to Matt, and then went back to the office to do paperwork.

At noon, my stomach was crying for food so I went over to the Shack. As I approached the Shack, I could hear ZZ Top's song "Leave Your Hat On" playing on the radio. I opened the door and cracked up laughing. Mo and Sexy Cathy were in the middle of the Shack practicing their bump-and-grinds.

Mo looked up and saw me. She said, "Come on, Meggie, you need practice, too."

I joined them and had just completed my third bump-and-grind when the door opened and in walked Big H. He looked at the three of us and cracked up laughing. It was the first time I ever saw him laugh. I looked over at Mo and Sexy Cathy and they didn't miss a beat, they just kept on bumping and grinding. Big H walked around the counter still laughing and poured himself a cup of coffee. He put a dollar down and gave us a last look before he walked out the door. Mo waved at him and he blushed. When the song ended, we all started laughing.

Mo said, "Well, at least he got a taste of what he's missin' out on."

I said, "You can say that again, Mo. You got the bump-and-grind down."

Sexy Cathy said, "I've never seen Big H laugh like that."

I said, "Me neither."

Mo said, "I have and it makes me melt. He's ten times more handsome when he laughs or smiles. He needs to do it more often."

She walked behind the counter and asked, "You girls

hungry?"

I said, "I'm starving."

Sexy Cathy said, "Me too. Kenny kept me up half the night last night."

Mo said, "Brag, brag, brag. You shouldn't be sayin' things like that around a horny, middle-aged woman. It's downright cruel."

I said, "Mo, you're gonna meet that Fisher Man tomorrow and he's going to be all over you."

Sexy Cathy said, "Oh, you finally are going out with that guy you've been telling me about?"

Mo said, "Yeah, but I ain't gettin' my hopes up."

I said, "Well, my hopes are up, and I'm keeping my fingers crossed for you, Mo."

Sexy Cathy said, "Me, too."

Mo said, "What are you gals in the mood for? I got a great special today—Chinese chicken salad with my own special dressing.

Cathy and I both said, "I'll have that."

My mouth started to water just thinking about it. God, if I wind up back in Philly, I'm going to have to get all of Mo's recipes before I go. Maybe I'll quit teaching and open my own sandwich shop.

Mo went behind the counter to make our salads.

Cathy asked, "How are things with you, Meggie?"

I said, "Okay. I'm going fishing tomorrow on the *Bonnie Blue.*"

Mo said, "Hey, catch me a big tuna, I'm running low."

I said, "I'll try. I'm really looking forward to it."

Sexy Cathy said, "You'll be in good hands. Bonnie will

take care of you. Kenny and I went with them one time and we had a great day on the water and caught some nice fish."

Mo asked, "When's your Gram comin' home? I can't wait to see her."

I said, "She should be home Sunday. I'm sure she'll make an appearance here sometime next week."

Mo put our salads in front of us and Cathy and I dug in. Food just shouldn't be this good. I need to get running again.

I went back to the office and worked like a dog to get caught up so I could take the day off tomorrow. I didn't close up shop until seven. I locked the door and ran into Tony in the parking lot on my way to the cottage.

"Hi, Tony."

He asked, "You're coming to my party, right?"

I said, "Yeah, Ian and I will be there. When's Helen flying in?"

"Tomorrow afternoon. I can't wait to see her. I bought her a another new bikini for the party."

I laughed and said, "She'll love that."

He said, "I've gotta keep the Princess happy. We've got the party Saturday night and then Paisano Sunday the next day."

"Whoa. You're taking her to Paisano Sunday again? Isn't that dangerous?"

He laughed and said, "Yeah, but she's worth the risk. I've had to tell my parents where I've been disappearing to every other weekend, so now they want to get to know her."

I said, "Well, they'll love her."

He winked at me and said, "Of course they will. Would you and Ian like to go? It might help to have some friends with us."

"I would love to, but I don't know what's going on with Ian. I'll take a rain check if that's okay?"

I could feel my eyes starting to well up.

I could tell by the expression on his face that he noticed.

He said, "I'm going over to Kelly's for a burger. You want to come?"

I thought about it for a second, shrugged my shoulders, and said, "Sure, why not?"

"Come on. I'll drive."

We walked to his truck and he opened the door for me. I jumped up into the truck, Tony got in and two minutes later we walked into Kelly's. It wasn't too busy so we were able to grab a booth. We both ordered burgers, Tony ordered a beer, and I ordered a Coke.

I told him, "I'm going fishing tomorrow, so I want to feel good in the morning."

He smiled and said, "I don't blame you. You have to have a good stomach to go offshore. It's supposed to be a stellar day tomorrow so you should be fine."

I noticed Pete the pick-up-line guy walking into the bar. He passed our booth and glanced our way. When he spotted me, he walked backward like Michael Jackson, stopped at our booth, and greeted me. "Hey, Red One."

I laughed and said, "Hi, Pete. How are you doing with your pick-up lines?"

He hung his head. "Not too good."

He looked at Tony and leaned over and whispered in my ear, "I thought you were going out with that lobster guy."

I said, "I am. This is Tony Maroni. He goes out with the

blond one." Pete's eyes popped. He said, "The goddess?"

Tony laughed and said, "The very one, and believe me, she's a goddess."

Pete shook his head like a wet dog and said, "Are you *the* Tony Maroni, the 'King of Love'?"

Tony and I looked at each other and burst out laughing.

Tony finally said, "Well, I've heard people call me that."

Pete said, "Hey, can you do a dude a favor and give me some tips? I'm desperate. I'm a bust with the ladies and it's not from lack of trying. Share your oh-so-great wisdom with a lowly commoner."

Tony looked at him and bit his lip trying not to laugh and hurt his feelings. I was doing everything I could to maintain my self-control.

Tony said, "Sure, but you have to keep this between us. I don't dole out my secrets to just anybody, but since you're a friend of the Red One and the Goddess, I feel it's my duty to help a guy in need."

Pete got a serious look on his face and put his hand over his heart and said, "Your secrets are safe with me, Oh Wise One."

I was on the edge of my seat waiting to hear what Tony would say to him. I felt Pete wasn't the only one who was going to learn something tonight.

Tony said, "Well, I was raised around a lot of women. Do you like women?"

Pete said, "I love women."

Tony said, "You not only have to love women, but you have to be a man who likes women, really and truly likes them. You have to like hanging out with them, you have to like listening to them. You have to worship them. Can you do that?"

Pete looked at Tony in awe and said, "I think so."

Tony said, "It's either all or nothing. Listening is the most important. They like to talk about their feelings and you have to give them what they need. You have to make them feel that what they say and feel is important to you. Women are the most beautiful, amazing creatures in the world and you have to believe it to the core of your being. Look at history. Men have fought wars for them, they've died for them. They've built castles for them. You have to love *all* women—old ones, middle-aged ones, young ones, pretty ones, and homely ones. I'm talking about all women. The most important thing is you have to respect them. If you don't respect them, they'll never trust you. If they don't trust you, they won't love you. Let me ask you a question. What's your most precious material possession?"

Pete thought about it for a minute and then said, "I'd have to say my surfboard?

Tony said, "Good. Do you take good care of your board?"

Pete said, "I take really good care of it. I wax it all the time and polish it so it rides smooth in the water."

Tony said, "Well, treat a women like you do your board and you'll be all set. Cherish her, worship her, rub her body with slow, soft strokes, and she'll be putty in your hands."

Pete said, "Oh my God. I'm finally getting it."

Tony said, "Don't come on too strong in the beginning. Don't talk too much about yourself, be a little mysterious. Let her be curious about you. Lure her in and she'll want to find out more about you."

Pete thought about this for a while and said, "I'm not good-looking like you, though. Will it work for me?"

Tony said, "Looks aren't everything and that works both ways. There are a lot of women who might not look like a goddess on the outside, but inside they are all goddesses waiting to be released by the right guy. In order to be that guy, you have to listen, respect, care, and worship. If you get lucky enough to gain their respect, you'll be able to worship every inch of them. Remember, their pleasure always comes first. You'll get yours in abundance if you do that."

Pete looked dazed. He asked Tony, "How can I ever thank you?"

Tony said, "Go forth and conquer, young man, and remember a gentleman is always a gentleman."

Pete got up from the booth and said, "My eternal thanks, Oh Wise One."

When he walked away, Tony rolled his eyes at me and we both started to laugh.

The waitress served our food.

I said, "Tony, you are too funny. I thought I was going to pee my pants. I've got to tell you, though, I liked what you said. If that kid follows your advice, he's going to be a happy man."

Tony got a serious look on his face and said, "I meant what I said, Meggie. I *do* love women. I enjoy their company, I respect them, and I really do think they're the most amazing creatures in the world."

I smiled at him and said, "I believe you. Tony, you get women, you really get us. I'm amazed. Helen is a lucky girl."

He said, "I'm the lucky one. Now what the hell is going

on with you, Red Hot?" Tell the 'Oh Wise One' why those beautiful baby blues of yours look so sad."

I immediately got choked up. I swallowed hard and said, "It's Ian. I don't know what to do about him. For the past week I've been on an emotional roller coaster. First I overheard a conversation he was having with some guy in the store who asked Ian if he got Gram to agree to sell him the marina yet."

Tony looked surprised. He said, "I didn't know he was interested in it."

"Neither did I. My first thought was that he was dating me to get on Gram's good side."

"I doubt that, Red Hot."

"I confronted him about it and he told me the truth, but I was surprised he never discussed it with me before. He said it never came up in conversation. I'm not sure I believe he was using me to get to Gram, but it made me doubt him. I only have a week left before I go back to Philly. Gram asked me to stay and run the marina. I would like to, but I'm hesitant because I'm not sure how Ian feels about me. He's never told me."

"But he's showed you in many ways, don't forget that."

"Maybe he's that way with all the girls he dates."

"Does Ian know your Gram wants you to stay?"

"That's the thing. I told him and he didn't say anything. He didn't encourage me one way or the other. I really believe that he was only into having a summer fling. If I stay and he dumps me, I would have to see him all the time and I don't know if I can do that. I'm in love with him and it would hurt too much."

Tony sat back and smiled at me. He said, "Meggie, I'm

sure he has feelings for you. Take it from the Wise One, he does. I think you should stay and see where it goes and I don't think you'll be disappointed. Remember what I said about the code. He's just making sure of his feelings before he lets them out of the bag. He's being extra careful with you because he cares."

"I hope you're right, Tony."

He winked at me and said, "If I'm not and he breaks your little heart, I've got some relatives who could make him sorry he ever darkened your doorstep."

I laughed. "Thanks for listening, Tony."

"You're welcome, Red Hot."

We chatted some more while we finished off our burgers.

As we got up to leave, we both turned around to see how Pete was making out in the back of the bar. He was standing near the dartboard talking to a petite brunette. He looked our way and Tony gave him a thumbs-up. Pete smiled and bowed.

Tony and I smiled at each other and laughed our way out to his truck.

When I got home, I checked my answering machine and there was a message from Helen to call her.

I dialed her number and she picked up on the second ring.

I said, "Hi, Hel, it's me."

"Hey you. I'm flying up tomorrow; I can't wait. Are you and Ian coming to the pool party?"

"Yep, it should be fun. I just had an interesting dinner with Tony."

She said, "Oh, that's nice. Where did you two go?"

"Kelly's and we ran into the pick-up-line artist, Pete."

"How's he making out, any luck?"

"No, but I think things are about to change for him. He asked Tony for some tips and Tony gave him a class in Women 101."

"Oh boy, I bet that was interesting."

"It was and I've got to hand it to Tony, he's a man who really gets women. He blew me away."

She laughed and asked, "What did he say?"

"He said we are all goddesses and need to be treated with respect. There was a lot more to it, but Tony really should teach a class and all men should be required to take it in high school. It should be a requirement like math and English. The world would be filled with happy women."

"I have to admit, he is amazing. I can't wait to see him."

"Things must be serious with you guys. He told me you're going to Paisano Sunday again."

"I'm a little nervous about that, but he's worth having my ass pinched a few more times. How are things going with Ian?"

"He's been up in Maine the last few days, but I'm supposed to see him tomorrow night. My Gram has asked me to stay and run the marina and I'm not sure what to do. I told Ian this and he had no comment. I don't know how he feels about me and I don't want to stay unless I know where I stand with him. I've had a great time with him, but the problem is I'm in love with him and I'm afraid I'll be broken-hearted if I stay. I've got to make up my mind this weekend. Gram needs to know and if I decide to stay I've gotta let the school know."

"Oh Meggie, I'm sure he has feelings for you. I think you should go for it. Stay up there and keep dating him and see where it goes. If I wind up moving up there, I want my best friend nearby."

"Tony basically said the same thing. I bored him with all my troubles over dinner. He's a good listener. I know a lot of men have trouble talking about their feelings, but I've got life-changing decisions to make. I imagine Tony tells you how he feels, doesn't he?

She laughed. "He does. I'm not used to it and at first I felt a little uncomfortable about it, but now I can't get enough. He's much better at expressing his feelings than I am."

"Consider yourself lucky."

"Maybe you can have a talk with Ian tomorrow night."

"I intend to. I don't know what our plans are for the evening, but I'm definitely going to talk to him."

"Go for it, Meggie. No guts, no glory."

"I'm going offshore fishing tomorrow and then I'm going to check out Mo's blind date for her. She's got a date with a guy she met on the net and he's picking her up at the marina. She wants me to scope him out for her before she gets on his boat."

"I hope he's a hot one for her."

"So do I. I'll see you on Saturday and let you know what I've decided. Thanks, Hel."

"Chin up, girlfriend. Bye."

I hung up and got ready for bed. Tomorrow will be a big day. God, I miss Ian.

CHAPTER NINETEEN

I walked out of the cottage and went over to the store to open up. Journey was coming in early to cover for me. To my surprise, I actually slept well last night and I feel great. I'm so excited about the fishing trip; it's kept my mind off Ian. Of course, he is always in the back of my mind, but I promised myself I wasn't going to think too much about him today. I'm going to enjoy myself on the high seas.

Journey showed up and I proceeded down to the docks to the *Bonnie Blue*. Everyone was already on board ready to go. The Murphy brothers took the bag I had packed with my super-duper sunscreen and a six pack of bottled water.

The Murphy brothers look so much alike they could be twins. Don is the younger one and Mikey a few years older. They're both in their thirties and have great bodies. They have the same brown hair, blue eyes, and strong chins. Through the grapevine, okay, thru Mo, I heard Mikey is divorced and Don has never been married. They smiled at me and Don heaved my bag up above in the cockpit.

Don asked, "Are you ready to catch a big fish, Meggie?"

I smiled and said, "I can't wait."

Jim was fooling around with the radios. He turned around and said, "Little lady, we're hoping you'll bring us luck today."

I said, "I hope so, too."

Bonnie came up from below with a cup of coffee in her hand. She spotted me and said, "Hey Meggie, want some joe?"

I smiled at her and said, "No thanks, I'm wired as it is. I'm so excited."

Jim said, "We have about a two-and-a-half-hour ride out before we drop the lines, so you can nap below or sit up here and watch the sunrise."

"I'm gonna watch the sunrise," I replied.

Bonnie said, "It's amazing to watch from the water."

I asked, "Where are we going?"

Jim held up his right hand and wiggled his fingers. "The Fingers. It's about 40 miles out, 20 miles south of Martha's Vineyard. They call it the Fingers because the depth contours are shaped like, guess what, fingers. It's a great fishing spot."

He started the engines and I took a seat up in the cockpit with Bonnie. The Murphy brothers sat on coolers in the back of the boat.

We pulled out of the harbor and through the channel between Jerusalem and Galilee. It was flat calm and I settled in to enjoy the views. Pretty soon all that was visible in every direction was water. An hour after we got out to sea, the sun rose and it was a spectacular sight. I was in heaven.

A little while later, Jim shouted at me, "Meggie, you've got to see this, look off starboard."

I turned to the right to see a big giant turtle swimming along. There is nothing better than observing sea creatures in their own element. We all watched the turtle swimming along happy as can be. Already I've had a great day. It was priceless.

An hour later, the Murphy brothers went down below and started to bring up the rods and reels. Bonnie and I helped as they placed them in the rod holders in the back of the boat. Don and Mikey started to rig the rods with different-colored lures, making sure they were all rigged up properly to the outriggers and the safety lines. Jim had told me that we would be trolling today and dragging plastic. When the guys were finished, seven rods were rigged up and we were ready to start fishing. Bonnie had the binoculars out and was on bait watch.

Ten minutes later, she said, "There's the bait—portside. Here, have a look, Meggie."

She handed me the binoculars and I took a look at the water. I had no idea what I was looking for.

I said, "I see a bubbling on the surface of the water."

She patted me on the back and said, "You're a natural fisherwoman. That's the bait moving. The big fish look for that and then they come up to eat. That's when we drop the lines and go for them."

The Murphys started to let line out and we were officially fishing. A few minutes later, I heard a click and zzzzzzzzzz sound.

Don said, "Fish on. You're up, Meggie."

I jumped up and Don handed me the rod.

He said, "Start reeling in, Meggie. Nice and easy."

I started reeling and by the time I got the fish to the boat, Mikey was holding a gaff and Don a large net.

Mikey said, "It looks like just a mushie."

I said, "What's a mushie?"

Don laughed and said, "Nothing you would enjoy eating.

It's oceanic bonito. They have a soft mouth and bloody meat, not too tasty. We're gonna let him see another day."

Mikey gently took the hook out the fish's mouth and tossed him back in. A couple more lines hit and we reeled in a few more mushies. We trolled around for another half-hour and then two rods hit. They were bent over.

Bonnie said, "Looks like we got two big ones."

She put a belt on me that had a rod holder attached and then put one on herself. Don handed me one rod and Bonnie the other one. We started to reel in the fish. It was a workout. It took us about five minutes to bring them to the boat, but it seemed a lot longer. I was working up a sweat. Bonnie got hers to the boat first and the guys scooped it up with a large net.

Jim said, "Nice mahi, Bonnie. Looks like a thirty-pounder."

I looked over at the fish flopping around the deck. Its skin was beautiful with different shades of blue, yellow, and green. Mikey held down the fish while Don took the hook out of its mouth and put it in the large cooler. Then they helped me with my fish, which was also a mahi, but not quite as big as Bonnie's.

Don took the hook out and I went over to open the cooler. I lifted the lid and Bonnie's mahi took a flying leap out of the cooler, up in the air, and over the side.

Everyone started laughing.

I said, "Oh my God. I'm so sorry."

Jim said, "That's a first. I guess that fish had other plans. Don't worry about it, Meggie, at least you'll have a good story to tell about your first offshore trip."

I started to laugh and I said, "I can't believe that happened."

Bonnie said, "I can't either. Too funny."

I could hear my fish banging around in the cooler. I said, "I kind of feel bad for the fish."

Bonnie said, "We only take our limit and we eat it all. Sometimes we just sportfish and tag the catch for the Marine Fisheries Service. It helps them keep track of the species population. One time we tagged a small tuna and got a postcard from the Fishery Service that it was caught two years later down in Venezuela."

I said, "That's cool."

The Murphys set the lines again and we continued to troll around. We could see a few other boats in the area.

Don jumped up and said, "Whale off the starboard side."

I looked out in the water and saw my first whale in the wild. It was gray and I could see it move through the water, its hump and tail resurfacing. We all enjoyed watching the whale until we heard a line hit and then it was back to fishing. Every time I heard a line hit, my adrenaline started pumping. Fishing, I think, runs two opposite ends of the spectrum. You go from being completely bored to totally excited in about two seconds flat.

Mikey went for the rod that was bent over; its tip was almost down to the water's edge.

Bonnie said, "You take it, Mikey, it looks like a big one."

Don fastened a rod holder around Mikey's waist and he started to reel it in. It kept taking more line and then he would reel it in again. This went on for about fifteen minutes.

Mikey said, "I think I'd better sit in the fighting chair. He sat and took the rod out of the belt at his waist and set it in the holder on the chair. Sweat poured down his face as he fought the fish and he was grunting from the strain.

Bonnie laughed and said to me, "It's like watching a woman have a baby."

I agreed and we continued to watch Mikey fight the fish. Finally he was making progress and the fish was almost to the boat. Jim and Don stood ready with gaffs and when the fish got to the boat, they gaffed it and hauled it on board. I stepped up in the cockpit to get out of the way and watch.

Don said, "It's a bluefin. What do you think Jim, a hundred twenty-five pounds?"

Jim smiled and said, "About. Nice fish, Mikey."

Mikey grinned from ear to ear. Bonnie and I watched as they removed the hook from the fish's mouth and stuck it in the cooler."

Bonnie said to me, "What do you think about offshore fishing?"

I said, "There's a lot more to it than I ever thought. This has been an experience."

We caught two small bluefin after that and decided to call it a day and head home. On our way back, a school of dolphins came by and rode the wake of the boat for a while. I think that was my favorite part of the trip.

We pulled up to the dock around five and I helped Bonnie clean the boat while the guys cleaned the fish. Don handed me two bags of fish, one with mahi and one with tuna.

I said, "I had a great day. Thank you all for showing me the ropes. Sorry about that mahi."

They all laughed.

Jim said, "You're welcome anytime, Meggie."

"Thanks."

I took the fish up to the cottage and went over to close up the store.

Journey was at the counter when I walked in. She said, "Hey, how was fishing?"

"Great. We caught a lot and I got to see all kinds of sea life, whales, dolphins, turtles. It was cool. How were things around here today?"

"Busy. I'm beat."

"Well, take off. I'm going to lock up."

When I was through, I went directly over to the Shack to meet Mo who was standing behind the counter.

I asked her, "Are you ready for your big date? Come out here and let me see how you look."

She let out a sigh, walked around the counter, and twirled. She had on light-blue cropped pants, a white T-shirt, and a jeans jacket. On her feet she wore a pair of navy canvas topsiders.

I said, "You look really nice. That's the perfect outfit for a boat ride."

She nodded, "That's what I was thinkin'." She shivered, "I've got butterflies bad. I've been dreadin' this date all week. I can't wait till it's over."

Surprised, I said, "I thought you really liked this guy. You've been e-mailing for weeks and you told me you got along really well."

"That's just it. Too well. He's too good to be true. I'm tellin' you, he'll have two teeth in his head."

I laughed, "Think positive. Hey, if he's a fisherman, how bad can he be? Every fisherman I've met around here's been really nice."

Mo said, "Well, you can put a cat in the oven, but that don't make him a biscuit. When the other guys turned out to be losers, it didn't bother me because I wasn't all that crazy about them anyway. This one I really like. I'll be disappointed if he turns out to be a dud."

I smiled at her and repeated, "Think positive. Let me go down to the dock and see if he's there yet. Maybe he'll be early and you can get the suspense over with."

"Thanks, Meggie."

"Be right back."

I walked down to the fuel dock and the only boat I saw was Big H's. Matt was fueling it up for him. I looked up and down the channel but didn't see any boats approaching from either side.

Big H asked, "Are you looking for someone, Meggie?"

I said, "Yeah. Mo has a blind date, and he's picking her up here. I'm supposed to check him out. She's afraid he'll pull up in a rust bucket and only have two teeth in his head."

Big H looked up and gave me a big, wide, toothy smile.

I looked him over and realized he was a bit dressed up for Big H. No fishing hat, no T-shirt with oil and fish blood stains. He had on khaki pants and a nice navy polo shirt. Suddenly the pieces fit. I thought to myself, no way.

I said, "Oh my God, you're him, aren't you? You're Fisher Man."

He laughed and said, "That's me."

"I'm so excited. Mo is gonna flip out. I can't believe it's you."

"Go get her. Tell her I have a full set of teeth, but don't tell her it's me."

"I'll be right back." I couldn't stop smiling. I couldn't wait to see Mo's reaction.

I walked in the Shack and she looked at me wide-eyed. She asked, "Is he there?"

"Yeah, he's there."

"Meggie, don't keep me in suspenders. What's he like? Will I like him?"

"You'll like him alright."

She asked, "Is he good-lookin'?"

"Very handsome, and he has a really nice boat."

"How about the teeth?"

I nodded. "He has good teeth and they look like they're his own."

She smiled and said, "Really?"

I laughed. "Really. I think you'll have a great time."

She grabbed her purse, and we walked out of the Shack.

There was no way I was going to miss this so I said, "I'll walk you down. I want to get another look at him."

Halfway down the dock, Mo grabbed my arm and said, "Just to be on the safe side, get the name and make of his boat in case I wind up fish food. I usually meet these Internet guys in public places."

I gave her arm a squeeze. "Stop worrying, you'll be fine."

We reached the end of the dock and Mo glanced around.

She turned to me and said, "He must've changed his mind. The only boat I see is Big H's."

Big H must have gone down below. He came up a few seconds later and looked up at us. Mo was gazing down the channel

Mo asked me, "Meggie, what did his boat look like?"

I pointed at Big H and said, "Mo, I want you to meet the Fisher Man."

Mo's jaw dropped and then slammed shut, her faced turned beet-red, her body tensed up, and her hands balled into fists. She stomped over to Big H's boat and climbed aboard.

She stood in front of him shaking and said, "I'm so angry with you. What the hell took you so long?"

Big H grabbed Mo and started kissing her like he was a drowning man. I stood and watched them for a minute, and then I felt like a voyeur, so I turned around and danced up the dock. Halfway up, I looked over and, as usual, Bob on the *Bite Me* had his camera out. I gave him a wiggle, punched my fist up in the air, and he snapped my picture.

By the time I got to the cottage, I had made up my mind. There was no way I was going back to Philly.

When I walked in, the phone was ringing. I ran to pick it up before the machine came on.

"Hello."

"Hi, Meggie. I hope we're still on for tonight?"

"Yes."

"I thought we would go out to dinner somewhere, if that's okay."

"I went fishing today with Jim and Bonnie and I have two big bags of fish. Maybe we should eat it while it's fresh."

"Okay. Bring some over here and I'll cook it on the grill?"

"Yeah, that sounds great. I'll bring some rice and I've got stuff for a salad, too."

"Then I guess I'll see you in a while."

"About an hour. Bye."

I took a quick shower and dressed in some capris and a

T-shirt. I packed up the dinner supplies and got in the car to drive over to Ian's. I'm a bit nervous about seeing him and telling him my decision. I hope he's happy about it.

Ian and Sam came out to greet me when I pulled in the driveway. Ian gave me a quick hug and peck on the cheek and then he grabbed the bag of groceries. I gave Sam a good scratch behind his ears and we all went into the house.

Ian smiled at me and said, "So, now you're an offshore fisherwoman."

"Yes, I am and I loved it."

I proceeded to tell him about my day and all about Big H and Mo.

Ian said, "It's about time those two got together."

I asked him, "How did you make out with the boat parts?"

"Great. I got what I needed and was back here by noon, did the repairs, and the boat's all set."

He came toward me and put his arms around me and gave me a tender kiss.

He said, "It feels like I haven't seen you in a long time. I've missed you."

I took a deep, calming breath and said, "I've made my decision about staying and running the marina."

He said, "Hold that thought. I'll be right back."

He went upstairs and came down a minute later. "It's a great night. Let's take a walk on the beach before we cook dinner."

"Sure."

You would think he'd be anxious to know what I was going to do.

We walked a little way down the beach. The sun was

starting to set, the beach was deserted, and the evening couldn't be more beautiful. I thought I would wait for him to ask me what I'd decided.

We were holding hands and he stopped.

He said, "Meggie, I need to talk to you about something."

My heart caught in my throat. Hesitantly, I said, "Okay."

He said, "I never told you about wanting to buy the marina because I didn't want you to think that was why I was dating you. Of course, that was a mistake and you found out from someone else when you should have learned that from me. I'm sorry about that. Believe me, the marina didn't even cross my mind when I asked you out. I wanted to ask you out the first time I saw you again, but I waited because I didn't want to hurt you. I wanted to make sure what I felt for you was the real thing."

My heart was beating so hard in my chest. I couldn't wait to hear what he said next.

He said, "Before you tell me what you've decided to do, I want to tell you how I feel. I love you. I haven't said it before because I've never said those three words to anyone and I wanted to be absolutely sure. I know this has happened to you many times before, but I hope this will be the last time."

He got down on one knee and reached in his pocket. He lifted his hand up, and in it shone a beautiful diamond ring.

"Meggie, I love you. I have from the moment I saw you standing on the dock that first day we saw each other again. I don't care if you stay and run the marina, or you teach, or if you just want to stay home and have kids. I just want you to stay. Will you marry me?"

I started to cry and knelt down in front of him. I said,

"Yes. Ian, I love you so much. Are you sure?"

"Meggie, I've never been so sure of anything in my life."

He slipped the ring on my finger, kissed me, and held me close to him for a long time.

He said, "Just out of curiosity. What had you decided to do?"

I said, "I decided to follow my heart and stay."

He said, "Let's go back to the house. I want you to see the ring in the light."

I was bursting with happiness. Back at his house, I got a good look at the ring. It was an antique, with a diamond that looked to be over a carat and set in white gold with a sapphire on each side of the diamond.

I said, "Oh, Ian. It's the most beautiful ring I've ever seen."

"That ring was my grandmother's. She left it to me and wanted me to give it to my wife. My grandparents had such a happy marriage, she thought it would be good luck. If you would like something more modern, I'll get you whatever you want."

"Ian, it's perfect and it has so much love associated with it. I wouldn't want anything else."

He smiled and said, "That's what I think, too." He pulled me to him and said, "Meggie, you've made me so happy."

"Ian, I promise, I'll always make you happy."

He said, "How about we make each other happy? I love you, Meggie the mess."

EPILOGUE

THE FOLLOWING JUNE

I walked out the back door of the store and looked around at all the boats. It's a beautiful day, and it just dawned on me a few minutes ago that it's exactly a year ago today that I showed up here to take over running the marina for Gram.

So much has changed, and yet some things have remained the same. Ian and I got married on Valentine's Day. We had a big wedding down in Philly. My mom arranged the whole thing, and it was beautiful. We got married in the church I grew up in, and then had a great reception at a hotel. Since Ian and I both have small families, we decided to invite everyone from the marina. Because it was out of town, we weren't expecting a lot of people to make it, but we hoped a few would. To our surprise, half of them replied that they were coming. Big H decided to charter a bus so they could all come down together. We booked rooms for them at the hotel. Ian and I were thrilled.

Of course, my maid of honor was Helen, and my bridesmaids were Laura, Ian's cousin Christine, and my other friends, Frannie and Sue. Ian's friend, Jake, was his best man and his groomsmen were my two brothers, Tony, and Ian's friend, Steve.

I was so proud of myself. I didn't shed a single tear during the ceremony. The reception was a blast. Mom picked a great band and everyone danced up a storm.

Ian took me to St. Barts for our honeymoon. We decided to go somewhere neither one of us had been before. The island was just as romantic as I'd hoped it would be. We had the best time. When we got back, I moved into Ian's house. My brothers and I decided that, instead of renting the cottage, we would just keep it available for whenever they or my parents want to visit. Ian and I have been so happy. We decided to wait a year and then start trying to have a family. I can't wait.

Mo is still running the Snack Shack and cooking up gossip. Except now, she is Mrs. Big H. Big H asked her to marry him in March. He said he wasn't the big-wedding type and asked her if she wouldn't mind if they just went to Vegas. She said that was fine with her as long as they didn't get married by an Elvis Impersonator. They were married at the chapel in the Venetian Hotel. He took her for a romantic gondola ride after the ceremony.

Mo told me the other day that the latest rumor is that Don Murphy is dating Lolly. The pole-dancing classes were so popular at the Dancing Queen Dance Studio that Dancing Kathy added three more classes. Lolly was able to give up her side job.

Helen and Tony became engaged in April. Their wedding will be down in Philly at the end of September. Hel is just finishing up a project. She will be up here permanently in two weeks. She's going to take the summer off and start looking for a job in Rhode Island after their honeymoon. The Maroni women have been making gravy and meatballs since the engagement was announced and are throwing a traditional Italian engagement party for them in a couple of weeks. Oh, and guess what? Tony renamed his boat. His boat is now called the *Hell-n-Back.*

Don't you just love happy endings?

THE END

ABOUT THE AUTHOR

Sammie Grace lives in Rhode Island with her husband and her diva dog Lucy. She is hard at work on her next book and her website www.sammiegrace.com, which should be up and running in the near future. If you would like to contact Sammie Grace, you can do so at sammiegrace@cox.net.